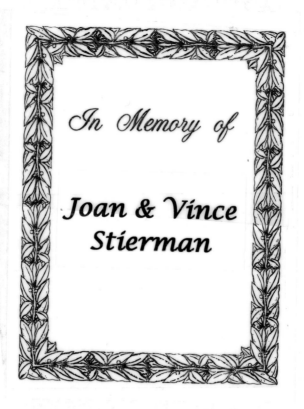

In Memory of

Joan & Vince
Stierman

EVERYMAN,
I WILL GO WITH THEE,
AND BE THY GUIDE,
IN THY MOST NEED
TO GO BY THY SIDE

ROBERT LOUIS STEVENSON

DR JEKYLL
AND
MR HYDE
AND OTHER STORIES

WITH AN INTRODUCTION
BY NICHOLAS RANCE

EVERYMAN'S LIBRARY
Alfred A. Knopf New York London Toronto
63

THIS IS A BORZOI BOOK
PUBLISHED BY ALFRED A. KNOPF

First included in Everyman's Library, 1925
This selection first published in Everyman's Library, 1992
Introduction, Bibliography and Chronology Copyright © 1992
by Everyman's Library
Typography by Peter B. Willberg
Tenth printing (US)

www.randomhouse.com/everymans
www.everymanslibrary.co.uk

ISBN: 978-0-679-40538-2 (US)
978-1-85715-063-6 (UK)

A CIP catalogue reference for this book is available from the
British Library

Library of Congress Cataloging-in-Publication Data
Stevenson, Robert Louis, 1850–1894.
[Strange case of Dr. Jekyll and Mr. Hyde]
Dr. Jekyll and Mr. Hyde/Robert Louis Stevenson.
p.   cm.—(Everyman's library)
ISBN 978-0-679-40538-2
I. Title.
PR5485.A1   1992   91-53216
823'.8–dc20   CIP

Book design by Barbara de Wilde and Carol Devine Carson

Printed and bound in Germany by GGP Media GmbH, Pössneck

C O N T E N T S

CONTENTS

INTRODUCTION

A stagnant month or so having elapsed after publication, Robert Louis Stevenson's Gothic novella, the *Strange Case of Dr Jekyll and Mr Hyde*, quickly compensated by becoming a best-seller and the new literary sensation. The publishing and commercial fortunes of Stevenson's story were appropriately quirky. Stevenson had submitted the story to Longman's in the thought of serial publication in *Longman's Magazine*. With acumen impressive in hindsight, Longman's decided to issue the story separately and in alternative formats: in cloth binding for the more sober market, but also a paper-covered edition, in the guise of a shilling shocker and priced accordingly. The book was ready in time to benefit by the boom in sales preceding Christmas, but booksellers were fully stocked and refused it. They were nearly as indifferent when Longman's resumed negotiations after Christmas. On 25 January 1886, however, apathy was dispelled by a review of the story in *The Times*. The review complimented Stevenson with a pregnant comparison which must have boosted sales. 'Slight as is the story, and supremely sensational, we remember nothing better since George Eliot's "Romola" than this delineation of a feeble but kindly nature steadily and inevitably succumbing to the sinister influences of besetting weaknesses.' Nearly forty thousand copies of *Dr Jekyll and Mr Hyde* were sold in Britain in the next six months; the story was also vastly popular in the United States, where a quarter of a million copies had been sold by the turn of the century. Press and pulpit pontificated about the story, and Jekyll and Hyde became household names even in households which had not heard of Stevenson.

The bibliographer and critic, Montague Summers, remarked of the vogue for the first wave of Gothic fiction, by Mrs Radcliffe and others, that 'readers, it is presumed, delighted in imaginary terrors whilst the horrors of the French Revolution were being enacted all about them'. In London in 1886, such horrors did not seem altogether remote. On 10 February in that year, according to the historian, Gareth

Stedman Jones, 'London was visited by something akin to the *grande peur*'. The 1870s had been marked by a renewed assent to early Victorian platitudes, suggesting that the poor had only themselves to blame, and that state intervention to relieve poverty was positively injurious, as discouraging or thwarting the blossoming of the virtue of independence. In the 1880s, improvidence and thriftlessness were still impugned, but such 'sins' were to be attributed to the pressures of city existence; they were to be seen as symptoms rather than causes. Following cyclical depression from 1884 and riots in 1886 and 1887, the Charity Organisation Society became increasingly isolated in fretting about the effects of indiscriminate charity, and the middle-class public anxious only to avert the spectre of revolution. Charles Booth's *Life and Labour of the People* began appearing from 1889, and uncovered and documented a chronic poverty beyond the scope of charity which would have to become the responsibility of the state. As Albert Fried and Richard Elman, editors of the Penguin selection from Booth's work, remark, 'Booth's evidence thus demolished the middle-class myth that poverty resulted from personal failure, vice, or improvidence. Despite himself, he implicitly lent support to the socialist argument that poverty was a collective, not an individual, responsibility.'

On 8 February 1886, there was a meeting of the unemployed in Trafalgar Square. The cry was for public works and protective tariffs as a remedy for unemployment. Following altercations between adherents of the Fair Trade League, which had called the meeting, and members of the Social Democratic Federation, whose leading figure, H. M. Hyndman, endearingly combined Marxism with playing cricket for Middlesex, the meeting became a riot. 'In a word, the West End was for a couple of hours in the hands of the mob,' commented *The Times*, which considered the situation more alarming than that in 1848. Of the following day, the newspaper remarked that 'such a state of excitement and alarm has rarely been experienced in the Metropolis'. On 10 February, there were recurrent rumours both of socialist meetings and of advancing mobs, and though the rumours were false, the crowds of unemployed excited by them were genuine. For

William Morris, the February scare was 'the first skirmish of revolution'. Tension continued through the rest of 1886 and through 1887, reaching a further climax on 13 November 1887, 'Bloody Sunday', when police attacked demonstrators in Trafalgar Square, injuring two hundred and killing three. As with the February scare of 1886, the West End was in panic for weeks afterwards.

In *Danse Macabre*, his critical analysis of horror fictions, the doyen of modern horror novelists, Stephen King, states flatly that 'the writer of horror fiction is neither more nor less than an agent of the status quo', but also remarks that 'the best horror films ... manage to be reactionary, anarchistic and revolutionary all at the same time', and there is not really a contradiction: anarchistic and revolutionary potentialities must be invoked in order to be contained. Leaving aside for the moment the issue of containment, we may consider the extent to which Stevenson's story invited being read as invoking aspects of the social crisis of 1886. Following G. K. Chesterton's lead, Owen Dudley Edwards and others have insisted that Stevenson's London in the story uncannily resembles the writer's native Edinburgh. There are echoes of the great scientific tradition of Edinburgh in Jekyll's subordination of moral considerations to his scientific ambition. More substantially, the geography of Stevenson's London is really that of Edinburgh. Mansions backing on to mean streets are typical of Edinburgh but not of London. 'Yet Stevenson firmly asserted the location of his work was in London,' remarks Mr Dudley Edwards, and though no doubt Stevenson was imaginatively more familiarized with the terrain of his native Edinburgh, perhaps he had a point.

Though *Dr Jekyll and Mr Hyde* provided fodder for sermons, the story might seem subversive of the concept of moral choice. We gather that Stevenson's wife, Fanny, disapproved of the first draft of the story as being merely sensational, when it might have been an allegory. Stevenson then burnt the first draft, perhaps in a fit of pique, and allegedly set about composing Fanny's allegory. But an incongruous element of determinism thwarts the allegory, so that instead of being provided with a guide to future action, the reader may be left feeling merely compromised by circumstance. This was the response to the story of John Addington Symonds, who had become friendly with Stevenson as a fellow-convalescent at Davos. Symonds pronounced in a letter to Stevenson, intriguingly if obscurely: 'the fact is that, viewed as an allegory, it touches one too closely'. He went on to expand. 'Physical and biological science on a hundred lines is reducing individual freedom to zero, and weakening the sense of responsibility. I doubt whether the artist should lend his genius to this grim argument.' Symonds had been discussing the story, along with a novel by Oliver Wendell Holmes, with Sir Thomas Lauder Brunton, a Scottish physiologist renowned for his work on the effects of drugs. 'I could see that, though a Christian, he held very feebly to the theory of human liberty; and these two books of fiction interested him, as *Dr Jekyll* does me, upon that point at issue.' Symonds enthused in comparison over the conclusion to Dostoevsky's *Crime and Punishment*, where the murderer, Raskolnikov, in Siberian exile, is converted to Christianity. 'How fine is that ending! Had you made your hero act thus, you would at least have saved the sense of human dignity.' *Dr Jekyll and Mr Hyde*, however, remained 'indeed a dreadful book because of a certain moral callousness, a want of sympathy, a shutting out of hope'.

Such a reading puts the story in touch with middle-class preoccupations in the 1880s, as the attribution of free will to the masses of the poor came to seem increasingly implausible. For an alleged allegory, there is an odd tendency in the story to present instances of anti-social behaviour as ineluctable. The Scottish lawyer, Utterson, is renowned for his own tolerance, but a similar tolerance is implicit in the commentary in the narration: 'in this character it was frequently his fortune to be the last reputable acquaintance and the last good influence in the lives of down-going men'. 'Down-going' does not suggest volition on the part of the men concerned. Enfield describes Hyde trampling the little girl as being not 'like a man; it was like some damned Juggernaut'. 'Juggernaut' means lord of the world, one of the titles of the god, Krishna, but refers more specifically to the annual custom of dragging the idol of the god in procession on a huge chariot, under the wheels of which devotees hurled themselves to be crushed. The god would seem innocent twice over of the deaths of the devotees, in that his idol is being dragged on a chariot, before which his worshippers insist on immolating themselves.

For the modern reader, connotations of an ineluctable 'return of the repressed' may attach to the name of 'Hyde'. The story pre-dates psychoanalysis. A few years later, F. W. H. Myers was to write an enthusiastic summary of the 'Preliminary Communication' with which Breuer and Freud anticipated and advertised *Studies on Hysteria*. The summary was published in *Proceedings of the Society for Psychical Research* in June 1893, 'so the first discoveries in what later became psychoanalysis were accessible to English readers within six months of their being announced,' remarks Freud's biographer, Ernest Jones; but the discoveries were too late to have influenced *Dr Jekyll and Mr Hyde*. Obviously, though, if Freud's theories were correct, the phenomenon of the 'return of the repressed' existed prior to being labelled, and Freud recurrently complimented poets, novelists and philosophers whose intuitions anticipated his theories.

Freud does not seem to have read *Dr Jekyll and Mr Hyde*, but doubtless would have been interested. In his 'Full Statement of the Case', Jekyll remarks: 'many a man would even have blazoned such irregularities as I was guilty of; but from the high views that I had set before me, I regarded and hid them with an almost morbid sense of shame. It was thus rather the exacting nature of my aspirations, than any particular degradation in my faults, that made me what I was ...' In *Civilization and Its Discontents*, Freud defines ethics 'as a therapeutic attempt – as an endeavour to achieve, by means of a command of the super-ego, something which has so far not been achieved by means of any other cultural activities'. Freud complains of 'the ethical demands of the cultural super-ego' in the same terms as of those of the super-ego of the individual.

It issues a command and does not ask whether it is possible for people to obey it. On the contrary, it assumes that a man's ego is psychologically capable of anything that is required of it, that his ego has unlimited mastery over his id. This is a mistake; and even in what are known as normal people the id cannot be controlled beyond certain limits. If more is demanded of a man, a revolt will be produced in him or a neurosis, or he will be made unhappy.

Of course, Jekyll is trying to cope with the problem in his own way by separating off his id in the form of Hyde, so that Jekyll may comply with ethical demands while allowing his id licence. Not surprisingly, however, even with the aid of potions, the attempt is a failure, and Jekyll half-reneges on his supposed discovery 'that man is not truly one, but truly two', in favour of a notion of identity or lack of identity that is much closer to Freud's own conception of the id, and in the light of which the thought of clean divorces between constituent elements can hardly be entertained. 'I say two, because the state of my own knowledge does not pass beyond that point. Others will follow, others will outstrip me on the same lines; and I hazard the guess that man will be ultimately known for a mere polity of multifarious, incongruous and independent denizens.'

There are recurrent allusions in the story to Hyde's stunted growth or to his appearing sub-human. Hyde is reported to be 'pale and dwarfish; he gave an impression of deformity, without any namable malformation...' 'Something troglodytic, shall we say?' muses Utterson. Clubbing to death Sir Danvers Carew, Hyde proceeds 'with ape-like fury', and not just his fury is ape-like. As Hyde's nature predominates over Jekyll's, the hand which Jekyll wakes to see on the bed-clothes is 'lean, corded, knuckly, of a dusky pallor, and thickly shaded with a swart growth of hair'. There is a respectable explanation at least of the dwarfishness in Jekyll's 'Full Statement of the Case'. The evil aspect of Jekyll's nature had been less developed and also less exhausted than the virtuous aspect. 'And hence, as I think, it came about that Edward Hyde was so much smaller, slighter and younger than Henry Jekyll.' On the other hand, social commentators in the 1880s constantly reported seeing Hyde-like creatures on the streets of London, so that Jekyll's interpretation in the 'Full Statement' may not be the last word.

The story has linked Hyde with the poor of London in

providing him with a house in Soho. Like the East End, the focus of middle-class anxieties, Soho was renowned for its slums. Utterson descends on Soho with a policeman:

As the cab drew up before the address indicated, the fog lifted a little and showed him a dingy street, a gin palace, a low French eating-house, many ragged children huddled in doorways, and many women of many different nationalities passing out, key in hand, to have a morning glass; and the next moment the fog settled down again upon that part, as brown as umber, and cut him off from his blackguardly surroundings. This was the home of Henry Jekyll's favourite; of a man who was heir to a quarter of a million sterling.

Such a choice of location seems pointed, and readers would have been liable to attribute similar looks to those of Hyde to his neighbours without prospects. In 1885, James Cantlie imputed the alleged degeneration of Londoners to a lack of ozone in the air. With difficulty he had managed to find a pure third-generation Londoner, who proceeded to confirm Cantlie's forebodings: 'height, 5 ft 1 in; age 21, chest measurement 28 in; his head measured across from tip of ear to tip of ear, 11 in ($1\frac{1}{2}$ in below the average). His aspect is pale, waxy; he is very narrow between the eyes and with a decided squint!' In 1886, the year in which *Dr Jekyll and Mr Hyde* became a popular literary sensation, Lord Brabazon advised: 'Let the reader walk through the wretched streets ... of the Eastern or Southern districts of London ... should he be of average height, he will find himself a head taller than those around him; he will see on all sides pale faces, stunted figures, debilitated forms, narrow chests, and all the outward signs of a low vital power.' The full title of the story is the 'Strange Case of Dr Jekyll and Mr Hyde'; evidently, however, at least in some respects, Hyde is not merely an isolated 'case'.

While allowing that the phenomenon described by the sociologists was a real one, Gareth Stedman Jones suggests that the theory of urban degeneration provided 'not in fact an adequate explanation of London poverty, but rather a mental landscape within which the middle class could recognize and articulate their own anxieties about urban existence'. The theory smoothed the way for the middle class to acknowledge the evidence that poverty was a problem of growing masses of the population, rather than the consequence of the imprudence or bad luck of isolated individuals. The terminology borrowed from Darwin absolved the middle class of responsibility or blame for the crisis. Life in the city was a battle in which the fittest survived. There was no justification for rigging conditions to eke out the existence of the unfit, as there had been none for cosseting those in the old category of undeserving poor, even though the state would have to intervene to solve the problem of swelling armies of the unfit. The images of Hyde as ape-like insist on him as being unfit, as being insufficiently evolved to meet the present conditions of existence. The story, however, is ambivalent in relation to the theory of urban degeneration. Though consoling in some respects, the theory did not preclude the rising armies of the unfit being an alarming spectacle. *Dr Jekyll and Mr Hyde* is thus in part, and particularly in conclusion, an ideological reworking of ideology. Paradoxically, but not surprisingly, in view of the meanderings to which ideology is prone, this involves a return to the simple moralism for the collapse of credence in which the theory of urban degeneration arose to compensate. There was applause in the pulpits and elsewhere since the doctrine that individuals were solely to blame for their miseries, exceptional cases of misfortune aside, was more comforting than the new theory which acknowledged the problem of mass poverty. The doctrine was also now manifestly vulnerable, but temporarily, while listening to a sermon or reading the story, that might be overlooked.

The project of separating Hyde from Jekyll, so that 'the unjust might go his way, delivered from the aspirations and remorse of his more upright twin; and the just could walk steadfastly and securely on his upward path, doing the good things in which he found pleasure, and no longer exposed to disgrace and penitence by the hands of this extraneous evil', might seem to the reader a typical Gothic extravagance. This, too, however, finds a local habitation and a name in the social history of the 1880s, and specifically in the housing crisis which first drew attention to the existence of mass poverty and so heralded the triumph of the theory of degeneration over that of demoralization. The focus of middle-class anxiety was less overcrowding than the way in which the housing crisis was forcing the 'respectable' working classes into proximity with the casual poor or 'residuum'. In 1883, George Sims declared that 'often is the family of an honest working man, compelled to take refuge in a thieves' kitchen ... there can be no question that numbers of habitual criminals would never have become such, had they not by force of circumstance been packed together with those who were hardened by crime'. The situation was to provoke increasing concern, since the 'respectable' working classes were suffering and 'agitators', at least, were abandoning distinctions between respectable and residuum in favour of the inclusive term, 'unemployed'. As Stedman Jones remarks, 'the dangerous possibility existed that the respectable working class, under the stress of prolonged unemployment, might throw in its lot with the casual poor'.

Lanyon comments in relation to Hyde on 'the odd, subjective disturbance caused by his neighbourhood. This bore some resemblance to incipient rigor, and was accompanied by a marked sinking of the pulse.' This is the force to contaminate of the degenerate residuum, and in this respect Stevenson's parable is implicitly gloomy: the residuum resists being dissociated from the respectable elements and ultimately corrupts them. If the residuum formed a revolutionary combination with hitherto respectable sectors of the working class, then philanthropists such as Jekyll would be next to be overrun. The story, which according to Stevenson was prompted by a dream, condenses this ultimate fear with fear of the preliminary of the respectable working classes being contaminated.

Jekyll is 'one of your fellows who do what they call good': Hyde is the 'man who was heir to a quarter of a million sterling'. The speculation concerning Jekyll's relations with Hyde reflects a standard version of middle-class attitudes in the 1880s to the agitated poor. 'He was wild when he was young; a long while ago, to be sure; but in the law of God there is no statute of limitations. Ah, it must be that; the ghost of some old sin, the cancer of some concealed disgrace; punishment coming, *pede claudo*, years after memory has forgotten and self-love condoned the fault.' In a well-known passage,

Beatrice Webb referred to a crisis of conscience among the middle class in the 1880s as prompting a concern with the condition of the poor.

The origin of the ferment is to be discovered in a new consciousness of sin among men of intellect and men of property ... The consciousness of sin was a collective or class consciousness; a growing uneasiness, amounting to conviction, that the industrial organization, which had yielded rent, interest and profits on a stupendous scale, had failed to provide a decent livelihood and tolerable conditions for a majority of the inhabitants of Great Britain.

This, however, was a relatively self-flattering perspective. The motivation was not guilt but fear, as is suggested by the lack of tenderness in contemporary descriptions of the poor, who were brutish, but evidently a threat: thus is Hyde depicted. The Mansion House appeal for the unemployed was launched in January 1886, but attracted little support until the February riot and subsequent panic, when a sense of sin encompassed even the Stock Exchange, a generous contributor. In the story, Jekyll steps up his philanthropic activities after Hyde has murdered Sir Danvers Carew: 'whilst he had always been known for charities, he was now no less distinguished for religion. He was busy ... he did good; his face seemed to open and brighten, as if with an inward consciousness of service ...'

Dr Jekyll and Mr Hyde is in much closer relation to the historical actuality of the 1880s than, say, an Agatha Christie novel of the 1930s is liable to be in relation to that of the Great Depression. Agatha Christie was a giantess among best-sellers, but whether such a degree of social evasiveness as we find in her fiction is characteristic of best-sellers is perhaps a moot point: as was suggested earlier, alarming potentialities must be invoked in order to be contained. Thus the popular appeal of *Dr Jekyll and Mr Hyde* may have derived as much from the story's daring proximity to prevalent anxieties as from administering balm: such daring made the balm more sweet. Social anxieties are expressed in a highly condensed way in a story of a specific and outlandish 'case', and better still, a case which is alleged to be not symptomatic of the 1880s in particular, thus

further diluting the shock of the new: 'strange as my circumstances were, the terms of this debate are as old and commonplace as man; much the same inducements and alarms cast the
die for any tempted and trembling sinner; and it fell out with
me, as it falls with so vast a majority of my fellows, that I chose
the better part and was found wanting in the strength to keep
to it'.

The other stories in this selection must be considered more
cursorily, but they are chosen as having at least a Gothic aura
in common with *Dr Jekyll and Mr Hyde* – 'Markheim' and
'Thrawn Janet' are stories of the supernatural, and even the
superficially more genial novella, *The Misadventures of John
Nicholson*, includes murder, robbery and madness – and also as
being similarly preoccupied with the issue worrying John
Addington Symonds: the sense of the reduction of individual
moral freedom to zero. That the issue is a speciality of late
nineteenth-century Gothic fiction – Rider Haggard's and
Bram Stoker's as well as Stevenson's – is presumably no
accident. Gothic is renowned for touching on themes which
realism cannot reach, especially when fears for the future are
involved, as in the major example of Mary Shelley's *Franken-
stein*; but also for distancing such fears, since they are evoked in
what purport to be mere supernatural or melodramatic tales:
as Franco Moretti has insisted, Gothic is at once expressive
and evasive.

'A Lodging for the Night' was the first of Stevenson's stories
to be published, in *Temple Bar* in October 1877. It shows
Stevenson as engaged with the issue of moral relativism before
his running preoccupation was liable to chime with the public
mood, since the economic prosperity of the 1870s allowed
early Victorian platitudes to stay intact. The character of
François Villon in the story is not implied to the amiable:
'Greed had made folds about his eyes, evil smiles had puckered
his mouth.The wolf and pig struggled together in his face.'
The question is whether the 'evil' is absolute, or forced on
Villon by circumstances and poverty in particular. Even-
tually, Villon is provided with his lodging for the night by the
lord of Brisetout. Brisetout claims to be an honourable soldier,
and Villon allows the claim, while conceding his own lack of

honour and that there is a gulf between them. He adds, however: 'If I had been born lord of Brisetout, and you had been the poor scholar Francis, would the difference have been any the less? Should not I have been warming my knees at this charcoal pan, and would not you have been groping for farthings in the snow? Should not I have been the soldier, and you the thief?' The debate continues, until Brisetout wearies of the subversive frankness of his self-invited guest and bids him be off, and contemporary readers may have felt that Brisetout achieved at least a draw, but the story is then bracingly daring in according Villon the last word: 'A very dull old gentleman ... I wonder what his goblets may be worth.'

'The Body-Snatcher', written in 1881, tends to be classed as a pot-boiler, and is undoubtedly bland and orthodox in comparison with 'A Lodging for the Night', but it is perhaps a moot point whether the story is conventional because a pot-boiler, or suggests itself as a pot-boiler in being merely conventional. If the latter, there may be other reasons by 1881 for adopting a conventional line. The story concludes with the body-snatchers unearthing a female corpse from the grave-yard, only to find that the corpse metamorphoses into that of a man whom one of them has murdered while the other connived at the murder, 'the body of the dead and long-dissected Grey'. Providence, at least, is alive and alert, and ready to punish the evil-doer. Even in this story, however, doubt is cast on evil as being an absolute moral category. It is by insidious stages that the protagonist, Fettes, is led to conniving at murder. This might still be consistent rather than inconsistent with endorsing moral absolutism. *The Times* invoked George Eliot's *Romola* in relation to Stevenson, and Tito Melema in *Romola* is a typical George Eliot reprobate progressing ineluctably from venial sins to less venial ones, in his own case, murder. The moral is to be perpetually all ears to the whispering voice of your conscience, or once deaf, always deaf, and the slippery slope beckons. Whether in *Romola* or 'The Body-Snatcher', however, this would imply that in effect sinners have only the one chance to exercise moral choice, which might be suspected of conceding dangerously much to the circumstantial heresy of François Villon in 'A Lodging for the Night'.

The kinship between the two doctrines is suggested in 'Markheim', written in 1885, in which providential machinery is accorded an even higher profile than in 'The Body-Snatcher', since the devil makes an appearance. The recent murderer, Markheim, defends himself in the face of super-natural prosecution: 'Hitherto I have been driven with revolt to what I would not; I was a bond-slave to poverty, driven and scourged.' The devil easily recuperates for morality this line in determinism. 'Fifteen years ago you would have started at theft. Three years back you would have blenched at the name of murder. Is there any crime, is there any cruelty or mean-ness, from which you still recoil? – five years from now I shall detect you in the fact! Downward, downward, lies your way; nor can anything but death avail to stop you.' Triumphantly, Markheim confutes both his own determinism and the conces-sions typical of the devil and George Eliot to the circumstan-tial heresy by demonstrating that there may be morality even after murder, refusing to take the devil's insidious tip to kill the maid who would detect the murder of her employer, and instead volunteering a confession: 'You had better go for the police ... I have killed your master.'

'Thrawn Janet', first published in the *Cornhill Magazine* in October 1881, would seem to insist on the existence of God and the devil, and the respective categories of virtue and vice, as against secular heresies. Janet having been ducked by the villagers to test whether she is a witch, the minister argues that she has never been the same afterwards because 'The folks' cruelty ... had gi'en her a stroke of the palsy.' The devil, however, has indeed possessed Janet, until exorcised by the minister, or so we gather. Janet's story is narrated in Scottish dialect by 'one of the older folk' who 'would warm into courage over his third tumbler, and recount the cause of the minister's strange looks and solitary life'. A more sophisticated or at any rate anglicized voice introduces the reminiscence, and thereafter supplies footnotes for presumably sophisticated readers who will not be inward with Scottish dialect or folklore. 'It was a common belief in Scotland that the devil appeared as a black man. This appears in several witch trials and I think in Law's *Memorials*, that delightful storehouse of the quaint and grisly.' Moreover, Janet is described as being precisely the kind of unfortunate or mild eccentric that in historical actuality attracted suspicion of being a witch; 'she had had a wean to a dragoon: she hadnae come forrit for maybe thretty year; and bairns had seen her mumblin' to hersel' up on Key's Loan in the gloamin', whilk was an unco time an' place for a God-fearin' woman'. Thus the tendency of the story as a whole is to leave the validity of the theological and moral fundamentalism of the narrator of Janet's history at least open to question, with perhaps the implication predominating that such beliefs, like those recorded in Law's *Memorials*, are merely 'quaint and grisly'.

The final story in this selection is *The Misadventures of John Nicholson*, published in 1887. The mood of the story is light-hearted compared with the Gothic intensity of the preceding tales, and it was conceived and published as a Christmas tale. It is also, however, an extended commentary on the lack of necessary connection between the careers of down-going men and any real guilt. Gothic fiction is expressive partly on condition of being evasive: the same is liable to be true of the Christmas tale, whose cheery connotations might provide cover for dealing with potentially dark themes. *The Misadventures of John Nicholson* is an intriguing corrective to 'The Body-Snatcher' and 'Markheim', with their insistence that the destiny of the individual is shaped by the display or lack of display of moral character. Like the mass of poor in the 1880s, John Nicholson demonstrates the possibility of being wretched without being sinful.

I dwell, even at the risk of tedium, on John's minutest errors, his case being so perplexing to the moralist; but we have done with them now, the roll is closed, the reader has the worst of our poor hero, and I leave him to judge for himself whether he or John has been the less deserving. Henceforth we have to follow the spectacle of a man who was a mere whip-top for calamity; on whose unmerited misadventures not even the humourist can look without pity, and not even the philosopher without alarm.

The protagonist suffering misadventures also strikes it rich on the Stock Exchange in San Francisco, which, however, no more than the misadventures, is implied to be attributable to moral character.

In an essay on 'The Politics of Stevenson', Christopher Harvie has suggested that 'the sombre subject-matter of the later novels was to some extent due to the interaction of Stevenson's own powerful personal preoccupations with those of a predominantly middle-class critical coterie and readership'. Stevenson's preoccupations with questions of morality and of the relation between destiny and moral character is evidently linked with his Scottish Calvinist inheritance. In the 1880s, however, such questions also preoccupied a middle-class public without such an inheritance. The best-selling status of *Dr Jekyll and Mr Hyde* in the mid-1880s, is thus to some degree a satire of circumstance akin to those which were to inform *The Misadventures of John Nicholson*. Alternatively, it might be thought that a wheel had come full circle. Engels wrote of Calvin: 'His predestination doctrine was the religious expression of the fact that in the commercial world of competition success or failure does not depend upon a man's activity or cleverness, but upon circumstances uncontrollable by him. It is not of him that willeth or of him that runneth, but of the mercy of unknown superior economic powers.'

Nicholas Rance

NICHOLAS RANCE is Senior Lecturer in English at Middlesex University and author of *The Historical Novel and Popular Politics in Nineteenth-Century England* and *Wilkie Collins and Other Sensation Novelists: Walking the Moral Hospital*.

SELECT BIBLIOGRAPHY

There is a significant diversity of interpretations of *Dr Jekyll and Mr Hyde*: I have added another one, rather than try to sum up what has gone before, but give some indication here of the critical range.

CALDER, JENNI, ed., *Stevenson and Victorian Scotland*, Edinburgh University Press, 1981. A collection of high-class critical and biographical essays, including Christopher Harvie's 'The Politics of Stevenson', referred to in the introduction.

DUDLEY EDWARDS, OWEN, *The Quest for Sherlock Holmes*, Penguin, 1984. Includes a stirring evocation of Stevenson's Edinburgh: Stevenson, as a contemporary young writer who was rapidly making a name, was a model and inspiration for the slightly junior native of Edinburgh, Arthur Conan Doyle.

FURNAS, J. C., *Voyage to Windward: The Life of Robert Louis Stevenson*, Faber and Faber, 1952. Though by no means the latest, the best biography of Stevenson.

MAIXNER, PAUL, ed., *Robert Louis Stevenson: The Critical Heritage*, Routledge & Kegan Paul, 1981. A most useful collection of early reviews and appreciations, including the correspondence between Stevenson and John Addington Symonds.

MILLER, KARL, *Doubles: Studies in Literary History*, Oxford University Press, 1985. Includes a chapter anticipating Elaine Showalter's more developed thesis that Jekyll and probably Stevenson were 'queer fellows'.

MORETTI, FRANCO, *Signs Taken for Wonders: Essays in the Sociology of Literary Form*, Verso, 1983. Includes a dazzling essay on nineteenth-century Gothic fiction.

PUNTER, DAVID, *The Literature of Terror: A History of Gothic Fictions from 1765 to the present day*, Longman, 1980. Useful on Gothic fiction generally, and approaches *Dr Jekyll and Mr Hyde* in the light of 'the particular difficulties encountered by English imperialism in its decline'.

SHOWALTER, ELAINE, *Sexual Anarchy: Gender and Culture at the 'Fin de Siècle'*, Bloomsbury, 1991. Includes a powerful chapter arguing for Jekyll as a closet homosexual.

STEDMAN JONES, GARETH, *Outcast London: A Study in the Relationship Between Classes in Victorian Society*, Oxford University Press, 1971. Not surprisingly, Stevenson is not mentioned, but the book provides a key to understanding the popular success of *Dr Jekyll and Mr Hyde*.

VEEDER, WILLIAM, and HIRSH, GORDON, eds., *Dr Jekyll and Mr Hyde after One Hundred Years*, University of Chicago Press, 1988. Theoretically sophisticated: both critic and ultimately the act of criticism emerge as sharing Jekyll's complexity as a 'mere polity of multifarious, incongruous and independent denizens'.

CHRONOLOGY

DATE	AUTHOR'S LIFE	LITERARY CONTEXT
1850	Edinburgh, 13th November: birth of Robert Louis (originally Lewis), son of Thomas Stevenson, joint-engineer to the Board of Northern Lighthouses.	First publication of Wordsworth's *Prelude*. Death of Wordsworth. Herbert Spencer: *Social Statics*. Dickens: *David Copperfield*. Hawthorne: *The Scarlet Letter*. Death of Balzac. Turgenev: *A Month in the Country*.
1851		Melville: *Moby-Dick*.
1853		
1854		Birth of Oscar Wilde. Dickens: *Hard Times*. Thoreau: *Walden*. Elizabeth Gaskell: *Mary Barton, A Tale of Manchester Life*.
1855		Trollope: *The Warden*. Lewes: *Life of Goethe*. Elizabeth Gaskell: *North and South*. Turgenev: *Russian Life in the Interior or the Experiences of a Sportsman*.
1856		Flaubert: *Madame Bovary*. Turgenev: *Rudin*. George Eliot translates Spinoza, *Ethics* (published by Chapman). Baudelaire: *Les Fleurs du mal*.
1857		Dickens: *Little Dorrit*.
1859		George Eliot: *Adam Bede*, first published novel. Darwin: *The Origin of Species*. J. S. Mill: *On Liberty*. Dickens: *A Tale of Two Cities*.
1860		George Eliot: *The Mill on the Floss*. Wilkie Collins: *The Woman in White* appears in volume form. Dickens: *Great Expectations*.

First Exhibition at the Crystal Palace. Don Pacifico. Californian gold rush.

Great Exhibition. Dismissal of Palmerston. French *coup d'état*. Livingstone reaches Zambesi.
Crimean War begins.

Palmerston becomes Prime Minister. Fall of Sebastopol. *Daily Telegraph* founded.

Western Union founded. Crimean War ends. Peace of Paris. Birth of Freud.

Defeat and return of Palmerston. Indian Mutiny. Divorce Act.

DATE	AUTHOR'S LIFE	LITERARY CONTEXT
1867	Enters Edinburgh University.	Turgenev: *Fathers and Sons* (translation Eugene Schuyler). Trollope: *The Last Chronicle of Barset.*
1871	Gives up engineering for law (April).	George Eliot: *Middlemarch.* Henry James: *Watch and Ward* – first novel – serialized in *Atlantic Monthly.* Dostoevsky: *The Devils.*
1872	Visits Germany with Sir Walter Simpson (July). Passes preliminary examinations for the Scottish bar (November).	Twain: *Roughing it.*
1873	Meets Sidney Colvin.	Twain: *The Guilded Age* in collaboration with C. Dudley Warner.
1874	France: Menton (April). Edinburgh and Swanston, London and Hampstead with Colvin (May–June). Resumes law classes in November.	Hardy: *Far From The Madding Crowd.*
1875	Meets W. E. Henley who becomes a close friend. Stevenson is admitted to Scottish bar (July). Returns to France and meets Mrs Fanny Van de Grift Osbourne. Returns to Edinburgh in September.	Henry James: *Roderick Hudson* and *A Passionate Pilgrim and other Tales.* Twain: *Old Times on the Mississippi.* Births of Thomas Mann and John Buchan.
1878	Paris (March). Edinburgh and Swanston (April-May). Publication of *An Inland Voyage.* London and Paris. Fanny Osbourne goes back to America (August). *Picturesque Notes on Edinburgh* (December).	Hardy: *The Return of the Native.* George Eliot finishes her work: *Problems of Life and Mind.* Henry James: *Daisy Miller* and *The Europeans.*
1879	Writing *Deacon Brodie* (January). France. *Travels with a Donkey in the Cévennes* (June). Embarks for America and spends the next months with Fanny Osbourne and her family (August).	George Meredith: *The Egoist.* George Eliot: *Impressions of Theophrastus Such* (essays). Henry James: *Hawthorne.* Ibsen: *A Doll's House.*
1880	Marries Fanny in San Francisco, 19th May. Returns to England with wife and stepson Lloyd (August).	Deaths of George Eliot and Flaubert. Henry Adams: *Democracy.* Dostoevsky: *The Brothers Karamazov.*

CHRONOLOGY

DATE	AUTHOR'S LIFE	LITERARY CONTEXT
1881	Meets John Addington Symonds. *Virginibus Puerisque* (April).	Wilde: *Poems.* Joel Chandler Harris: *Uncle Remus, His Songs and Sayings.* James: *The Portrait of a Lady.* Deaths of Dostoevsky and Carlisle.
1882	*Familiar Studies of Men and Books* (April). *New Arabian Nights* (August). Goes to South of France to look for a residence, with Bob Stevenson; is rejoined by Fanny at Marseilles (September).	Death of Trollope.
1883	Spends the year in France. *The Silverado Squatters* and *Treasure Island* (December).	Maupassant: *Une Vie.* Nietzsche: *Thus Spoke Zarathustra.*
1884	Excursion to Nice, where Stevenson is taken ill (January). Returns to Hyères (February). Outbreak of cholera at Hyères; returns to London at the end of the month (July). *Admiral Guinea.*	Twain: *The Adventures of Huckleberry Finn.*
1885	*A Child's Garden of Verses* (March). *More New Arabian Nights*, with Fanny (May). *Prince Otto* (November).	W. D. Howells: *The Rise of Silas Lapham.* Maupassant: *Bel Ami.*
1886	*Strange Case of Dr Jekyll and Mr Hyde* (January). *Kidnapped* (July).	Henry James: *Princess Casamassima* and *The Bostonians.* Hardy: *The Mayor of Casterbridge.*
1887	Death of Thomas Stevenson. *Underwoods.* Sails for America with Fanny, Lloyd and Mrs Thomas Stevenson. Arrives in New York City, 7 August. *Memories and Portraits. The Merry Men* (December).	Walter Pater: *Imaginary Portraits.*
1888	San Francisco. Sets out on first South Seas voyage, aboard the *Casco*, 28 June. The Marquesas Islands (July-August). The Sandwich Islands (December). *The Black Arrow*, a historical romance.	Wilde: *The Happy Prince and other Tales.* Henry James: *The Aspern Papers.* William Morris: *A Dream of John Ball.*

CHRONOLOGY

HISTORICAL EVENTS

Invention of the incandescent lamp. 'Otto' bicycle patented. Tsar
Alexander II assassinated.

Deaths of Garibaldi and Darwin. Married Women's Property Act.

Deaths of Marx, Wagner, Turgenev and Manet. Fabian Society. Maxim
gun.

Oscar Hammerstein invents the first Practical Cigar Rolling Machine. The
first Negro plays Major League baseball. First Oxford Chair of English.
Third Reform Bill.

Fall of Khartoum. Salisbury becomes Prime Minister.

Meeting of the unemployed in Trafalgar Square becomes a riot
(8 February). Gladstone becomes Prime Minister. First Home Rule for
Ireland Bill. Greenwich bomb outrage. Cunninghame Graham becomes
MP. Liberal split.

Queen Victoria's Golden Jubilee. 'Bloody Sunday' (police attack
demonstrators in Trafalgar Square: 200 injured and 3 killed). Graham
arrested. Independent Labour Party.

Match girls' strike in London. Gladstone's First Home Rule Bill defeated.
Wilhelm II becomes Kaiser.

DATE	AUTHOR'S LIFE	LITERARY CONTEXT
1889	Honolulu (June). *The Wrong Box* with Lloyd Osbourne. Sets out on second cruise, aboard the *Equator*, to the Gilbert Islands. *The Master of Ballantrae* (September). Samoa. Purchases estate in Upolu (December).	Wilde: *The Portrait of Mr W.H.* Twain: *A Connecticut Yankee at King Arthur's Court.* Charles Booth: *Life and Labour of the People* begins publication.
1890	Sydney (February). *Father Damien: an open letter to the Reverend Dr Hyde of Honolulu* (March). Third cruise, aboard the *Janet Nicoll*, to Gilberts, Marshalls and other islands (April–August). Week's stay, August, at Noumea, New Caledonia, while wife and stepson continue cruise. Settles in Samoa (October).	Wilde: *The Picture of Dorian Gray* and *The Critic as Artist.* Henry James: *The Tragic Muse.* Death of Newman.
1891	Excursion to Sydney, to meet mother returning from Scotland (January). *Ballads*.	Hardy: *Tess of the D'Urbervilles.* Gissing: *New Grub Street* and *The Odd Women.* Shaw: *Quintessence of Ibsenism.* Howells: *A Modern Instance.* Birth of Neil Gunn.
1892	*Across the Plains* (April). *A Footnote to History* (August).	Wilde: *Lady Windermere's Fan* published and *Salome* banned. Birth of Hugh MacDiarmid, pseudonym of Christopher Murray Grieve.
1893	Sydney (February). *Island Nights' Entertainments* (April). Outbreak of war in Samoa (August). Honolulu. *David Balfour* (September–October). *Catriona* (sequel to *Kidnapped*).	Stephen Crane: *The Red Badge of Courage.* Wilde: *A Woman of No Importance.*
1894	*The Ebb-Tide*, with Lloyd Osbourne (September). Dies from a brain haemorrhage, 3 December, while working on his unfinished masterpiece, *Weir of Hermiston* (1896).	Twain: *The Tragedy of Pudd'nhead Wilson.* Wilde: *Salome* and *The Sphynx.* Kipling: *The Jungle Book.*

CHRONOLOGY

HISTORICAL EVENTS

Large central area of the Indian territory opened; huge land rush. Eiffel Tower built. Death of Browning. Birth of Hitler. Dock strike.

Fall of Bismarck. Deaths of Van Gogh, Cardinal Newman, César Franck. Parnell resigns as Irish Nationalist leader.

Death of Parnell. Free elementary education. US International Copyright Bill: improved authors' finances.

Ellis Island established as a receiving station for immigrants. Death of Tennyson.

Severe financial panics. Keir Hardie forms Independent Labour Party. Karl Benz' four-wheeled car. Deaths of Maupassant and Tschaikovsky.

Dreyfus affair. Nicholas II becomes Tsar. Gladstone resigns, having split Liberals over Home Rule.

STRANGE CASE OF
DR. JEKYLL AND MR. HYDE

STRANGE CASE OF
DR. JEKYLL AND MR. HYDE

Story of the Door

MR. UTTERSON the lawyer was a man of a rugged countenance, that was never lighted by a smile; cold, scanty and embarrassed in discourse; backward in sentiment; lean, long, dusty, dreary, and yet somehow lovable. At friendly meetings, and when the wine was to his taste, something eminently human beaconed from his eye; something indeed which never found its way into his talk, but which spoke not only in these silent symbols of the after-dinner face, but more often and loudly in the acts of his life. He was austere with himself; drank gin when he was alone, to mortify a taste for vintages; and though he enjoyed the theatre, had not crossed the doors of one for twenty years. But he had an approved tolerance for others; sometimes wondering, almost with envy, at the high pressure of spirits involved in their misdeeds; and in any extremity inclined to help rather than to reprove. "I incline to Cain's heresy," he used to say quaintly: "I let my brother go to the devil in his own way." In this character, it was frequently his fortune to be the last reputable acquaintance and the last good influence in the lives of down-going men. And to such as these, so long as they came about his chambers, he never marked a shade of change in his demeanour.

No doubt the feat was easy to Mr. Utterson; for he was undemonstrative at the best, and even his friendships seemed to be founded in a similar catholicity of good-nature. It is the mark of a modest man to accept his friendly circle ready-made from the hands of opportunity; and that was the lawyer's way. His friends were those of his own blood, or those whom he had known the longest; his affections, like ivy, were the growth of time, they implied no aptness in the object. Hence, no doubt, the bond that united him to Mr. Richard Enfield, his distant kinsman, the well-known man about town. It was a nut to crack for many, what these two could see in each other or what subject they could find in common. It was reported by those who encountered them in their Sunday walks that they said nothing, looked singularly dull, and would hail with obvious relief the appearance of a friend. For all that, the two men put the greatest store by these excursions, counted them the chief jewel of each week, and not only set aside occasions of pleasure, but even resisted the calls of business, that they might enjoy them uninterrupted.

It chanced on one of these rambles that their way led them down a by-street in a busy quarter of London. The street was small, and what is called quiet, but it drove a thriving trade on the week-days. The inhabitants were all doing well, it seemed, and all emulously hoping to do better still, and laying out the surplus of their gains in coquetry; so that the shop-fronts stood along that thoroughfare with an air of invitation, like rows of smiling saleswomen. Even on Sunday, when it veiled its more florid charms and lay comparatively empty of passage, the street shone out in contrast to its dingy neighbourhood, like a fire in a forest; and with its freshly painted shutters, well-polished brasses, and general cleanliness and gaiety of note, instantly caught and pleased the eye of the passenger.

Two doors from one corner on the left hand going east, the line was broken by the entry of a court; and just at that point a certain sinister block of building thrust forward its gable on the street. It was two stories high; showed no window, nothing but a door on the lower story and a blind forehead of discoloured wall on the upper; and bore in every feature the marks of prolonged and sordid negligence. The door, which was equipped with neither bell nor knocker, was blistered and distained. Tramps slouched into the recess and struck matches on the panels; children kept shop upon the steps; the schoolboy had tried his knife on the mouldings; and for close on a generation no one had appeared to drive away these random visitors or to repair their ravages.

Mr. Enfield and the lawyer were on the other side of the by-street, but when they came abreast of the entry, the former lifted up his cane and pointed.

"Did you ever remark that door?" he asked; and when his companion had replied in the affirmative, "it is connected in my mind," added he, "with a very odd story."

"Indeed?" said Mr. Utterson, with a slight change of voice, "and what was that?"

"Well, it was this way," returned Mr. Enfield: "I was coming home from some place at the end of the world, about three o'clock of a black winter morning, and my way lay through a part of town where there was literally nothing to be seen but lamps. Street after street, and all the folks asleep – street after street, all lighted up as if for a procession and all as empty as a church – till at last I got into that state of mind when a man listens and listens and begins to long for the sight of a policeman. All at once I saw two figures: one a little man who was stumping along eastward at a good walk, and the other a girl of maybe eight or ten, who was running as hard as she was able down a cross street. Well, sir, the two ran into one another naturally enough at the corner; and then came the horrible part of the thing; for the man trampled calmly over the child's body and left her screaming on the ground. It sounds nothing to hear, but it was hellish to see. It wasn't like a man; it was like some damned Juggernaut. I gave a view-holloa, took to my heels, collared my gentleman, and brought him back to where there was already quite a group about the screaming child. He was perfectly cool, and made no resistance, but gave me one look so ugly that it brought out the sweat on me like running. The people who had turned out were the girl's own family; and pretty soon, the doctor, for whom she had been sent, put in his appearance. Well,

the child was not much the worse, more frightened,
according to the Sawbones; and there you might have
supposed would be an end to it. But there was one curious circumstance. I had taken a loathing to my gentleman at first sight. So had the child's family, which was
only natural. But the doctor's case was what struck me.
He was the usual cut-and-dry apothecary, of no particular
age and colour, with a strong Edinburgh accent, and
about as emotional as a bagpipe. Well, sir, he was like the
rest of us; every time he looked at my prisoner, I saw that
Sawbones turn sick and white with the desire to kill him.
I knew what was in his mind, just as he knew what was in
mine; and killing being out of the question, we did the
next best. We told the man we could and would make
such a scandal out of this as should make his name stink
from one end of London to the other. If he had any
friends or any credit, we undertook that he should lose
them. And all the time, as we were pitching it in red-hot,
we were keeping the women off him as best we could,
for they were as wild as harpies. I never saw a circle of
such hateful faces; and there was the man in the middle,
with a kind of black, sneering coolness – frightened, too,
I could see that – but carrying it off, sir, really like Satan.
'If you choose to make capital out of this accident,' said
he, 'I am naturally helpless. No gentleman but wishes to
avoid a scene,' says he. 'Name your figure.' Well, we
screwed him up to a hundred pounds for the child's family; he would have clearly liked to stick out; but there
was something about the lot of us that meant mischief,
and at last he struck. The next thing was to get the
money; and where do you think he carried us but to that
place with the door? – whipped out a key, went in, and
presently came back with the matter of ten pounds in
gold and a cheque for the balance on Coutts's, drawn
payable to bearer and signed with a name that I can't
mention, though it's one of the points of my story, but it
was a name at least very well known and often printed.
The figure was stiff; but the signature was good for more

than that, if it was only genuine. I took the liberty of
pointing out to my gentleman that the whole business
looked apocryphal, and that a man does not, in real life,
walk into a cellar-door at four in the morning and come
out of it with another man's cheque for close upon a hundred pounds. But he was quite easy and sneering. 'Set
your mind at rest,' says he, 'I will stay with you till the
banks open and cash the cheque myself.' So we all set
off, the doctor, and the child's father, and our friend and
myself, and passed the rest of the night in my chambers;
and next day, when we had breakfasted, went in a body
to the bank. I gave in the cheque myself, and said I had
every reason to believe it was a forgery. Not a bit of it.
The cheque was genuine."

"Tut-tut," said Mr. Utterson.

"I see you feel as I do," said Mr. Enfield. "Yes, it's a
bad story. For my man was a fellow that nobody could
have to do with, a really damnable man; and the person
that drew the cheque is the very pink of the proprieties,
celebrated too, and (what makes it worse) one of your
fellows who do what they call good. Blackmail, I suppose; an honest man paying through the nose for some of
the capers of his youth. Black Mail House is what I call
that place with the door, in consequence. Though even
that, you know, is far from explaining all," he added, and
with the words fell into a vein of musing.

From this he was recalled by Mr. Utterson asking
rather suddenly: "And you don't know if the drawer of
the cheque lives there?"

"A likely place, isn't it?" returned Mr. Enfield. "But I
happened to have noticed his address; he lives in some
square or other."

"And you never asked about – the place with the
door?" said Mr. Utterson.

"No, sir: I had a delicacy," was the reply. " I feel very
strongly about putting questions; it partakes too much of
the style of the day of judgment. You start a question,
and it's like starting a stone. You sit quietly on the top of

a hill; and away the stone goes, starting others; and presently some bland old bird (the last you would have thought of) is knocked on the head in his own back-garden and the family have to change their name. No, sir, I make it a rule of mine: the more it looks like Queer Street, the less I ask."

"A very good rule too," said the lawyer.

"But I have studied the place for myself," continued Mr. Enfield. "It seems scarcely a house. There is no other door, and nobody goes in or out of that one but, once in a great while, the gentleman of my adventure. There are three windows looking on the court on the first floor; none below; the windows are always shut, but they're clean. And then there is a chimney which is generally smoking; so somebody must live there. Yet it's not so sure; for the buildings are so packed together about that court that it's hard to say where one ends and another begins."

The pair walked on again for a while in silence; and then, "Enfield," said Mr. Utterson, "that's a good rule of yours."

"Yes, I think it is," returned Enfield.

"But for all that," continued the lawyer, "there's one point I want to ask: I want to ask the name of that man who walked over the child."

"Well," said Mr. Enfield, "I can't see what harm it would do. He was a man of the name of Hyde."

"H'm," said Mr. Utterson. "What sort of a man is he to see?"

"He is not easy to describe. There is something wrong with his appearance; something displeasing, something downright detestable. I never saw a man I so disliked, and yet I scarce know why. He must be deformed some-where; he gives a strong feeling of deformity, although I couldn't specify the point. He's an extraordinary-looking man, and yet I really can name nothing out of the way. No, sir; I can make no hand of it; I can't describe him. And it's not want of memory; for I declare I can see him this moment."

Mr. Utterson again walked some way in silence and obviously under a weight of consideration. "You are sure he used a key?" he inquired at last.

"My dear sir – " began Enfield, surprised out of himself.

"Yes, I know," said Utterson; "I know it must seem strange. The fact is, if I do not ask you the name of the other party it is because I know it already. You see, Richard, your tale has gone home. If you have been inexact in any point, you had better correct it."

"I think you might have warned me," returned the other with a touch of sullenness. "But I have been pedantically exact, as you call it. The fellow had a key; and what's more, he has it still. I saw him use it not a week ago."

Mr. Utterson sighed deeply but said never a word; and the young man presently resumed. "Here is another lesson to say nothing," said he. "I am ashamed of my long tongue. Let us make a bargain never to refer to this again."

"With all my heart," said the lawyer. "I shake hands on that, Richard."

Search for Mr. Hyde

THAT evening Mr. Utterson came home to his bachelor house in sombre spirits and sat down to dinner without relish. It was his custom of a Sunday, when this meal was over, to sit close by the fire, a volume of some dry divinity on his reading-desk, until the clock of the neighbouring church rang out the hour of twelve, when he would go soberly and gratefully to bed. On this night, however, as soon as the cloth was taken away, he took up a candle and went into his business-room. There he opened his safe, took from the most private part of it a document endorsed on the envelope as Dr. Jekyll's Will, and sat down with a clouded brow to study its contents. The will was holograph, for Mr. Utterson, though he took charge of it now that it was made, had refused to lend the least assistance in the making of it; it provided not only that, in case of the decease of Henry Jekyll, M.D., D.C.L., LL.D., F.R.S., &c., all his possessions were to pass into the hands of his "friend and benefactor Edward Hyde," but that in case of Dr. Jekyll's "disappearance or unexplained absence for any period exceeding three calendar months," the said Edward Hyde should step into the said Henry Jekyll's shoes without further delay and free from any burthen or obligation, beyond the payment of a few small sums to the members of the doctor's household. This document had long been the lawyer's eyesore. It offended him both as a lawyer and as a lover of the sane and customary sides of life, to whom the fanciful was the immodest. And hitherto it was his ignorance of Mr. Hyde that had swelled his indignation; now, by a sudden turn, it was his knowledge. It was already bad enough when the name was but a name of which he could learn no more. It was worse when it began to be clothed upon with detestable attributes; and out of the shifting, insubstantial mists that had so long baffled his eye, there leaped up the sudden, definite presentment of a fiend.

"I thought it was madness," he said, as he replaced the obnoxious paper in the safe, "and now I begin to fear it is disgrace."

With that he blew out his candle, put on a greatcoat, and set forth in the direction of Cavendish Square, that citadel of medicine, where his friend, the great Dr. Lanyon, had his house and received his crowding patients. "If any one knows, it will be Lanyon," he had thought.

The solemn butler knew and welcomed him; he was subjected to no stage of delay, but ushered direct from the door to the dining-room, where Dr. Lanyon sat alone over his wine. This was a hearty, healthy, dapper, red-faced gentleman, with a shock of hair prematurely white, and a boisterous and decided manner. At sight of Mr. Utterson, he sprang up from his chair and welcomed him with both hands. The geniality, as was the way of the man, was somewhat theatrical to the eye; but it reposed on genuine feeling. For these two were old friends, old mates both at school and college, both thorough respecters of themselves and of each other, and, what does not always follow, men who thoroughly enjoyed each other's company.

After a little rambling talk, the lawyer led up to the subject which so disagreeably preoccupied his mind.

"I suppose, Lanyon," said he, "you and I must be the two oldest friends that Henry Jekyll has?"

"I wish the friends were younger," chuckled Dr. Lanyon. "But I suppose we are. And what of that? I see little of him now."

"Indeed?" said Utterson. "I thought you had a bond of common interest."

"We had," was the reply. "But it is more than ten years

since Henry Jekyll became too fanciful for me. He began to go wrong, wrong in mind; and though of course I continue to take an interest in him for old sake's sake, as they say, I see and I have seen devilish little of the man. Such unscientific balderdash," added the doctor, flushing suddenly purple, "would have estranged Damon and Pythias."

This little spirt of temper was somewhat of a relief to Mr. Utterson. "They have only differed on some point of science," he thought; and being a man of no scientific passions (except in the matter of conveyancing) he even added: "It is nothing worse than that!" He gave his friend a few seconds to recover his composure, and then approached the question he had come to put. "Did you ever come across a protégé of his – one Hyde?" he asked.

"Hyde," repeated Lanyon. "No. Never heard of him. Since my time."

That was the amount of information that the lawyer carried back with him to the great, dark bed on which he tossed to and fro, until the small hours of the morning began to grow large. It was a night of little ease to his toiling mind, toiling in mere darkness and besieged by questions.

Six o'clock struck on the bells of the church that was so conveniently near to Mr. Utterson's dwelling, and still he was digging at the problem. Hitherto it had touched him on the intellectual side alone; but now his imagination also was engaged, or rather enslaved; and as he lay and tossed in the gross darkness of the night and the curtained room, Mr. Enfield's tale went by before his mind in a scroll of lighted pictures. He would be aware of the great field of lamps of a nocturnal city; then of the figure of a man walking swiftly; then of a child running from the doctor's; and then these met, and that human Juggernaut trod the child down and passed on regardless of her screams. Or else he would see a room in a rich house, where his friend lay asleep, dreaming and smiling at his dreams; and then the door of that room would be opened, the curtains of the bed plucked apart, the sleeper recalled, and lo! there would stand by his side a figure to whom power was given, and even at that dead hour he must rise and do its bidding. The figure in these two phases haunted the lawyer all night; and if at any time he dozed over, it was but to see it glide more stealthily through sleeping houses, or move the more swiftly and still the more swiftly, even to dizziness, through wider labyrinths of lamplighted city, and at every street corner crush a child and leave her screaming. And still the figure had no face by which he might know it; even in his dreams, it had no face, or one that baffled him and melted before his eyes; and thus it was that there sprang up and grew apace in the lawyer's mind a singularly strong, almost an inordinate, curiosity to behold the features of the real Mr. Hyde. If he could but once set eyes on him, he thought the mystery would lighten and perhaps roll altogether away, as was the habit of mysterious things when well examined. He might see a reason for his friend's strange preference or bondage (call it which you please) and even for the startling clauses of the will. And at least it would be a face worth seeing: the face of a man who was without bowels of mercy: a face which had but to show itself to raise up, in the mind of the unimpressionable Enfield, a spirit of enduring hatred.

From that time forward, Mr. Utterson began to haunt the door in the by-street of shops. In the morning before office hours, at noon when business was plenty and time scarce, at night under the face of the fogged city moon, by all lights and at all hours of solitude or concourse, the lawyer was to be found on his chosen post.

"If he be Mr. Hyde," he had thought, "I shall be Mr. Seek."

And at last his patience was rewarded. It was a fine dry night; frost in the air; the streets as clean as a ball-room floor; the lamps, unshaken by any wind, drawing a regular pattern of light and shadow. By ten o'clock, when the shops were closed, the by-street was very solitary and, in spite of the low growl of London from all round, very silent. Small sounds carried far; domestic sounds out of the houses were clearly audible on either side of the roadway; and the rumour of the approach of any passenger preceded him by a long time. Mr. Utterson had been some minutes at his post, when he was aware of an odd, light footstep drawing near. In the course of his nightly patrols he had long grown accustomed to the quaint effect with which the footfalls of a single person, while he is still a great way off, suddenly spring out distinct from the vast hum and clatter of the city. Yet his attention had never before been so sharply and decisively arrested; and it was with a strong, superstitious prevision of success that he withdrew into the entry of the court.

The steps drew swiftly nearer, and swelled out suddenly louder as they turned the end of the street. The lawyer, looking forth from the entry, could soon see what manner of man he had to deal with. He was small and very plainly dressed, and the look of him, even at that distance, went somehow strongly against the watcher's inclination. But he made straight for the door, crossing the roadway to save time; and as he came, he drew a key from his pocket like one approaching home.

Mr. Utterson stepped out and touched him on the shoulder as he passed. "Mr. Hyde, I think?"

Mr. Hyde shrank back with a hissing intake of the breath. But his fear was only momentary; and though he did not look the lawyer in the face, he answered coolly enough: "That is my name. What do you want?"

"I see you are going in," returned the lawyer. "I am an old friend of Dr. Jekyll's – Mr. Utterson of Gaunt Street – you must have heard my name; and meeting you so conveniently, I thought you might admit me."

"You will not find Dr. Jekyll; he is from home," replied Mr. Hyde, blowing in the key. And then suddenly, but still without looking up, "How did you know me?" he asked.

"On your side," said Mr. Utterson, "will you do me a favour?"

"With pleasure," replied the other. "What shall it be?"

"Will you let me see your face?" asked the lawyer.

Mr. Hyde appeared to hesitate, and then, as if upon some sudden reflection, fronted about with an air of defiance; and the pair stared at each other pretty fixedly for a few seconds. "Now I shall know you again," said Mr. Utterson. "It may be useful."

"Yes," returned Mr. Hyde, "it is as well we have met; and à *propos*, you should have my address." And he gave a number of a street in Soho.

"Good God!" thought Mr. Utterson, "can he too have been thinking of the will?" But he kept his feelings to himself and only grunted in acknowledgment of the address.

"And now," said the other, "how did you know me?"

"By description," was the reply.

"Whose description?"

"We have common friends," said Mr. Utterson.

"Common friends?" echoed Mr. Hyde, a little hoarsely. "Who are they?"

"Jekyll, for instance," said the lawyer.

"He never told you," cried Mr. Hyde, with a flush of anger. "I did not think you would have lied."

"Come," said Mr. Utterson, "that is not fitting language."

The other snarled aloud into a savage laugh; and the next moment, with extraordinary quickness, he had unlocked the door and disappeared into the house.

The lawyer stood awhile when Mr. Hyde had left him, the picture of disquietude. Then he began slowly to mount the street, pausing every step or two and putting his hand to his brow like a man in mental perplexity. The problem he was thus debating as he walked was one of a class that is rarely solved. Mr. Hyde was pale and dwarfish. He gave an impression of deformity without any nameable malformation, he had a displeasing smile, he had borne himself to the lawyer with a sort of murderous mixture of timidity and boldness, and he spoke with a husky, whispering and somewhat broken voice; all these were points against him, but not all of these together could explain the hitherto unknown disgust, loathing, and fear with which Mr. Utterson regarded him. "There must be something else," said the perplexed gentleman. "There *is* something more, if I could find a name for it. God bless me, the man seems hardly human! Something troglodytic, shall we say? or can it be the old story of Dr. Fell? or is it the mere radiance of a foul soul that thus transpires through, and transfigures, its clay continent? The last, I think; for O my poor old Harry Jekyll, if ever I read Satan's signature upon a face, it is on that of your new friend."

Round the corner from the by-street there was a square of ancient, handsome houses, now for the most part decayed from their high estate and let in flats and chambers to all sorts and conditions of men: map-engravers, architects, shady lawyers, and the agents of obscure enterprises. One house, however, second from the corner, was still occupied entire; and at the door of this, which wore a great air of wealth and comfort, though it was now plunged in darkness except for the fan-light, Mr. Utterson stopped and knocked. A well-dressed elderly servant opened the door.

"Is Dr. Jekyll at home, Poole?" asked the lawyer.

"I will see, Mr. Utterson," said Poole, admitting the visitor, as he spoke, into a large, low-roofed, comfortable hall, paved with flags, warmed (after the fashion of a country house) by a bright, open fire, and furnished with costly cabinets of oak. "Will you wait here by the fire, sir? or shall I give you a light in the dining-room?"

"Here, thank you," said the lawyer, and he drew near and leaned on the tall fender. This hall, in which he was now left alone, was a pet fancy of his friend the doctor's; and Utterson himself was wont to speak of it as the pleasantest room in London. But to-night there was a shudder in his blood; the face of Hyde sat heavy on his memory; he felt (what was rare with him) a nausea and distaste of life; and in the gloom of his spirits, he seemed to read a menace in the flickering of the firelight on the polished cabinets and the uneasy starting of the shadow on the roof. He was ashamed of his relief, when Poole presently returned to announce that Dr. Jekyll was gone out.

"I saw Mr. Hyde go in by the old dissecting-room door, Poole," he said. "Is that right, when Dr. Jekyll is from home?"

"Quite right, Mr. Utterson, sir," replied the servant. "Mr. Hyde has a key."

"Your master seems to repose a great deal of trust in that young man, Poole," resumed the other musingly.

"Yes, sir, he do indeed," said Poole. "We have all orders to obey him."

"I do not think I ever met Mr. Hyde?" asked Utterson.

"O dear no, sir. He never *dines* here," replied the butler. "Indeed, we see very little of him on this side of the house; he mostly comes and goes by the laboratory."

"Well, good-night, Poole."

"Good-night, Mr. Utterson."

And the lawyer set out homeward with a very heavy heart. "Poor Harry Jekyll," he thought, "my mind misgives me he is in deep waters! He was wild when he was young; a long while ago, to be sure; but in the law of God there is no statute of limitations. Ay, it must be that; the ghost of some old sin, the cancer of some concealed disgrace: punishment coming, *pede claudo*, years after memory has forgotten and self-love condoned the fault." And the lawyer, scared by the thought, brooded awhile on his own past, groping in all the corners of memory, lest by chance some Jack-in-the-Box of an old iniquity should leap to light there. His past was fairly blameless; few men could read the rolls of their life with less apprehension; yet he was humbled to the dust by the many ill things he had done, and raised up again into a sober and fearful gratitude by the many that he had come so near to doing, yet avoided. And then, by a return on his former subject, he conceived a spark of hope. "This Master Hyde, if he were studied," thought he, "must have secrets of his own: black secrets, by the look of him; secrets compared to which poor Jekyll's worst would be like sunshine. Things cannot continue as they are. It turns me cold to think of this creature stealing like a thief to Harry's bedside; poor Harry, what a wakening! And the danger of it; for if this Hyde suspects the existence of the will, he may grow impatient to inherit. Ay, I must put my shoulder to the wheel – if Jekyll will but let me," he added, "if Jekyll will only let me." For once more he saw before his mind's eye, as clear as a transparency, the strange clauses of the will.

Dr. Jekyll was Quite at Ease

A FORTNIGHT later, by excellent good fortune, the doctor gave one of his pleasant dinners to some five or six old cronies, all intelligent, reputable men, and all judges of good wine; and Mr. Utterson so contrived that he remained behind after the others had departed. This was no new arrangement, but a thing that had befallen many scores of times. Where Utterson was liked, he was liked well. Hosts loved to detain the dry lawyer, when the light-hearted and the loose-tongued had already their foot on the threshold; they liked to sit awhile in his unobtrusive company, practising for solitude, sobering their minds in the man's rich silence after the expense and strain of gaiety. To this rule Dr. Jekyll was no exception; and as he now sat on the opposite side of the fire – a large, well-made, smooth-faced man of fifty, with something of a slyish cast perhaps, but every mark of capacity and kindness – you could see by his looks that he cherished for Mr. Utterson a sincere and warm affection.

"I have been wanting to speak to you, Jekyll," began the latter. "You know that will of yours?"

A close observer might have gathered that the topic was distasteful; but the doctor carried it off gaily. "My poor Utterson," said he, "you are unfortunate in such a client. I never saw a man so distressed as you were by my will; unless it were that hide-bound pedant, Lanyon, at what he called my scientific heresies. Oh, I know he's a good fellow – you needn't frown – an excellent fellow, and I always mean to see more of him; but a hide-bound pedant for all that; an ignorant, blatant pedant. I was never more disappointed in any man than Lanyon."

"You know I never approved of it," pursued Utterson,

ruthlessly disregarding the fresh topic.

"My will? Yes, certainly, I know that," said the doctor, a trifle sharply. "You have told me so."

"Well, I tell you so again," continued the lawyer. "I have been learning something of young Hyde."

The large handsome face of Dr. Jekyll grew pale to the very lips, and there came a blackness about his eyes. "I do not care to hear more," said he. "This is a matter I thought we had agreed to drop."

"What I heard was abominable," said Utterson.

"It can make no change. You do not understand my position" returned the doctor, with a certain incoherency of manner. "I am painfully situated, Utterson; my position is a very strange – a very strange one. It is one of those affairs that cannot be mended by talking."

"Jekyll," said Utterson, "you know me: I am a man to be trusted. Make a clean breast of this in confidence; and I make no doubt I can get you out of it."

"My good Utterson," said the doctor, "this is very good of you, this is downright good of you, and I cannot find words to thank you in. I believe you fully; I would trust you before any man alive – ay, before myself, if I could make the choice; but indeed it isn't what you fancy; it is not so bad as that; and just to put your good heart at rest, I will tell you one thing: the moment I choose, I can be rid of Mr. Hyde. I give you my hand upon that; and I thank you again and again; and I will just add one little word, Utterson, that I'm sure you'll take in good part: this is a private matter, and I beg of you to let it sleep."

Utterson reflected a little, looking in the fire.

"I have no doubt you are perfectly right," he said at last, getting to his feet.

"Well, but since we have touched upon this business, and for the last time I hope," continued the doctor, "there is one point I should like you to understand. I have really a very great interest in poor Hyde. I know you have seen him; he told me so; and I fear he was rude.

But I do sincerely take a great, a very great interest in that young man; and if I am taken away, Utterson, I wish you to promise me that you will bear with him and get his rights for him. I think you would, if you knew all; and it would be a weight off my mind if you would promise."

"I can't pretend that I shall ever like him," said the lawyer.

"I don't ask that," pleaded Jekyll, laying his hand upon the other's arm; "I only ask for justice; I only ask you to help him for my sake, when I am no longer here."

Utterson heaved an irrepressible sigh. "Well," said he, "I promise."

The Carew Murder Case

NEARLY a year later, in the month of October 18 – , London was startled by a crime of singular ferocity, rendered all the more notable by the high position of the victim. The details were few and startling. A maidservant living alone in a house not far from the river had gone upstairs to bed about eleven. Although a fog rolled over the city in the small hours, the early part of the night was cloudless, and the lane, which the maid's window overlooked, was brilliantly lit by the full moon. It seems she was romantically given, for she sat down upon her box, which stood immediately under the window, and fell into a dream of musing. Never (she used to say, with streaming tears, when she narrated that experience), never had she felt more at peace with all men or thought more kindly of the world. And as she so sat she became aware of an aged and beautiful gentleman with white hair drawing near along the lane: and advancing to meet him another and very small gentleman, to whom at first she paid less attention. When they had come within speech (which was just under the maid's eyes) the older man bowed and accosted the other with a very pretty manner of politeness. It did not seem as if the subject of his address were of great importance; indeed, from his pointing, it sometimes appeared as if he were only inquiring his way; but the moon shone on his face as he spoke, and the girl was pleased to watch it, it seemed to breathe such an innocent and old-world kindness of disposition, yet with something high too, as of a wellfounded self-content. Presently her eye wandered to the other, and she was surprised to recognise in him a certain Mr. Hyde, who had once visited her master, and for whom she had conceived a dislike. He had in his hand a heavy cane, with which he was trifling; but he answered never a word, and seemed to listen with an ill-contained impatience. And then all of a sudden he broke out in a great flame of anger, stamping with his foot, brandishing the cane, and carrying on (as the maid described it) like a madman. The old gentleman took a step back, with the air of one very much surprised and a trifle hurt; and at that Mr. Hyde broke out of all bounds and clubbed him to the earth. And next moment, with ape-like fury, he was trampling his victim under foot, and hailing down a storm of blows, under which the bones were audibly shattered and the body jumped upon the roadway. At the horror of these sights and sounds the maid fainted.

It was two o'clock when she came to herself and called for the police. The murderer was gone long ago; but there lay his victim in the middle of the lane, incredibly mangled. The stick with which the deed had been done, although it was of some rare and very tough and heavy wood, had broken in the middle under the stress of this insensate cruelty; and one splintered half had rolled in the neighbouring gutter – the other, without doubt, had been carried away by the murderer. A purse and a gold watch were found upon the victim; but no cards or papers, except a sealed and stamped envelope, which he had been probably carrying to the post, and which bore the name and address of Mr. Utterson.

This was brought to the lawyer the next morning before he was out of bed; and he had no sooner seen it, and been told the circumstances, than he shot out a solemn lip. "I shall say nothing till I have seen the body," said he; "this may be very serious. Have the kindness to wait while I dress." And with the same grave coun-tenance he hurried through his breakfast and drove to the police station, whither the body had been carried. As soon as he came into the cell he nodded.

"Yes," said he, "I recognise him. I am sorry to say that this is Sir Danvers Carew."

"Good God, sir," exclaimed the officer, "is it possible?" And the next moment his eye lighted up with professional ambition. "This will make a deal of noise," he said. "And perhaps you can help us to the man." And he briefly narrated what the maid had seen, and showed the broken stick.

Mr. Utterson had already quailed at the name of Hyde; but, when the stick was laid before him he could doubt no longer; broken and battered as it was, he recognised it for one that he had himself presented many years before to Henry Jekyll.

"Is this Mr. Hyde a person of small stature?" he inquired.

"Particularly small and particularly wicked-looking, is what the maid calls him," said the officer.

Mr. Utterson reflected; and then, raising his head, "If you will come with me in my cab," he said, "I think I can take you to his house."

It was by this time about nine in the morning, and the first fog of the season. A great chocolate-coloured pall lowered over heaven, but the wind was continually charging and routing these embattled vapours; so that as the cab crawled from street to street, Mr. Utterson beheld a marvellous number of degrees and hues of twilight; for here it would be dark like the back-end of evening; and there would be a glow of a rich, lurid brown, like the light of some strange conflagration; and here, for a moment, the fog would be quite broken up, and a haggard shaft of daylight would glance in between the swirling wreaths. The dismal quarter of Soho seen under these changing glimpses, with its muddy ways, and slatternly passengers, and its lamps, which had never been extinguished or had been kindled afresh to combat this mournful re-invasion of darkness, seemed, in the lawyer's eyes, like a district of some city in a nightmare. The thoughts of his mind, besides, were of the gloomiest dye; and when he glanced at the companion of his drive, he was conscious of some touch of that terror of

the law and the law's officers which may at times assail
the most honest.

As the cab drew up before the address indicated, the
fog lifted a little, and showed him a dingy street, a gin-
palace, a low French eating-house, a shop for the retail of
penny numbers and twopenny salads, many ragged children huddled in the doorways, and many women of
many different nationalities passing out, key in hand, to
have a morning glass; and the next moment the fog settled down again upon that part, as brown as umber, and
cut him off from his blackguardly surroundings. This was
the home of Henry Jekyll's favourite; of a man who was
heir to a quarter of a million sterling.

An ivory-faced and silvery-haired old woman opened
the door. She had an evil face, smoothed by hypocrisy;
but her manners were excellent. Yes, she said, this was
Mr. Hyde's, but he was not at home; he had been in that
night very late, but had gone away again in less than an
hour; there was nothing strange in that; his habits were
very irregular, and he was often absent; for instance, it
was nearly two months since she had seen him till yesterday.

"Very well then, we wish to see his rooms," said the
lawyer; and when the woman began to declare it was
impossible, "I had better tell you who this person is," he
added. "This is Inspector Newcomen of Scotland Yard."

A flash of odious joy appeared upon the woman's face.
"Ah!" said she, "he is in trouble! What has he done?"

Mr. Utterson and the inspector exchanged glances.
"He don't seem a very popular character," observed the
latter. "And now, my good woman, just let me and this
gentleman have a look about us."

In the whole extent of the house, which but for the
old woman remained otherwise empty, Mr. Hyde had
only used a couple of rooms; but these were furnished
with luxury and good taste. A closet was filled with wine;
the plate was of silver, the napery elegant; a good picture
hung upon the walls, a gift (as Utterson supposed) from

Henry Jekyll, who was much of a connoisseur; and the carpets were of many plies and agreeable in colour. At this moment, however, the rooms bore every mark of having been recently and hurriedly ransacked; clothes lay about the floor, with their pockets inside out; lockfast drawers stood open; and on the hearth there lay a pile of grey ashes, as though many papers had been burned. From these embers the inspector disinterred the butt-end of a green cheque-book, which had resisted the action of the fire; the other half of the stick was found behind the door; and as this clinched his suspicions, the officer declared himself delighted. A visit to the bank, where several thousand pounds were found to be lying to the murderer's credit, completed his gratification.

"You may depend upon it, sir," he told Mr. Utterson: "I have him in my hand. He must have lost his head, or he never would have left the stick or, above all, burned the cheque-book. Why, money's life to the man. We have nothing to do but wait for him at the bank, and get out the handbills."

This last, however, was not so easy of accomplishment; for Mr. Hyde had numbered few familiars – even the master of the servant-maid had only seen him twice; his family could nowhere be traced; he had never been photographed; and the few who could describe him differed widely, as common observers will. Only on one point were they agreed; and that was the haunting sense of unexpressed deformity with which the fugitive impressed his beholders.

Incident of the Letter

IT was late in the afternoon when Mr. Utterson found his
way to Dr. Jekyll's door, where he was at once admitted
by Poole, and carried down by the kitchen offices and
across a yard which had once been a garden to the building which was indifferently known as the laboratory or
the dissecting-rooms. The doctor had bought the house
from the heirs of a celebrated surgeon; and, his own tastes
being rather chemical than anatomical, had changed
the destination of the block at the bottom of the garden.
It was the first time that the lawyer had been received
in that part of his friend's quarters; and he eyed the dingy
windowless structure with curiosity, and gazed round
with a distasteful sense of strangeness as he crossed the
theatre, once crowded with eager students and now
lying gaunt and silent, the tables laden with chemical
apparatus, the floor strewn with crates and littered with
packing straw, and the light falling dimly through the
foggy cupola. At the farther end, a flight of stairs mounted
to a door covered with red baize; and through this,
Mr. Utterson was at last received into the doctor's cabinet.
It was a large room, fitted round with glass presses,
furnished, among other things, with a cheval-glass
and a business-table, and looking out upon the court by
three dusty windows barred with iron. The fire burned
in the grate; a lamp was set lighted on the chimney shelf,
for even in the houses the fog began to lie thickly; and
there, close up to the warmth, sat Dr. Jekyll, looking
deadly sick; he did not rise to meet his visitor, but held out
a cold hand and bade him welcome in a changed voice.

"And now," said Mr. Utterson, as soon as Poole had
left them, "you have heard the news?"

The doctor shuddered. "They were crying it in the square," he said. "I heard them in my dining-room."

"One word," said the lawyer. "Carew was my client, but so are you, and I want to know what I am doing. You have not been mad enough to hide this fellow?"

"Utterson, I swear to God," cried the doctor, "I swear to God I will never set eyes on him again. I bind my honour to you that I am done with him in this world. It is all at an end. And indeed he does not want my help; you do not know him as I do; he is safe, he is quite safe; mark my words, he will never more be heard of."

The lawyer listened gloomily; he did not like his friend's feverish manner. "You seem pretty sure of him," said he; "and for your sake, I hope you may be right. If it came to a trial your name might appear."

"I am quite sure of him," replied Jekyll; "I have grounds for certainty that I cannot share with any one. But there is one thing on which you may advise me. I have – I have received a letter; and I am at a loss whether I should show it to the police. I should like to leave it in your hands, Utterson; you would judge wisely, I am sure; I have so great a trust in you."

"You fear, I suppose, that it might lead to his detection?" asked the lawyer.

"No," said the other. "I cannot say that I care what becomes of Hyde; I am quite done with him. I was thinking of my own character, which this hateful business has rather exposed."

Utterson ruminated awhile; he was surprised at his friend's selfishness, and yet relieved by it. "Well," said he at last, "let me see the letter."

The letter was written in an odd, upright hand and signed "Edward Hyde": and it signified, briefly enough, that the writer's benefactor, Dr. Jekyll, whom he had long so unworthily repaid for a thousand generosities, need labour under no alarm for his safety, as he had means of escape on which he placed a sure dependence. The lawyer liked this letter well enough; it put a better colour on the intimacy than he had looked for; and he blamed himself for some of his past suspicions.

"Have you the envelope?" he asked.

"I burned it," replied Jekyll, "before I thought what I was about. But it bore no postmark. The note was handed in."

"Shall I keep this and sleep upon it?" asked Utterson.

"I wish you to judge for me entirely," was the reply. "I have lost confidence in myself."

"Well, I shall consider," returned the lawyer. – "And now one word more: it was Hyde who dictated the terms in your will about that disappearance?"

The doctor seemed seized with a qualm of faintness; he shut his mouth tight and nodded.

"I knew it," said Utterson. "He meant to murder you. You have had a fine escape"

"I have had what is far more to the purpose," returned the doctor solemnly: "I have had a lesson – O God, Utterson, what a lesson I have had!" And he covered his face for a moment with his hands.

On his way out, the lawyer stopped and had a word or two with Poole. "By the by," said he, "there was a letter handed in to-day: what was the messenger like?" But Poole was positive nothing had come except by post; "and only circulars by that," he added.

This news sent off the visitor with his fears renewed. Plainly the letter had come by the laboratory door; possibly indeed, it had been written in the cabinet; and if that were so, it must be differently judged, and handled with the more caution. The newsboys, as he went, were crying themselves hoarse along the footways: "Special edition. Shocking murder of an M.P." That was the funeral oration of one friend and client; and he could not help a certain apprehension lest the good name of another should be sucked down in the eddy of the scandal. It was, at least, a ticklish decision that he had to make; and, self-reliant as he was by habit, he began to cherish a longing for advice. It was not to be had directly;

but perhaps, he thought, it might be fished for.

Presently after, he sat on one side of his own hearth, with Mr. Guest, his head clerk, upon the other, and midway between, at a nicely calculated distance from the fire, a bottle of a particular old wine that had long dwelt unsunned in the foundations of his house. The fog still slept on the wing above the drowned city, where the lamps glimmered like carbuncles; and through the muffle and smother of these fallen clouds, the procession of the town's life was still rolling on through the great arteries with a sound as of a mighty wind. But the room was gay with firelight. In the bottle the acids were long ago resolved; the imperial dye had softened with time, as the colour grows richer in stained windows; and the glow of hot autumn afternoons on hillside vineyards was ready to be set free and to disperse the fogs of London. Insensibly the lawyer melted. There was no man from whom he kept fewer secrets than Mr. Guest; and he was not always sure that he kept as many as he meant. Guest had often been on business to the doctor's; he knew Poole; he could scarce have failed to hear of Mr. Hyde's familiarity about the house; he might draw conclusions: was it not as well, then, that he should see a letter which put that mystery to rights? and above all since Guest, being a great student and critic of handwriting, would consider the step natural and obliging? The clerk, besides, was a man of counsel; he would scarce read so strange a document without dropping a remark; and by that remark Mr. Utterson might shape his future course.

"This is a sad business about Sir Danvers," he said.

"Yes, sir, indeed. It has elicited a great deal of public feeling," returned Guest. "The man, of course, was mad."

"I should like to hear your views on that," replied Utterson. "I have a document here in his handwriting; it is between ourselves, for I scarce know what to do about it; it is an ugly business at the best. But there it is; quite in your way: a murderer's autograph."

Guest's eyes brightened, and he sat down at once and studied it with passion. "No, sir," he said; "not mad; but it is an odd hand."

"And by all accounts a very odd writer," added the lawyer.

Just then the servant entered with a note.

"Is that from Dr. Jekyll, sir?" inquired the clerk. "I thought I knew the writing. Anything private, Mr. Utterson?"

"Only an invitation to dinner. Why? do you want to see it?"

"One moment. I thank you, sir;" and the clerk laid the two sheets of paper alongside and sedulously compared their contents. "Thank you, sir," he said at last, returning both; "it's a very interesting autograph."

There was a pause, during which Mr. Utterson struggled with himself. "Why did you compare them, Guest?" he inquired suddenly.

"Well, sir," returned the clerk, "there's a rather singular resemblance; the two hands are in many points identical: only differently sloped."

"Rather quaint," said Utterson.

"It is, as you say, rather quaint," returned Guest.

"I wouldn't speak of this note, you know," said the master.

"No, sir," said the clerk. "I understand."

But no sooner was Mr. Utterson alone that night than he locked the note into his safe, where it reposed from that time forward. "What!" he thought. "Henry Jekyll forge for a murderer!" And his blood ran cold in his veins.

Remarkable Incident of Dr. Lanyon

TIME ran on; thousands of pounds were offered in reward, for the death of Sir Danvers was resented as a public injury; but Mr. Hyde had disappeared out of the ken of the police as though he had never existed. Much of his past was unearthed, indeed, and all disreputable: tales came out of the man's cruelty, at once so callous and violent, of his vile life, of his strange associates, of the hatred that seemed to have surrounded his career; but of his present whereabouts, not a whisper. From the time he had left the house in Soho on the morning of the murder, he was simply blotted out; and gradually, as time drew on, Mr. Utterson began to recover from the hotness of his alarm, and to grow more at quiet with himself. The death of Sir Danvers was, to his way of thinking, more than paid for by the disappearance of Mr. Hyde. Now that that evil influence had been withdrawn, a new life began for Dr. Jekyll. He came out of his seclusion, renewed relations with his friends, became once more their familiar guest and entertainer; and whilst he had always been known for charities, he was now no less distinguished for religion. He was busy, he was much in the open air, he did good; his face seemed to open and brighten, as if with an inward consciousness of service; and for more than two months the doctor was at peace.

On the 8th of January Utterson had dined at the doctor's with a small party; Lanyon had been there; and the face of the host had looked from one to the other as in the old days when the trio were inseparable friends. On the 12th, and again on the 14th, the door was shut against the lawyer. "The doctor was confined to the house," Poole said, "and saw no one." On the 15th he tried again, and was again refused; and having now been used for the last two months to see his friend almost daily, he found this return of solitude to weigh upon his spirits. The fifth night he had in Guest to dine with him; and the sixth he betook himself to Dr. Lanyon's.

There at least he was not denied admittance; but when he came in, he was shocked at the change which had taken place in the doctor's appearance. He had his death-warrant written legibly upon his face. The rosy man had grown pale; his flesh had fallen away; he was visibly balder and older; and yet it was not so much these tokens of a swift physical decay that arrested the lawyer's notice, as a look in the eye and quality of manner that seemed to testify to some deep-seated terror of the mind. It was unlikely that the doctor should fear death; and yet that was what Utterson was tempted to suspect. "Yes," he thought; "he is a doctor, he must know his own state and that his days are counted; and the knowledge is more than he can bear." And yet when Utterson remarked on his ill-looks, it was with an air of great firmness that Lanyon declared himself a doomed man.

"I have had a shock," he said, "and I shall never recover. It is a question of weeks. Well, life has been pleasant; I liked it; yes, sir, I used to like it. I sometimes think if we knew all we should be more glad to get away."

"Jekyll is ill too," observed Utterson. "Have you seen him?"

But Lanyon's face changed, and he held up a trembling hand. "I wish to see or hear no more of Dr. Jekyll," he said in a loud, unsteady voice. "I am quite done with that person; and I beg that you will spare me any allusion to one whom I regard as dead."

"Tut-tut," said Mr. Utterson; and then, after a considerable pause, "Can't I do anything?" he inquired. "We are three very old friends, Lanyon; we shall not live to make others."

"Nothing can be done," returned Lanyon; "ask himself."

"He will not see me," said the lawyer.

"I am not surprised at that," was the reply. "Some day, Utterson, after I am dead, you may perhaps come to learn the right and wrong of this. I cannot tell you. And in the meantime, if you can sit and talk with me of other things, for God's sake, stay and do so; but if you cannot keep clear of this accursed topic, then, in God's name, go, for I cannot bear it."

As soon as he got home, Utterson sat down and wrote to Jekyll, complaining of his exclusion from the house, and asking the cause of this unhappy break with Lanyon; and the next day brought him a long answer, often very pathetically worded, and sometimes darkly mysterious in drift. The quarrel with Lanyon was incurable. "I do not blame our old friend," Jekyll wrote, "but I share his view that we must never meet. I mean from henceforth to lead a life of extreme seclusion; you must not be surprised, nor must you doubt my friendship, if my door is often shut even to you. You must suffer me to go my own dark way. I have brought on myself a punishment and a danger that I cannot name. If I am the chief of sinners, I am the chief of sufferers also. I could not think that this earth contained a place for sufferings and terrors so unmanning; and you can but do one thing, Utterson, to lighten this destiny, and that is to respect my silence." Utterson was amazed; the dark influence of Hyde had been withdrawn, the doctor had returned to his old tasks and amities; a week ago, the prospect had smiled with every promise of a cheerful and an honoured age; and now in a moment, friendship and peace of mind and the whole tenor of his life were wrecked. So great and unprepared a change pointed to madness; but in view of Lanyon's manner and words, there must lie for it some deeper ground.

A week afterwards Dr. Lanyon took to his bed, and in something less than a fortnight he was dead. The night after the funeral, at which he had been sadly affected, Utterson locked the door of his business-room, and sitting there by the light of a melancholy candle, drew out and set before him an envelope addressed by the hand and sealed with the seal of his dead friend. "PRIVATE: for the hands of G. J. Utterson ALONE, and in case of his predecease *to be destroyed unread,*" so it was emphatically superscribed; and the lawyer dreaded to behold the contents. "I have buried one friend to-day," he thought: "what if this should cost me another?" And then he condemned the fear as a disloyalty, and broke the seal. Within there was another enclosure, likewise sealed, and marked upon the cover as "not to be opened till the death or disappearance of Dr. Henry Jekyll." Utterson could not trust his eyes. Yes, it was disappearance; here again, as in the mad will which he had long ago restored to its author, here again were the idea of a disappearance and the name of Henry Jekyll bracketed. But in the will that idea had sprung from the sinister suggestion of the man Hyde; it was set there with a purpose all too plain and horrible. Written by the hand of Lanyon, what should it mean? A great curiosity came on the trustee, to disregard the prohibition and dive at once to the bottom of these mysteries; but professional honour and faith to his dead friend were stringent obligations; and the packet slept in the inmost corner of his private safe.

It is one thing to mortify curiosity, another to conquer it; and it may be doubted if, from that day forth, Utterson desired the society of his surviving friend with the same eagerness. He thought of him kindly; but his thoughts were disquieted and fearful. He went to call indeed; but he was perhaps relieved to be denied admittance; perhaps, in his heart, he preferred to speak with Poole upon the doorstep and surrounded by the air and sounds of the open city, rather than to be admitted into that house of voluntary bondage, and to sit and speak with its inscrutable recluse. Poole had, indeed, no very pleasant news to communicate. The doctor, it appeared, now more than ever confined himself to the cabinet over the laboratory, where he would sometimes even sleep; he was out of spirits, he had grown very silent, he did not read; it seemed as if he had something on his mind. Utterson became so used to the unvarying character of these reports, that he fell off little by little in the frequency of his visits.

Incident at the Window

It chanced on Sunday, when Mr. Utterson was on his usual walk with Mr. Enfield, that their way lay once again through the by-street; and that when they came in front of the door, both stopped to gaze on it.

"Well," said Enfield, "that story's at an end at least. We shall never see more of Mr. Hyde."

"I hope not," said Utterson. "Did I ever tell you that I once saw him, and shared your feeling of repulsion?"

"It was impossible to do the one without the other," returned Enfield. "And by the way, what an ass you must have thought me, not to know that this was a back way to Dr. Jekyll's! It was partly your own fault that I found it out, even when I did."

"So you found it out, did you?" said Utterson. "But if that be so, we may step into the court and take a look at the windows. To tell you the truth, I am uneasy about poor Jekyll; and even outside, I feel as if the presence of a friend might do him good."

The court was very cool and a little damp, and full of premature twilight, although the sky, high up overhead, was still bright with sunset. The middle one of the three windows was half-way open; and sitting close beside it, taking the air with an infinite sadness of mien, like some disconsolate prisoner, Utterson saw Dr. Jekyll.

"What! Jekyll!" he cried. "I trust you are better."

"I am very low, Utterson," replied the doctor drearily, "very low. It will not last long, thank God."

"You stay too much indoors," said the lawyer. "You should be out, whipping up the circulation like Mr. Enfield and me. (This is my cousin – Mr. Enfield – Dr. Jekyll.) Come now; get your hat and take a quick turn with us."

"You are very good," sighed the other. "I should like to very much; but no, no, no, it is quite impossible; I dare not. But indeed, Utterson, I am very glad to see you; this is really a great pleasure; I would ask you and Mr. Enfield up, but the place is really not fit."

"Why then," said the lawyer good-naturedly, "the best thing we can do is to stay down here and speak with you from where we are."

"That is just what I was about to venture to propose," returned the doctor, with a smile. But the words were hardly uttered, before the smile was struck out of his face and succeeded by an expression of such abject terror and despair as froze the very blood of the two gentlemen below. They saw it but for a glimpse, for the window was instantly thrust down; but that glimpse had been sufficient, and they turned and left the court without a word. In silence, too, the by-street; and it was not until they had come into a neighbouring thoroughfare, where even upon a Sunday there were still some stirrings of life, that Mr. Utterson at last turned and looked at his companion. They were both pale; and there was an answering horror in their eyes.

"God forgive us, God forgive us!" said Mr. Utterson.

But Mr. Enfield only nodded his head very seriously, and walked on once more in silence.

The Last Night

MR. UTTERSON was sitting by his fireside one evening after dinner, when he was surprised to receive a visit from Poole.

"Bless me, Poole, what brings you here?" he cried; and then, taking a second look at him, "What ails you?" he added, "is the doctor ill?"

"Mr. Utterson," said the man, "there is something wrong."

"Take a seat, and here is a glass of wine for you," said the lawyer. "Now, take your time, and tell me plainly what you want."

"You know the doctor's ways, sir," replied Poole, "and how he shuts himself up. Well, he's shut up again in the cabinet; and I don't like it, sir – I wish I may die if I like it. Mr. Utterson, sir, I'm afraid."

"Now, my good man," said the lawyer, "be explicit. What are you afraid of?"

"I've been afraid for about a week," returned Poole, doggedly disregarding the question, "and I can bear it no more."

The man's appearance amply bore out his words; his manner was altered for the worse; and except for the moment when he had first announced his terror, he had not once looked the lawyer in the face. Even now, he sat with the glass of wine untasted on his knee, and his eyes directed to a corner of the floor. "I can bear it no longer," he repeated.

"Come," said the lawyer, "I see you have some good reason, Poole; I see there is something seriously amiss. Try to tell me what it is."

"I think there's been foul play," said Poole hoarsely.

"Foul play!" cried the lawyer, a good deal frightened, and rather inclined to be irritated in consequence. "What foul play? What does the man mean?"

"I daren't say, sir," was the answer; "but will you come along with me and see for yourself?"

Mr. Utterson's only answer was to rise and get his hat and greatcoat; but he observed with wonder the greatness of the relief that appeared upon the butler's face, and perhaps with no less, that the wine was still untasted when he set it down to follow.

It was a wild, cold, seasonable night of March, with a pale moon, lying on her back as though the wind had tilted her, and a flying wrack of the most diaphanous and lawny texture. The wind made talking difficult, and flecked the blood into the face. It seemed to have swept the streets unusually bare of passengers, besides; for Mr. Utterson thought he had never seen that part of London so deserted. He could have wished it otherwise; never in his life had he been conscious of so sharp a wish to see and touch his fellow-creatures; for, struggle as he might, there was borne in upon his mind a crushing anticipation of calamity. The square, when they got there, was all full of wind and dust, and the thin trees in the garden were lashing themselves along the railing. Poole, who had kept all the way a pace or two ahead, now pulled up in the middle of the pavement, and, in spite of the biting weather, took off his hat and mopped his brow with a red pocket-handkerchief. But for all the hurry of his coming, these were not the dews of exertion that he wiped away, but the moisture of some strangling anguish; for his face was white, and his voice, when he spoke, harsh and broken.

"Well, sir," he said, "here we are, and God grant there be nothing wrong."

"Amen, Poole," said the lawyer.

Thereupon the servant knocked in a very guarded manner; the door was opened on the chain; and a voice asked from within, "Is that you, Poole?"

"It's all right," said Poole. "Open the door."

The hall, when they entered it, was brightly lighted up; the fire was built high; and about the hearth the whole of the servants, men and women, stood huddled together like a flock of sheep. At the sight of Mr. Utterson, the housemaid broke into hysterical whimpering; and the cook, crying out "Bless God! it's Mr. Utterson," ran forward as if to take him in her arms.

"What, what? Are you all here?" said the lawyer peevishly. "Very irregular, very unseemly; your master would be far from pleased."

"They're all afraid," said Poole.

Blank silence followed, no one protesting; only the maid lifted up her voice and now wept loudly.

"Hold your tongue!" Poole said to her, with a ferocity of accent that testified to his own jangled nerves; and indeed, when the girl had so suddenly raised the note of her lamentation, they had all started and turned towards the inner door with faces of dreadful expectation. "And now," continued the butler, addressing the knife-boy, "reach me a candle, and we'll get this through hands at once." And then he begged Mr. Utterson to follow him, and led the way to the back-garden.

"Now, sir," said he, "you come as gently as you can. I want you to hear, and I don't want you to be heard. And see here, sir, if by any chance he was to ask you in, don't go."

Mr. Utterson's nerves, at this unlooked-for termination, gave a jerk that nearly threw him from his balance; but he re-collected his courage and followed the butler into the laboratory building and through the surgical theatre, with its lumber of crates and bottles, to the foot of the stair. Here Poole motioned him to stand on one side and listen; while he himself, setting down the candle and making a great and obvious call on his resolution, mounted the steps and knocked with a somewhat uncertain hand on the red baize of the cabinet door.

"Mr. Utterson, sir, asking to see you," he called; and, even as he did so, once more violently signed to the lawyer to give ear.

A voice answered from within : "Tell him I cannot see any one," it said complainingly.

"Thank you, sir," said Poole, with a note of something like triumph in his voice; and taking up his candle, he led Mr. Utterson back across the yard and into the great kitchen, where the fire was out and the beetles were leaping on the floor.

"Sir," he said, looking Mr. Utterson in the eyes, "was that my master's voice?"

"It seems much changed," replied the lawyer, very pale, but giving look for look.

"Changed? Well, yes, I think so," said the butler. "Have I been twenty years in this man's house, to be deceived about his voice? No, sir; master's made away with; he was made away with eight days ago, when we heard him cry out upon the name of God; and *who's* in there instead of him, and *why* it stays there, is a thing that cries to Heaven, Mr. Utterson!"

"This is a very strange tale, Poole; this is rather a wild tale, my man," said Mr. Utterson, biting his finger. "Suppose it were as you suppose, supposing Dr. Jekyll to have been – well, murdered, what could induce the murderer to stay? That won't hold water; it doesn't commend itself to reason."

"Well, Mr. Utterson, you are a hard man to satisfy, but I'll do it yet," said Poole. "All this last week (you must know) him, or it, or whatever it is that lives in that cabinet, has been crying night and day for some sort of medicine and cannot get it to his mind. It was sometimes his way – the master's, that is – to write his orders on a sheet of paper and throw it on the stair. We've had nothing else this week back; nothing but papers, and a closed door, and the very meals left there to be smuggled in when nobody was looking. Well, sir, every day, ay, and twice and thrice in the same day, there have been orders and complaints, and I have been sent flying to all the wholesale chemists in town. Every time I brought the stuff back, there would be another paper telling me to return it, because it was not pure, and another order to a different firm. This drug is wanted bitter bad, sir, whatever for."

"Have you any of these papers?" asked Mr. Utterson.

Poole felt in his pocket and handed out a crumpled note, which the lawyer, bending nearer to the candle, carefully examined. Its contents ran thus: "Dr. Jekyll presents his compliments to Messrs. Maw. He assures them that their last sample is impure, and quite useless for his present purpose. In the year 18 – , Dr. J. purchased a somewhat large quantity from Messrs. M. He now begs them to search with the most sedulous care, and should any of the same quality be left, to forward it to him at once. Expense is no consideration. The importance of this to Dr. J. can hardly be exaggerated."

So far the letter had run composedly enough, but here, with a sudden splutter of the pen, the writer's emotion had broken loose. "For God's sake," he had added, "find me some of the old."

"This is a strange note," said Mr. Utterson; and then sharply, "How do you come to have it open?"

"The man at Maw's was main angry, sir, and he threw it back to me like so much dirt," returned Poole.

"This is unquestionably the doctor's hand, do you know?" resumed the lawyer.

I thought it looked like it," said the servant rather sulkily; and then, with another voice, "But what matters hand-of-write?" he said. "I've seen him!"

"Seen him?" repeated Mr. Utterson. "Well?"

"That's it!" said Poole. "It was this way. I came suddenly into the theatre from the garden. It seems he had slipped out to look for this drug, or whatever it is; for the cabinet door was open, and there he was at the far end of the room digging among the crates. He looked up when I came in, gave a kind of cry, and whipped upstairs into the cabinet. It was but for one minute that I saw him, but the hair stood up on my head like quills. Sir, if that was my master, why had he a mask upon his face? If it was my master, why did he cry out like a rat, and run from me? I have served him long enough. And then ...", the man paused and passed his hand over his face.

"These are all very strange circumstances," said Mr. Utterson, "but I think I begin to see daylight. Your master, Poole, is plainly seized with one of those maladies that both torture and deform the sufferer; hence, for aught I know, the alteration of his voice; hence the mask and his avoidance of his friends; hence his eagerness to find this drug, by means of which the poor soul retains some hope of ultimate recovery – God grant that he be not deceived. There is my explanation; it is sad enough, Poole, ay, and appalling to consider; but it is plain and natural, hangs well together, and delivers us from all exorbitant alarms."

"Sir," said the butler, turning to a sort of mottled pallor, "that thing was not my master, and there's the truth. My master" – here he looked round him and began to whisper – "is a tall, fine build of a man, and this was more of a dwarf." Utterson attempted to protest. "O sir," cried Poole, "do you think I do not know my master after twenty years? do you think I do not know where his head comes to in the cabinet door, where I saw him every morning of my life? No, sir, that thing in the mask was never Dr. Jekyll – God knows what it was, but it was never Dr. Jekyll; and it is the belief of my heart that there was murder done."

"Poole," replied the lawyer, "if you say that, it will become my duty to make certain. Much as I desire to spare your master's feelings, much as I am puzzled by this note which seems to prove him to be still alive, I shall consider it my duty to break in that door."

"Ah, Mr. Utterson, that's talking!" cried the butler.

"And now comes the second question," resumed Utterson: "Who is going to do it?"

"Why, you and me, sir," was the undaunted reply.

"That is very well said," returned the lawyer; "and whatever comes of it, I shall make it my business to see you are no loser."

"There is an axe in the theatre," continued Poole; "and you might take the kitchen poker for yourself."

The lawyer took that rude but weighty instrument into his hand, and balanced it. "Do you know, Poole," he said, looking up, "that you and I are about to place ourselves in a position of some peril?"

"You may say so, sir, indeed," returned the butler.

"It is well, then, that we should be frank," said the other. "We both think more than we have said; let us make a clean breast. This masked figure that you saw, did you recognise it?"

"Well, sir, it went so quick, and the creature was so doubled up, that I could hardly swear to that," was the answer. "But if you mean, was it Mr. Hyde? – why, yes, I think it was! You see, it was much of the same bigness; and it had the same quick light way with it; and then who else could have got in by the laboratory door? You have not forgot, sir, that at the time of the murder he had still the key with him? But that's not all. I don't know, Mr. Utterson, if ever you met this Mr. Hyde?"

"Yes," said the lawyer, "I once spoke with him."

"Then you must know as well as the rest of us that there was something queer about that gentleman – something that gave a man a turn – I don't know rightly how to say it, sir, beyond this: that you felt it in your marrow kind of cold and thin."

"I own I felt something of what you describe," said Mr. Utterson.

"Quite so, sir," returned Poole. "Well, when that masked thing like a monkey jumped from among the chemicals and whipped into the cabinet, it went down my spine like ice. Oh, I know it's not evidence, Mr. Utterson; I'm book-learned enough for that; but a man has his feelings, and I give you my Bible-word it was Mr. Hyde!"

"Ay, ay," said the lawyer. "My fears incline to the same point. Evil, I fear, founded – evil was sure to come – of that connection. Ay, truly, I believe you; I believe poor Harry is killed; and I believe his murderer (for what purpose, God alone can tell) is still lurking in his victim's room. Well, let our name be vengeance. Call Bradshaw."

"The footman came at the summons, very white and nervous.

"Pull yourself together, Bradshaw," said the lawyer. "This suspense, I know, is telling upon all of you; but it is now our intention to make an end of it. Poole, here, and I are going to force our way into the cabinet. If all is well, my shoulders are broad enough to bear the blame. Meanwhile, lest anything should really be amiss, or any malefactor seek to escape by the back, you and the boy must go round the corner with a pair of good sticks, and take your post at the laboratory door. We give you ten minutes to get to your stations."

As Bradshaw left, the lawyer looked at his watch. "And now, Poole, let us get to ours," he said; and taking the poker under his arm, he led the way into the yard. The scud had banked over the moon, and it was now quite dark. The wind, which only broke in puffs and draughts into that deep well of building, tossed the light of the candle to and fro about their steps, until they came into the shelter of the theatre, where they sat down silently to wait. London hummed solemnly all around; but nearer at hand, the stillness was only broken by the sound of a footfall moving to and fro along the cabinet floor.

"So it will walk all day, sir," whispered Poole; "ay, and the better part of the night. Only when a new sample comes from the chemist, there's a bit of a break. Ah, it's an ill-conscience that's such an enemy to rest! Ah, sir, there's blood foully shed in every step of it! But hark again, a little closer – put your heart in your ears, Mr. Utterson, and tell me, is that the doctor's foot?"

The steps fell lightly and oddly, with a certain swing, for all they went so slowly; it was different indeed from the heavy creaking tread of Henry Jekyll. Utterson sighed. "Is there never anything else?" he asked.

46

Poole nodded. "Once," he said. "Once I heard it weeping!"

"Weeping? how that?" said the lawyer, conscious of a sudden chill of horror.

"Weeping like a woman or a lost soul," said the butler. "I came away with that upon my heart that I could have wept too."

But now the ten minutes drew to an end. Poole disinterred the axe from under a stack of packing straw; the candle was set upon the nearest table to light them to the attack; and they drew near with bated breath to where that patient foot was still going up and down, up and down, in the quiet of the night.

"Jekyll," cried Utterson, with a loud voice, "I demand to see you." He paused a moment, but there came no reply. "I give you fair warning, our suspicions are aroused, and I must and shall see you," he resumed; "if not by fair means, then by foul – if not of your consent, then by brute force!"

"Utterson," said the voice, "for God's sake have mercy!"

"Ah, that's not Jekyll's voice – it's Hyde's!" cried Utterson. "Down with the door, Poole."

Poole swung the axe over his shoulder; the blow shook the building, and the red baize door leaped against the lock and hinges. A dismal screech, as of mere animal terror, rang from the cabinet. Up went the axe again, and again the panels crashed and the frame bounded; four times the blow fell; but the wood was tough and the fittings were of excellent workmanship; and it was not until the fifth, that the lock burst in sunder and the wreck of the door fell inwards on the carpet.

The besiegers, appalled by their own riot and the stillness that had succeeded, stood back a little and peered in. There lay the cabinet before their eyes in the quiet lamplight, a good fire glowing and chattering on the hearth, the kettle singing its thin strain, a drawer or two open, papers neatly set forth on the business-table, and, nearer the fire, the things laid out for tea: the quietest room, you would have said, and, but for the glazed presses full of chemicals, the most commonplace that night in London.

Right in the midst there lay the body of a man sorely contorted, and still twitching. They drew near on tiptoe, turned it on its back, and beheld the face of Edward Hyde. He was dressed in clothes far too large for him, clothes of the doctor's bigness; the cords of his face still moved with a semblance of life, but life was quite gone; and by the crushed phial in the hand and the strong smell of kernels that hung upon the air, Utterson knew that he was looking on the body of a self-destroyer.

"We have come too late," he said sternly, "whether to save or punish. Hyde is gone to his account; and it only remains for us to find the body of your master."

The far greater proportion of the building was occupied by the theatre, which filled almost the whole ground story and was lighted from above, and by the cabinet, which formed an upper story at one end and looked upon the court. A corridor joined the theatre to the door on the by-street; and with this, the cabinet communicated separately by a second flight of stairs. There were besides a few dark closets and a spacious cellar. All these they now thoroughly examined. Each closet needed but a glance, for all were empty, and all, by the dust that fell from their doors, had stood long unopened. The cellar, indeed, was filled with crazy lumber, mostly dating from the times of the surgeon who was Jekyll's predecessor; but even as they opened the door, they were advertised of the uselessness of further search, by the fall of a perfect mat of cobweb which had for years sealed up the entrance. Nowhere was there any trace of Henry Jekyll, dead or alive.

Poole stamped on the flags of the corridor. "He must be buried here," he said, hearkening to the sound.

"Or he may have fled," said Utterson, and he turned to examine the door in the by-street. It was locked; and lying near by on the flags, they found the key, already stained with rust.

"This does not look like use," observed the lawyer.

"Use!" echoed Poole. "Do you not see, sir, it is broken? much as if a man had stamped on it."

"Ay," continued Utterson, "and the fractures, too, are rusty." The two men looked at each other with a scare. "This is beyond me, Poole," said the lawyer. "Let us go back to the cabinet."

They mounted the stair in silence, and, still with an occasional awe-struck glance at the dead body, proceeded more thoroughly to examine the contents of the cabinet. At one table there were traces of chemical work, various measured heaps of some white salt being laid on glass saucers, as though for an experiment in which the unhappy man had been prevented.

"That is the same drug that I was always bringing him," said Poole; and even as he spoke, the kettle with a startling noise boiled over.

This brought them to the fireside, where the easy-chair was drawn cosily up, and the tea-things stood ready to the sitter's elbow, the very sugar in the cup. There were several books on a shelf; one lay beside the tea-things open, and Utterson was amazed to find it a copy of a pious work, for which Jekyll had several times expressed a great esteem, annotated, in his own hand, with startling blasphemies.

Next, in the course of their review of the chamber, the searchers came to the cheval-glass, into whose depths they looked with an involuntary horror. But it was so turned as to show them nothing but the rosy glow playing on the roof, the fire sparkling in a hundred repetitions along the glazed front of the presses, and their own pale and fearful countenances stooping to look in.

"This glass have seen some strange things, sir," whispered Poole.

"And surely none stranger than itself," echoed the lawyer in the same tones. "For what did Jekyll" – he

caught himself up at the word with a start, and then con-
quering the weakness: "what could Jekyll want with it?"
he said.

"You may say that!" said Poole.

Next they turned to the business-table. On the desk,
among the neat array of papers, a large envelope was
uppermost, and bore, in the doctor's hand, the name of
Mr. Utterson. The lawyer unsealed it, and several enclos-
ures fell to the floor. The first was a will, drawn in the
same eccentric terms as the one which he had returned
six months before, to serve as a testament in case of
death and as a deed of gift in case of disappearance; but,
in place of the name of Edward Hyde, the lawyer, with
indescribable amazement, read the name of Gabriel John
Utterson. He looked at Poole, and then back at the
paper, and last of all at the dead malefactor stretched
upon the carpet.

"My head goes round," he said. "He has been all
these days in possession; he had no cause to like me; he
must have raged to see himself displaced; and he has not
destroyed this document."

He caught up the next paper; it was a brief note in the
doctor's hand, and dated at the top. "O Poole!" the
lawyer cried, "he was alive and here this day. He cannot
have been disposed of in so short a space, he must be still
alive, he must have fled! And then, why fled? and how?
and in that case, can we venture to declare this suicide?
Oh, we must be careful. I foresee that we may yet
involve your master in some dire catastrophe."

"Why don't you read it, sir?" asked Poole.

"Because I fear," replied the lawyer solemnly. "God
grant I have no cause for it!" and with that he brought
the paper to his eyes and read as follows:

"My dear Utterson, – When this shall fall into your
hands, I shall have disappeared, under what circumstances I have not the penetration to foresee, but my
instinct and all the circumstances of my nameless situ-

ation tell me that the end is sure, and must be early. Go
then, and first read the narrative which Lanyon warned
me he was to place in your hands; and if you care to hear
more, turn to the confession of

"Your unworthy and unhappy friend,

"HENRY JEKYLL."

"There was a third enclosure?" asked Utterson.

"Here sir," said Poole, and gave into his hands a considerable packet sealed in several places.

The lawyer put it in his pocket. "I would say nothing
of this paper. If your master has fled or is dead, we may at
least save his credit. It is now ten; I must go home and
read these documents in quiet; but I shall be back before
midnight, when we shall send for the police."

They went out, locking the door of the theatre behind
them; and Utterson, once more leaving the servants gathered about the fire in the hall, trudged back to his office
to read the two narratives in which this mystery was now
to be explained.

Dr. Lanyon's Narrative

ON the ninth of January, now four days ago, I received by the evening delivery a registered envelope, addressed in the hand of my colleague and old school-companion, Henry Jekyll. I was a good deal surprised by this; for we were by no means in the habit of correspondence; I had seen the man, dined with him, indeed, the night before; and I could imagine nothing in our intercourse that should justify the formality of registration. The contents increased my wonder; for this is how the letter ran: –

"10th December, 18 –

"Dear Lanyon, – You are one of my oldest friends; and although we may have differed at times on scientific questions, I cannot remember, at least on my side, any break in our affection. There was never a day when, if you had said to me, 'Jekyll, my life, my honour, my reason, depend upon you,' I would not have sacrificed my fortune or my left hand to help you. Lanyon, my life, my honour, my reason, are all at your mercy; if you fail me to-night, I am lost. You might suppose, after this preface, that I am going to ask you for something dishonourable to grant. Judge for yourself.

"I want you to postpone all other engagements for tonight – ay, even if you were summoned to the bedside of an emperor; to take a cab, unless your carriage should be actually at the door; and with this letter in your hand for consultation, to drive straight to my house. Poole, my butler, has his orders; you will find him waiting your arrival with a locksmith. The door of my cabinet is then to be forced; and you are to go in alone; to open the glazed press (letter E) on the left hand, breaking the lock if it be shut; and to draw out, *with all its contents as they stand*, the fourth drawer from the top or (which is the same thing) the third from the bottom. In my extreme distress of mind I have a morbid fear of misdirecting you; but even if I am in error, you may know the right drawer by its contents: some powders, a phial, and a paper book. This drawer I beg of you to carry back with you to Cavendish Square exactly as it stands.

"That is the first part of the service: now for the second. You should be back, if you set out at once on the receipt of this, long before midnight; but I will leave you that amount of margin, not only in the fear of one of those obstacles that can neither be prevented nor foreseen, but because an hour when your servants are in bed is to be preferred for what will then remain to do. At midnight, then, I have to ask you to be alone in your consulting-room, to admit with your own hand into the house a man who will present himself in my name, and to place in his hands the drawer that you will have brought with you from my cabinet. Then you will have played your part and earned my gratitude completely. Five minutes afterwards, if you insist upon an explanation, you will have understood that these arrangements are of capital importance; and that by the neglect of one of them, fantastic as they must appear, you might have charged your conscience with my death or the shipwreck of my reason.

"Confident as I am that you will not trifle with this appeal, my heart sinks and my hand trembles at the bare thought of such a possibility. Think of me at this hour, in a strange place, labouring under a blackness of distress that no fancy can exaggerate, and yet well aware that, if you will but punctually serve me, my troubles will roll away like a story that is told. Serve me, my dear Lanyon, and save

"Your friend,
"H. J.

"*P.S.* – I had already sealed this up when a fresh terror struck upon my soul. It is possible that the post office may fail me, and this letter not come into your hands until to-morrow morning. In that case, dear Lanyon, do my errand when it shall be most convenient for you in the course of the day; and once more expect my messenger at midnight. It may then already be too late; and if that night passes without event, you will know that you have seen the last of Henry Jekyll."

Upon the reading of this letter I made sure my colleague was insane; but till that was proved beyond the possibility of doubt, I felt bound to do as he requested. The less I understood of this farrago, the less I was in a position to judge of its importance; and an appeal so worded could not be set aside without a grave responsibility. I rose accordingly from table, got into a hansom, and drove straight to Jekyll's house. The butler was awaiting my arrival; he had received by the same post as mine a registered letter of instruction, and had sent at once for a locksmith and a carpenter. The tradesmen came while we were yet speaking; and we moved in a body to old Dr. Denman's surgical theatre, from which (as you are doubtless aware) Jekyll's private cabinet is most conveniently entered. The door was very strong, the lock excellent; the carpenter avowed he would have great trouble and have to do much damage, if force were to be used; and the locksmith was near despair. But this last was a handy fellow, and after two hours' work the door stood open. The press marked E was unlocked; and I took out the drawer, had it filled up with straw and tied in a sheet, and returned with it to Cavendish Square.

Here I proceeded to examine its contents. The powders were neatly enough made up, but not with the nicety of the dispensing chemist; so that it was plain they were of Jekyll's private manufacture; and when I opened one of the wrappers, I found what seemed to me a simple, crystalline salt of a white colour. The phial, to which

I next turned my attention, might have been about half-full of a blood-red liquor, which was highly pungent to the sense of smell and seemed to me to contain phosphorus and some volatile ether. At the other ingredients I could make no guess. The book was an ordinary version-book, and contained little but a series of dates. These covered a period of many years, but I observed that the entries ceased nearly a year ago, and quite abruptly. Here and there a brief remark was appended to a date, usually no more than a single word: "double" occurring perhaps six times in a total of several hundred entries; and once very early in the list, and followed by several marks of exclamation, "total failure! ! !" All this, though it whetted my curiosity, told me little that was definite. Here was a phial of some tincture, a paper of some salt, and a record of a series of experiments that had led (like too many of Jekyll's investigations) to no end of practical usefulness. How could the presence of these articles in my house affect either the honour, the sanity, or the life of my flighty colleague? If his messenger could go to one place, why could he not go to another? And even granting some impediment, why was this gentleman to be received by me in secret? The more I reflected, the more convinced I grew that I was dealing with a case of cerebral disease; and though I dismissed my servants to bed, I loaded an old revolver that I might be found in some posture of self-defence.

Twelve o'clock had scarce rung out over London, ere the knocker sounded very gently on the door. I went myself at the summons, and found a small man crouching against the pillars of the portico.

"Are you come from Dr. Jekyll?" I asked.

He told me "yes" by a constrained gesture; and when I had bidden him enter, he did not obey me without a searching backward glance into the darkness of the square. There was a policeman not far off, advancing with his bull's-eye open; and at the sight I thought my visitor started and made greater haste.

These particulars struck me, I confess, disagreeably; and as I followed him into the bright light of the consulting-room, I kept my hand ready on my weapon. Here, at last, I had a chance of clearly seeing him. I had never set eyes on him before, so much was certain. He was small, as I have said; I was struck besides with the shocking expression of his face, with his remarkable combination of great muscular activity and great apparent debility of constitution, and – last but not least – with the odd, subjective disturbance caused by his neighbourhood. This bore some resemblance to incipient rigor, and was accompanied by a marked sinking of the pulse. At the time, I set it down to some idiosyncratic, personal distaste, and merely wondered at the acuteness of the symptoms; but I have since had reason to believe the cause to lie much deeper in the nature of man, and to turn on some nobler hinge than the principle of hatred.

This person (who had thus, from the first moment of his entrance, struck in me what I can only describe as a disgustful curiosity) was dressed in a fashion that would have made an ordinary person laughable: his clothes, that is to say, although they were of rich and sober fabric, were enormously too large for him in every measurement – the trousers hanging on his legs and rolled up to keep them from the ground, the waist of the coat below his haunches and the collar sprawling wide upon his shoulders. Strange to relate, this ludicrous accoutrement was far from moving me to laughter. Rather, as there was something abnormal and misbegotten in the very essence of the creature that now faced me – something seizing, surprising, and revolting – this fresh disparity seemed but to fit in with and to reinforce it; so that to my interest in the man's nature and character there was added a curiosity as to his origin, his life, his fortune and status in the world.

These observations, though they have taken so great a space to be set down in, were yet the work of a few seconds. My visitor was, indeed, on fire with sombre excitement.

"Have you got it?" he cried. "Have you got it?" And so lively was his impatience that he even laid his hand upon my arm and sought to shake me.

I put him back, conscious at his touch of a certain icy pang along my blood. "Come, sir," said I. "You forget that I have not yet the pleasure of your acquaintance. Be seated, if you please." And I showed him an example, and sat down myself in my customary seat and with as fair an imitation of my ordinary manner to a patient as the lateness of the hour, the nature of my pre-occupations, and the horror I had of my visitor, would suffer me to muster.

"I beg your pardon, Dr. Lanyon," he replied civilly enough. "What you say is very well founded; and my impatience has shown its heels to my politeness. I come here at the instance of your colleague, Dr. Henry Jekyll, on a piece of business of some moment; and I understood ..." he paused and put his hand to his throat, and I could see, in spite of his collected manner, that he was wrestling against the approaches of the hysteria – "I understood, a drawer ..."

But here I took pity on my visitor's suspense, and some perhaps on my own growing curiosity.

"There it is, sir," said I, pointing to the drawer, where it lay on the floor behind a table and still covered with the sheet.

He sprang to it, and then paused, and laid his hand upon his heart; I could hear his teeth grate with the convulsive action of his jaws; and his face was so ghastly to see that I grew alarmed both for his life and reason.

"Compose yourself," said I.

He turned a dreadful smile to me, and as if with the decision of despair, plucked away the sheet. At sight of the contents he uttered one loud sob of such immense relief that I sat petrified. And the next moment, in a voice that was already fairly well under control, "Have you a graduated glass?" he asked.

I rose from my place with something of an effort and gave him what he asked.

He thanked me with a smiling nod, measured out a few minims of the red tincture and added one of the powders. The mixture, which was at first of a reddish hue, began, in proportion as the crystals melted, to brighten in colour, to effervesce audibly, and to throw off small fumes of vapour. Suddenly and at the same moment, the ebullition ceased and the compound changed to a dark purple, which faded again more slowly to a watery green. My visitor, who had watched these metamorphoses with a keen eye, smiled, set down the glass upon the table, and then turned and looked upon me with an air of scrutiny.

"And now," said he, "to settle what remains. Will you be wise? will you be guided? will you suffer me to take this glass in my hand and to go forth from your house without further parley? or has the greed of curiosity too much command of you? Think before you answer, for it shall be done as you decide. As you decide, you shall be left as you were before, and neither richer nor wiser, unless the sense of service rendered to a man in mortal distress may be counted as a kind of riches of the soul. Or, if you shall so prefer to choose, a new province of knowledge and new avenues to fame and power shall be laid open to you, here, in this room, upon the instant; and your sight shall be blasted by a prodigy to stagger the unbelief of Satan."

"Sir" said I, affecting a coolness that I was far from truly possessing, "you speak enigmas, and you will perhaps not wonder that I hear you with no very strong impression of belief. But I have gone too far in the way of inexplicable services to pause before I see the end."

"It is well," replied my visitor. "Lanyon, you remember your vows: what follows is under the seal of our profession. And now, you who have so long been bound to the most narrow and material views, you who have denied the virtue of transcendental medicine, you who have derided your superiors – behold!"

He put the glass to his lips and drank at one gulp. A

cry followed; he reeled, staggered, clutched at the table and held on, staring with injected eyes, gasping with open mouth; and as I looked there came, I thought, a change – he seemed to swell – his face became suddenly black and the features seemed to melt and alter – and the next moment I had sprung to my feet and leaped back against the wall, my arm raised to shield me from that prodigy, my mind submerged in terror.

"O God!" I screamed, and "O God!" again and again; for there before my eyes – pale and shaken, and half fainting, and groping before him with his hands, like a man restored from death – there stood Henry Jekyll!

What he told me in the next hour I cannot bring my mind to set on paper. I saw what I saw, I heard what I heard, and my soul sickened at it; and yet now when that sight has faded from my eyes, I ask myself if I believe it, and I cannot answer. My life is shaken to its roots; sleep has left me; the deadliest terror sits by me at all hours of the day and night; I feel that my days are numbered, and that I must die; and yet I shall die incredulous. As for the moral turpitude that man unveiled to me, even with tears of penitence, I cannot, even in memory, dwell on it without a start of horror. I will say but one thing, Utterson, and that (if you can bring your mind to credit it) will be more than enough. The creature who crept into my house that night was, on Jekyll's own confession, known by the name of Hyde, and hunted for in every corner of the land as the murderer of Carew.

HASTIE LANYON.

Henry Jekyll's Full Statement of the Case

I WAS born in the year 18 – to a large fortune, endowed besides with excellent parts, inclined by nature to industry, fond of the respect of the wise and good among my fellow-men, and thus, as might have been supposed, with every guarantee of an honourable and distinguished future. And indeed the worst of my faults was a certain impatient gaiety of disposition such as has made the happiness of many, but such as I found it hard to reconcile with my imperious desire to carry my head high, and wear a more than commonly grave countenance before the public. Hence it came about that I concealed my pleasures; and that when I reached years of reflection, and began to look round me and take stock of my progress and position in the world, I stood already committed to a profound duplicity of life. Many a man would have even blazoned such irregularities as I was guilty of; but from the high views that I had set before me, I regarded and hid them with an almost morbid sense of shame. It was thus rather the exacting nature of my aspirations than any particular degradation in my faults, that made me what I was, and, with even a deeper trench than in the majority of men, severed in me those provinces of good and ill which divide and compound man's dual nature. In this case, I was driven to reflect deeply and inveterately on that hard law of life, which lies at the root of religion and is one of the most plentiful springs of distress. Though so profound a double-dealer, I was in no sense a hypocrite; both sides of me were in dead earnest; I was no more myself when I laid aside restraint and plunged in shame, than when I laboured, in the eye of day, at the furtherance of knowledge or the relief of sorrow and suffering. And it chanced that the direction of my scientific studies, which led wholly towards the mystic and the transcendental, reacted and shed a strong light on this consciousness of the perennial war among my members. With every day, and from both sides of my intelligence, the moral and the intellectual, I thus drew steadily nearer to that truth, by whose partial discovery I have been doomed to such a dreadful ship-wreck: that man is not truly one, but truly two. I say two, because the state of my own knowledge does not pass beyond that point. Others will follow, others will outstrip me on the same lines; and I hazard the guess that man will be ultimately known for a mere polity of multifari-ous, incongruous and independent denizens. I for my part, from the nature of my life, advanced infallibly in one direction, and in one direction only. It was on the moral side, and in my own person, that I learned to recognise the thorough and primitive duality of man; I saw that of the two natures that contended in the field of my consciousness, even if I could rightly be said to be either, it was only because I was radically both; and from an early date, even before the course of my scientific dis-coveries had begun to suggest the most naked possibility of such a miracle, I had learned to dwell with pleasure, as a beloved day-dream, on the thought of the separation of these elements. If each, I told myself, could but be housed in separate identities, life would be relieved of all that was unbearable; the unjust might go his way, deliv-ered from the aspirations and remorse of his more upright twin; and the just could walk steadfastly and securely on his upward path, doing the good things in which he found his pleasure, and no longer exposed to disgrace and penitence by the hands of this extraneous evil. It was the curse of mankind that these incongruous fagots were thus bound together – that in the agonised womb of consciousness these polar twins should be con-tinuously struggling. How, then, were they dissociated?

I was so far in my reflections when, as I have said, a

side-light began to shine upon the subject from the laboratory table. I began to perceive more deeply than it has ever yet been stated, the trembling immateriality, the mist-like transience, of this seemingly so solid body in which we walk attired. Certain agents I found to have the power to shake and to pluck that fleshy vestment, even as a wind might toss the curtains of a pavilion. For two good reasons, I will not enter deeply into this scientific branch of my confession. First, because I have been made to learn that the doom and burthen of our life is bound for ever on man's shoulders, and when the attempt is made to cast it off, it but returns upon us with more unfamiliar and more awful pressure. Second, because as my narrative will make, alas! too evident, my discoveries were incomplete. Enough, then, that I not only recognised my natural body for the mere aura and effulgence of certain of the powers that made up my spirit, but managed to compound a drug by which these powers should be dethroned from their supremacy, and a second form and countenance substituted, none the less natural to me because they were the expression, and bore the stamp, of lower elements in my soul.

I hesitated long before I put this theory to the test of practice. I knew well that I risked death; for any drug that so potently controlled and shook the very fortress of identity, might by the least scruple of an overdose or at the least inopportunity in the moment of exhibition, utterly blot out that immaterial tabernacle which I looked to it to change. But the temptation of a discovery so singular and profound at last overcame the suggestions of alarm. I had long since prepared my tincture; I purchased at once, from a firm of wholesale chemists, a large quantity of a particular salt which I knew, from my experiments, to be the last ingredient required; and late one accursed night, I compounded the elements, watched them boil and smoke together in the glass, and when the ebullition had subsided, with a strong glow of courage drank off the potion.

The most racking pangs succeeded; a grinding in the bones, deadly nausea, and a horror of the spirit that cannot be exceeded at the hour of birth or death. Then these agonies began swiftly to subside, and I came to myself as if out of a great sickness. There was something strange in my sensations, something indescribably new and, from its very novelty, incredibly sweet. I felt younger, lighter, happier in body; within I was conscious of a heady recklessness, a current of disordered sensual images running like a mill-race in my fancy, a solution of the bonds of obligation, an unknown but not an innocent freedom of the soul. I knew myself, at the first breath of this new life, to be more wicked, tenfold more wicked, sold a slave to my original evil; and the thought, in that moment, braced and delighted me like wine. I stretched out my hands, exulting in the freshness of these sensations; and in the act I was suddenly aware that I had lost in stature.

There was no mirror, at that date, in my room; that which stands beside me as I write was brought there later on, and for the very purpose of these transformations. The night, however, was far gone into the morning – the morning, black as it was, was nearly ripe for the conception of the day – the inmates of my house were locked in the most rigorous hours of slumber; and I determined, flushed as I was with hope and triumph, to venture in my new shape as far as to my bedroom. I crossed the yard, wherein the constellations looked down upon me, I could have thought, with wonder, the first creature of that sort that their unsleeping vigilance had yet disclosed to them; I stole through the corridors, a stranger in my own house; and, coming to my room, I saw for the first time the appearance of Edward Hyde.

I must here speak by theory alone, saying not that which I know, but that which I suppose to be most probable. The evil side of my nature, to which I had now transferred the stamping efficacy, was less robust and less developed than the good which I had just deposed.

Again, in the course of my life, which had been, after all, nine-tenths a life of effort, virtue, and control, it had been much less exercised and much less exhausted. And hence, as I think, it came about that Edward Hyde was so much smaller, slighter, and younger than Henry Jekyll. Even as good shone upon the countenance of the one, evil was written broadly and plainly on the face of the other. Evil besides (which I must still believe to be the lethal side of man) had left on that body an imprint of deformity and decay. And yet when I looked upon that ugly idol in the glass, I was conscious of no repugnance, rather of a leap of welcome. This too, was myself. It seemed natural and human. In my eyes it bore a livelier image of the spirit, it seemed more express and single, than the imperfect and divided countenance I had been hitherto accustomed to call mine. And in so far I was doubtless right. I have observed that when I bore the semblance of Edward Hyde, none could come near to me at first without a visible misgiving of the flesh. This, as I take it, was because all human beings, as we meet them, are commingled out of good and evil: and Edward Hyde, alone in the ranks of mankind, was pure evil.

I lingered but a moment at the mirror: the second and conclusive experiment had yet to be attempted; it yet remained to be seen if I had lost my identity beyond redemption and must flee before daylight from a house that was no longer mine; and, hurrying back to my cabinet, I once more prepared and drank the cup, once more suffered the pangs of dissolution, and came to myself once more with the character, the stature, and the face of Henry Jekyll.

That night I had come to the fatal cross roads. Had I approached my discovery in a more noble spirit, had I risked the experiment while under the empire of generous or pious aspirations, all must have been otherwise, and from these agonies of death and birth I had come forth an angel instead of a fiend. The drug had no discriminating action; it was neither diabolical nor divine; it but shook the doors of the prison-house of my disposition; and like the captives of Philippi, that which stood within ran forth. At that time my virtue slumbered; my evil, kept awake by ambition, was alert and swift to seize the occasion; and the thing that was projected was Edward Hyde. Hence, although I had now two characters as well as two appearances, one was wholly evil, and the other was still the old Henry Jekyll, that incongruous compound of whose reformation and improvement I had already learned to despair. The movement was thus wholly toward the worse.

Even at that time I had not yet conquered my aversion to the dryness of a life of study. I would still be merrily disposed at times; and as my pleasures were (to say the least) undignified, and I was not only well known and highly considered, but growing towards the elderly man, this incoherency of my life was daily growing more unwelcome. It was on this side that my new power tempted me until I fell in slavery. I had but to drink the cup, to doff at once the body of the noted professor, and to assume, like a thick cloak, that of Edward Hyde. I smiled at the notion; it seemed to me at the time to be humorous; and I made my preparations with the most studious care. I took and furnished that house in Soho, to which Hyde was tracked by the police; and engaged as housekeeper a creature whom I well knew to be silent and unscrupulous. On the other side, I announced to my servants that a Mr. Hyde (whom I described) was to have full liberty and power about my house in the square; and to parry mishaps, I even called and made myself a familiar object, in my second character. I next drew up that will to which you so much objected; so that if anything befell me in the person of Doctor Jekyll, I could enter on that of Edward Hyde without pecuniary loss. And thus fortified, as I supposed, on every side, I began to profit by the strange immunities of my position.

Men have before hired bravos to transact their crimes, while their own person and reputation sat under shelter.

I was the first that ever did so for his pleasures. I was the first that could thus plod in the public eye with a load of genial respectability, and in a moment, like a schoolboy, strip off these lendings and spring headlong into the sea of liberty. But for me, in my impenetrable mantle, the safety was complete. Think of it – I did not even exist! Let me but escape into my laboratory-door, give me but a second or two to mix and swallow the draught that I had always standing ready; and whatever he had done, Edward Hyde would pass away like the stain of breath upon a mirror; and there in his stead, quietly at home, trimming the midnight lamp in his study, a man who could afford to laugh at suspicion, would be Henry Jekyll.

The pleasures which I made haste to seek in my disguise were, as I have said, undignified; I would scarce use a harder term. But in the hands of Edward Hyde they soon began to turn towards the monstrous. When I would come back from these excursions, I was often plunged into a kind of wonder at my vicarious depravity. This familiar that I called out of my own soul, and sent forth alone to do his good pleasure, was a being inherently malign and villainous; his every act and thought centred on self; drinking pleasure with bestial avidity from any degree of torture to another; relentless like a man of stone. Henry Jekyll stood at times aghast before the acts of Edward Hyde; but the situation was apart from ordinary laws, and insidiously relaxed the grasp of conscience. It was Hyde, after all, and Hyde alone, that was guilty. Jekyll was no worse; he woke again to his good qualities seemingly unimpaired; he would even make haste, where it was possible, to undo the evil done by Hyde. And thus his conscience slumbered.

Into the details of the infamy at which I thus connived (for even now I can scarce grant that I committed it) I have no design of entering; I mean but to point out the warnings and the successive steps with which my chastisement approached. I met with one accident which, as it brought on no consequence, I shall no more than mention. An act of cruelty to a child aroused against me the anger of a passer-by, whom I recognised the other day in the person of your kinsman; the doctor and the child's family joined him; there were moments when I feared for my life; and at last, in order to pacify their too just resentment, Edward Hyde had to bring them to the door, and pay them in a cheque drawn in the name of Henry Jekyll. But this danger was easily eliminated from the future, by opening an account at another bank in the name of Edward Hyde himself; and when, by sloping my own hand backward, I had supplied my double with a signature, I thought I sat beyond the reach of fate.

Some two months before the murder of Sir Danvers, I had been out for one of my adventures, had returned at a late hour, and woke the next day in bed with somewhat odd sensations. It was in vain I looked about me; in vain I saw the decent furniture and tall proportions of my room in the square; in vain that I recognised the pattern of the bed-curtains and the design of the mahogany frame; something still kept insisting that I was not where I was, that I had not wakened where I seemed to be, but in the little room in Soho where I was accustomed to sleep in the body of Edward Hyde. I smiled to myself, and, in my psychological way, began lazily to inquire into the elements of this illusion, occasionally, even as I did so, dropping back into a comfortable morning doze. I was still so engaged when, in one of my more wakeful moments, my eye fell upon my hand. Now the hand of Henry Jekyll (as you have often remarked) was professional in shape and size: it was large, firm, white, and comely. But the hand which I now saw, clearly enough, in the yellow light of a mid-London morning, lying half shut on the bed-clothes, was lean, corded, knuckly, of a dusky pallor, and thickly shaded with a swart growth of hair. It was the hand of Edward Hyde.

I must have stared upon it for near half a minute, sunk as I was in the mere stupidity of wonder, before terror woke up in my breast as sudden and startling as the crash of cymbals; and bounding from my bed, I rushed to the mirror. At the sight that met my eyes my blood was changed into something exquisitely thin and icy. Yes, I had gone to bed Henry Jekyll, I had awakened Edward Hyde. How was this to be explained? I asked myself; and then, with another bound of terror – how was it to be remedied? It was well on in the morning; the servants were up; all my drugs were in the cabinet – a long journey, down two pairs of stairs, through the back passage, across the open court and through the anatomical theatre, from where I was then standing horror-struck. It might indeed be possible to cover my face; but of what use was that, when I was unable to conceal the alteration in my stature? And then, with an overpowering sweetness of relief, it came back upon my mind that the servants were already used to the coming and going of my second self. I had soon dressed, as well as I was able, in clothes of my own size: had soon passed through the house, where Bradshaw stared and drew back at seeing Mr. Hyde at such an hour and in such a strange array; and ten minutes later Dr. Jekyll had returned to his own shape, and was sitting down, with a darkened brow, to make a feint of breakfasting.

Small indeed was my appetite. This inexplicable incident, this reversal of my previous experience, seemed, like the Babylonian finger on the wall, to be spelling out the letters of my judgment; and I began to reflect more seriously than ever before on the issues and possibilities of my double existence. That part of me which I had the power of projecting had lately been much exercised and nourished; it had seemed to me of late as though the body of Edward Hyde had grown in stature, as though (when I wore that form) I were conscious of a more generous tide of blood; and I began to spy a danger that, if this were much prolonged, the balance of my nature might be permanently overthrown, the power of voluntary change be forfeited, and the character of Edward Hyde become irrevocably mine. The power of the drug had not always been equally displayed. Once, very early in my career, it had totally failed me; since then I had been obliged on more than one occasion to double, and once, with infinite risk of death, to treble the amount; and these rare uncertainties had cast hitherto the sole shadow on my contentment. Now, however, and in the light of that morning's accident, I was led to remark that whereas, in the beginning, the difficulty had been to throw off the body of Jekyll, it had of late gradually but decidedly transferred itself to the other side. All things therefore seemed to point to this: that I was slowly losing hold of my original and better self, and becoming slowly incorporated with my second and worse.

Between these two, I now felt I had to choose. My two natures had memory in common, but all other faculties were most unequally shared between them. Jekyll (who was composite) now with the most sensitive apprehensions, now with a greedy gusto, projected and shared in the pleasures and adventures of Hyde; but Hyde was indifferent to Jekyll, or but remembered him as the mountain bandit remembers the cavern in which he conceals himself from pursuit. Jekyll had more than a father's interest; Hyde had more than a son's indifference. To cast in my lot with Jekyll was to die to those appetites which I had long secretly indulged, and had of late begun to pamper. To cast it in with Hyde was to die to a thousand interests and aspirations, and to become, at a blow and for ever, despised and friendless. The bargain might appear unequal; but there was still another consideration in the scales; for while Jekyll would suffer smartingly in the fires of abstinence, Hyde would be not even conscious of all that he had lost. Strange as my circumstances were, the terms of this debate are as old and commonplace as man; much the same inducements and alarms cast the die for any tempted and trembling sinner; and it fell out with me, as it falls with so vast a majority of my fellows, that I chose the better part, and was found wanting in the strength to keep to it.

Yes, I preferred the elderly and discontented doctor, surrounded by friends and cherishing honest hopes; and bade a resolute farewell to the liberty, the comparative youth, the light step, leaping pulses, and secret pleasures, that I had enjoyed in the disguise of Hyde. I made this choice perhaps with some unconscious reservation, for I neither gave up the house in Soho, nor destroyed the clothes of Edward Hyde, which still lay ready in my cabinet. For two months, however, I was true to my determination; for two months I led a life of such severity as I had never before attained to, and enjoyed the compensations of an approving conscience. But time began at last to obliterate the freshness of my alarm; the praises of conscience began to grow into a thing of course; I began to be tortured with throes and longings, as of Hyde struggling after freedom; and at last, in an hour of moral weakness, I once again compounded and swallowed the transforming draught.

I do not suppose that, when a drunkard reasons with himself upon his vice, he is once out of five hundred times affected by the dangers that he runs through his brutish, physical insensibility; neither had I, long as I had considered my position, made enough allowance for the complete moral insensibility and insensate readiness to evil, which were the leading characters of Edward Hyde. Yet it was by these that I was punished. My devil had been long caged, he came out roaring. I was conscious, even when I took the draught, of a more unbridled, a more furious propensity to ill. It must have been this, I suppose, that stirred in my soul that tempest of impatience with which I listened to the civilities of my unhappy victim; I declare at least, before God, no man morally sane could have been guilty of that crime upon so pitiful a provocation; and that I struck in no more reasonable spirit than that in which a sick child may break a plaything. But I had voluntarily stripped myself of all those balancing instincts, by which even the worst of us continues to walk with some degree of steadiness among temptations; and in my case, to be tempted, however slightly, was to fall.

Instantly the spirit of hell awoke in me and raged. With a transport of glee I mauled the unresisting body, tasting delight from every blow; and it was not till weariness had begun to succeed, that I was suddenly, in the top fit of my delirium, struck through the heart by a cold thrill of terror. A mist dispersed; I saw my life to be forfeit; and fled from the scene of these excesses, at once glorying and trembling, my lust of evil gratified and stimulated, my love of life screwed to the topmost peg. I ran to the house in Soho, and (to make assurance doubly sure) destroyed my papers; thence I set out through the lamplit streets, in the same divided ecstasy of mind, gloating on my crime, light-headedly devising others in the future, and yet still hastening and still hearkening in my wake for the steps of the avenger. Hyde had a song upon his lips as he compounded the draught, and as he drank it, pledged the dead man. The pangs of transformation had not done tearing him, before Henry Jekyll, with streaming tears of gratitude and remorse, had fallen upon his knees and lifted his clasped hands to God. The veil of self-indulgence was rent from head to foot, I saw my life as a whole: I followed it up from the days of childhood, when I had walked with my father's hand, and through the self-denying toils of my professional life, to arrive again and again, with the same sense of unreality, at the damned horrors of the evening. I could have screamed aloud; I sought with tears and prayers to smother down the crowd of hideous images and sounds with which my memory swarmed against me; and still, between the petitions, the ugly face of my iniquity stared into my soul. As the acuteness of this remorse began to die away, it was succeeded by a sense of joy. The problem of my conduct was solved. Hyde was thenceforth impossible; whether I would or not, I was now confined to the better part of my existence; and oh how I rejoiced to think it! with what willing humility I embraced anew the restrictions of natural life! with what sincere renunciation I locked the door by which I had so often gone and come, and ground the key under my heel!

The next day came the news that the murder had been overlooked, that the guilt of Hyde was patent to the world, and that the victim was a man high in public estimation. It was not only a crime, it had been a tragic folly. I think I was glad to know it; I think I was glad to have my better impulses thus buttressed and guarded by the terrors of the scaffold. Jekyll was now my city of refuge; let but Hyde peep out an instant, and the hands of all men would be raised to take and slay him.

I resolved in my future conduct to redeem the past; and I can say with honesty that my resolve was fruitful of some good. You know yourself how earnestly in the last months of last year, I laboured to relieve suffering; you know that much was done for others, and that the days passed quietly, almost happily for myself. Nor can I truly say that I wearied of this beneficent and innocent life; I think instead that I daily enjoyed it more completely; but I was still cursed with my duality of purpose; and as the first edge of my penitence wore off, the lower side of me, so long indulged, so recently chained down, began to growl for licence. Not that I dreamed of resuscitating Hyde; the bare idea of that would startle me to frenzy: no, it was in my own person that I was once more tempted to trifle with my conscience; and it was as an ordinary secret sinner that I at last fell before the assaults of temptation.

There comes an end to all things; the most capacious measure is filled at last; and this brief condescension to evil finally destroyed the balance of my soul. And yet I was not alarmed; the fall seemed natural, like a return to the old days before I had made my discovery. It was a fine, clear, January day, wet under foot where the frost had melted, but cloudless overhead; and the Regent's Park was full of winter chirrupings and sweet with spring odours. I sat in the sun on a bench; the animal within me licking the chops of memory; the spiritual side a little drowsed, promising subsequent penitence, but not yet moved to begin. After all, I reflected, I was like my neighbours; and then I smiled, comparing myself with other men, comparing my active goodwill with the lazy cruelty of their neglect. And at the very moment of that vainglorious thought a qualm came over me, a horrid nausea and the most deadly shuddering. These passed away, and left me faint; and then, as in its turn the faintness subsided, I began to be aware of a change in the temper of my thoughts, a greater boldness, a contempt of danger, a solution of the bonds of obligation. I looked down; my clothes hung formlessly on my shrunken limbs; the hand that lay on my knee was corded and hairy. I was once more Edward Hyde. A moment before I had been safe of all men's respect, wealthy, beloved – the cloth laying for me in the dining-room at home; and now I was the common quarry of mankind, hunted, houseless, a known murderer, thrall to the gallows.

My reason wavered, but it did not fail me utterly. I have more than once observed that, in my second character, my faculties seemed sharpened to a point and my spirits more tensely elastic; thus it came about that, where Jekyll perhaps might have succumbed, Hyde rose to the importance of the moment. My drugs were in one of the presses of my cabinet; how was I to reach them? That was the problem that (crushing my temples in my hands) I set myself to solve. The laboratory door I had closed. If I sought to enter by the house, my own servants would consign me to the gallows. I saw I must employ another hand, and thought of Lanyon. How was he to be reached? how persuaded? Supposing that I escaped capture in the streets, how was I to make my way into his presence? and how should I, an unknown and displeasing visitor, prevail on the famous physician to rifle the study of his colleague, Dr. Jekyll? Then I remembered that of my original character, one part remained to me: I could write my own hand; and once I had conceived that kindling spark, the way that I must follow became lighted up from end to end.

Thereupon I arranged my clothes as best I could, and summoning a passing hansom, drove to a hotel in Portland Street, the name of which I chanced to remember. At my appearance (which was indeed comical enough, however tragic a fate these garments covered) the driver could not conceal his mirth. I gnashed my teeth upon him with a gust of devilish fury; and the smile withered from his face – happily for him – yet more happily for myself, for in another instant I had certainly dragged him from his perch. At the inn, as I entered, I looked about me with so black a countenance as made the attendants tremble; not a look did they exchange in my presence; but obsequiously took my orders, led me to a private room, and brought me wherewithal to write. Hyde in danger of his life was a creature new to me: shaken with inordinate anger, strung to the pitch of murder, lusting to inflict pain. Yet the creature was astute; mastered his fury with a great effort of the will; composed his two important letters, one to Lanyon and one to Poole; and that he might receive actual evidence of their being posted, sent them out with directions that they should be registered.

Thenceforward, he sat all day over the fire in the private room, gnawing his nails; there he dined, sitting alone with his fears, the waiter visibly quailing before his eye; and then, when the night was fully come, he set forth in the corner of a closed cab, and was driven to and fro about the streets of the city. He, I say – I cannot say, I. That child of Hell had nothing human; nothing lived in him but fear and hatred. And when at last, thinking the driver had begun to grow suspicious, he discharged the cab and ventured on foot, attired in his misfitting clothes, an object marked out for observation, into the midst of the nocturnal passengers, these two base passions raged within him like a tempest. He walked fast, hunted by his

fears, chattering to himself, skulking through the less frequented thoroughfares, counting the minutes that still
divided him from midnight. Once a woman spoke to
him, offering, I think, a box of lights. He smote her in the
face, and she fled.

When I came to myself at Lanyon's, the horror of my
old friend perhaps affected me somewhat: I do not know;
it was at least but a drop in the sea to the abhorrence with
which I looked back upon these hours. A change had
come over me. It was no longer the fear of the gallows, it
was the horror of being Hyde that racked me. I received
Lanyon's condemnation partly in a dream; it was partly in
a dream that I came home to my own house and got into
bed. I slept after the prostration of the day, with a stringent and profound slumber which not even the night-
mares that wrung me could avail to break. I awoke in the
morning shaken, weakened, but refreshed. I still hated
and feared the thought of the brute that slept within me,
and I had not, of course, forgotten the appalling dangers
of the day before; but I was once more at home, in my
own house and close to my drugs; and gratitude for my
escape shone so strong in my soul that it almost rivalled
the brightness of hope.

I was stepping leisurely across the court after breakfast, drinking the chill of the air with pleasure, when I
was seized again with those indescribable sensations that
heralded the change; and I had but the time to gain the
shelter of my cabinet, before I was once again raging and
freezing with the passions of Hyde. It took on this occasion a double dose to recall me to myself; and alas! six
hours after, as I sat looking sadly in the fire, the pangs
returned, and the drug had to be re-administered. In
short, from that day forth it seemed only by a great effort
as of gymnastics, and only under the immediate stimula-
tion of the drug, that I was able to wear the countenance
of Jekyll. At all hours of the day and night I would be
taken with the premonitory shudder; above all, if I slept,
or even dozed for a moment in my chair, it was always as

Hyde that I awakened. Under the strain of this continually impending doom and by the sleeplessness to which I now condemned myself, ay, even beyond what I had thought possible to man, I became, in my own person, a creature eaten up and emptied by fever, languidly weak both in body and mind, and solely occupied by one thought: the horror of my other self. But when I slept, or when the virtue of the medicine wore off, I would leap almost without transition (for the pangs of transformation grew daily less marked) into the possession of a fancy brimming with images of terror, a soul boiling with causeless hatreds, and a body that seemed not strong enough to contain the raging energies of life. The powers of Hyde seemed to have grown with the sickliness of Jekyll. And certainly the hate that now divided them was equal on each side. With Jekyll, it was a thing of vital instinct. He had now seen the full deformity of that creature that shared with him some of the phenomena of consciousness, and was co-heir with him to death: and beyond these links of community, which in themselves made the most poignant part of his distress, he thought of Hyde, for all his energy of life, as of something not only hellish but inorganic. This was the shocking thing; that the slime of the pit seemed to utter cries and voices; that the amorphous dust gesticulated and sinned; that what was dead, and had no shape, should usurp the offices of life. And this again, that that insurgent horror was knit to him closer than a wife, closer than an eye; lay caged in his flesh, where he heard it mutter and felt it struggle to be born; and at every hour of weakness, and in the confidence of slumber, prevailed against him, and deposed him out of life. The hatred of Hyde for Jekyll was of a different order. His terror of the gallows drove him continually to commit temporary suicide, and return to his subordinate station of a part instead of a person; but he loathed the necessity, he loathed the despondency into which Jekyll was now fallen, and he resented the dislike with which he was himself regarded. Hence the ape-like tricks that he would play me, scrawling in my own hand blasphemies on the pages of my books, burning the letters and destroying the portrait of my father; and indeed, had it not been for his fear of death, he would long ago have ruined himself in order to involve me in the ruin. But his love of life is wonderful; I go further: I, who sicken and freeze at the mere thought of him, when I recall the abjection and passion of this attachment, and when I know how he fears my power to cut him off by suicide, I find it in my heart to pity him.

It is useless, and the time awfully fails me, to prolong this description; no one has ever suffered such torments, let that suffice; and yet even to these, habit brought – no, not alleviation – but a certain callousness of soul, a certain acquiescence of despair; and my punishment might have gone on for years, but for the last calamity which has now fallen, and which has finally severed me from my own face and nature. My provision of the salt, which had never been renewed since the date of the first experiment, began to run low. I sent out for a fresh supply, and mixed the draught; the ebullition followed, and the first change of colour, not the second; I drank it and it was without efficiency. You will learn from Poole how I have had London ransacked; it was in vain; and I am now persuaded that my first supply was impure, and that it was that unknown impurity which lent efficacy to the draught.

About a week has passed, and I am now finishing this statement under the influence of the last of the old powders. This, then, is the last time, short of a miracle, that Henry Jekyll can think his own thoughts or see his own face (now how sadly altered!) in the glass. Nor must I delay too long to bring my writing to an end; for if my narrative has hitherto escaped destruction, it has been by a combination of great prudence and great good luck. Should the throes of change take me in the act of writing it, Hyde will tear it in pieces; but if some time shall have elapsed after I have laid it by, his wonderful selfishness and circumscription to the moment will probably save it once again from the action of his ape-like spite. And indeed the doom that is closing on us both has already changed and crushed him. Half an hour from now, when I shall again and for ever re-indue that hated personality, I know how I shall sit shuddering and weeping in my chair, or continue, with the most strained and fearstruck ecstasy of listening, to pace up and down this room (my last earthly refuge) and give ear to every sound of menace. Will Hyde die upon the scaffold? or will he find the courage to release himself at the last moment? God knows; I am careless; this is my true hour of death, and what is to follow concerns another than myself. Here then, as I lay down the pen and proceed to seal up my confession, I bring the life of that unhappy Henry Jekyll to an end.

THE BODY-SNATCHER

THE BODY-SNATCHER

EVERY night in the year, four of us sat in the small parlour of the George at Debenham – the undertaker, and the landlord, and Fettes, and myself. Sometimes there would be more; but blow high, blow low, come rain or snow or frost, we four would be each planted in his own particular arm-chair. Fettes was an old drunken Scotchman, a man of education obviously, and a man of some property, since he lived in idleness. He had come to Debenham years ago, while still young, and by a mere continuance of living had grown to be an adopted townsman. His blue camlet cloak was a local antiquity, like the church-spire. His place in the parlour at the George, his absence from church, his old, crapulous, disreputable vices, were all things of course in Debenham. He had some vague Radical opinions and some fleeting infidelities, which he would now and again set forth and emphasise with tottering slaps upon the table. He drank rum – five glasses regularly every evening; and for the greater portion of his nightly visit to the George sat, with his glass in his right hand, in a state of melancholy alcoholic saturation. We called him the Doctor, for he was supposed to have some special knowledge of medicine, and had been known, upon a pinch, to set a fracture or reduce a dislocation; but beyond these slight particulars, we had no knowledge of his character and antecedents.

One dark winter night – it had struck nine some time before the landlord joined us – there was a sick man in the George, a great neighbouring proprietor suddenly struck down with apoplexy on his way to Parliament; and the great man's still greater London doctor had been telegraphed to his bedside. It was the first time that such a thing had happened in Debenham, for the railway was but newly open, and we were all proportionately moved by the occurrence.

"He's come," said the landlord, after he had filled and lighted his pipe.

"He?" said I. "Who? – not the doctor?"

"Himself," replied our host.

"What is his name?"

"Doctor Macfarlane," said the landlord.

Fettes was far through his third tumbler, stupidly fuddled, now nodding over, now staring mazily around him; but at the last word he seemed to awaken, and repeated the name "Macfarlane" twice, quietly enough the first time, but with sudden emotion at the second.

"Yes," said the landlord, "that's his name, Doctor Wolfe Macfarlane."

Fettes became instantly sober; his eyes awoke, his voice became clear, loud, and steady, his language forcible and earnest. We were all startled by the transformation, as if a man had risen from the dead.

"I beg your pardon," he said, "I am afraid I have not been paying much attention to your talk. Who is this Wolfe Macfarlane?" And then, when he had heard the landlord out, "It cannot be, it cannot be," he added; "and yet I would like well to see him face to face."

"Do you know him, Doctor?" asked the undertaker, with a gasp.

"God forbid!" was the reply. "And yet the name is a strange one; it were too much to fancy two. Tell me, landlord, is he old?"

"Well," said the host, "he's not a young man, to be sure, and his hair is white; but he looks younger than you."

"He is older, though; years older. But," with a slap upon the table, "it's the rum you see in my face – rum and sin. This man, perhaps, may have an easy conscience and a good digestion. Conscience! Hear me speak. You would think I was some good, old, decent Christian, would you not? But no, not I; I never canted. Voltaire might have canted if he'd stood in my shoes; but the brains" – with a rattling fillip on his bald head – "the brains were clear and active, and I saw and made no deductions."

"If you know this doctor," I ventured to remark, after a somewhat awful pause, "I should gather that you do not share the landlord's good opinion."

Fettes paid no regard to me.

"Yes," he said, with sudden decision, " I must see him face to face."

There was another pause, and then a door was closed rather sharply on the first floor, and a step was heard upon the stair.

"That's the doctor," cried the landlord. "Look sharp, and you can catch him."

It was but two steps from the small parlour to the door of the old George Inn; the wide oak staircase landed almost in the street; there was room for a Turkey rug and nothing more between the threshold and the last round of the descent; but this little space was every evening brilliantly lit up, not only by the light upon the stair and the great signal lamp below the sign, but by the warm radiance of the bar-room window. The George thus brightly advertised itself to passers-by in the cold street. Fettes walked steadily to the spot, and we, who were hanging behind, beheld the two men meet, as one of them had phrased it, face to face. Dr. Macfarlane was alert and vigorous. His white hair set off his pale and placid, although energetic, countenance. He was richly dressed in the finest of broadcloth and the whitest of linen, with a great gold watch-chain, and studs and spectacles of the same precious material. He wore a broadfolded tie, white and speckled with lilac, and he carried on his arm a comfortable driving-coat of fur. There was no doubt but he became his years, breathing, as he did, of wealth and consideration; and it was a surprising contrast to see our parlour sot – bald, dirty, pimpled, and robed in his old camlet cloak – confront him at the bottom of the stairs.

"Macfarlane!" he said somewhat loudly, more like a herald than a friend.

The great doctor pulled up short on the fourth step, as though the familiarity of the address surprised and somewhat shocked his dignity.

"Toddy Macfarlane!" repeated Fettes.

The London man almost staggered. He stared for the swiftest of seconds at the man before him, glanced behind him with a sort of scare, and then in a startled whisper, "Fettes!" he said, "you!"

"Ay", said the other, "me! Did you think I was dead too? We are not so easy shut of our acquaintance."

"Hush, hush!" exclaimed the doctor "Hush, hush! this meeting is so unexpected – I can see you are unmanned. I hardly knew you, I confess, at first; but I am overjoyed – overjoyed to have this opportunity. For the present it must be how-d'ye-do and good-bye in one, for my fly is waiting, and I must not fail the train; but you shall – let me see – yes – you shall give me your address, and you can count on early news of me. We must do something for you Fettes. I fear you are out at elbows; but we must see to that for auld lang syne, as once we sang at suppers."

"Money!" cried Fettes; "money from you! The money that I had from you is lying where I cast it in the rain."

Dr. Macfarlane had talked himself into some measure of superiority and confidence, but the uncommon energy of this refusal cast him back into his first confusion.

A horrible, ugly look came and went across his almost venerable countenance. "My dear fellow," he said, "be it as you please; my last thought is to offend you. I would intrude on none. I will leave you my address, however –"

"I do not wish it – I do not wish to know the roof that shelters you," interrupted the other. "I heard your name; I feared it might be you; I wished to know if, after all, there were a God; I know now that there is none. Begone!"

He still stood in the middle of the rug, between the stair and doorway; and the great London physician, in order to escape, would be forced to step to one side. It was plain that he hesitated before the thought of this humiliation. White as he was, there was a dangerous glitter in his spectacles; but while he still paused uncertain, he became aware that the driver of his fly was peering in from the street at this unusual scene and caught a glimpse at the same time of our little body from the parlour, huddled by the corner of the bar. The presence of so many witnesses decided him at once to flee. He crouched together, brushing on the wainscot, and made a dart like a serpent, striking for the door. But his tribulation was not entirely at an end, for even as he was passing Fettes clutched him by the arm and these words came in a whisper, and yet painfully distinct, "Have you seen it again?"

The great rich London doctor cried out aloud with a sharp, throttling cry; he dashed his questioner across the open space, and, with his hands over his head, fled out of the door like a detected thief. Before it had occurred to one of us to make a movement the fly was already rattling toward the station. The scene was over like a dream, but the dream had left proofs and traces of its passage. Next day the servant found the fine gold spectacles broken on the threshold, and that very night we were all standing breathless by the bar-room window, and Fettes at our side, sober, pale, and resolute in look.

"God protect us, Mr. Fettes!" said the landlord, coming first into possession of his customary senses. "What in the universe is all this? These are strange things you have been saying."

Fettes turned toward us; he looked us each in succession in the face. "See if you can hold your tongues," said he. "That man Macfarlane is not safe to cross; those that have done so already have repented it too late."

And then, without so much as finishing his third glass, far less waiting for the other two, he bade us good-bye and went forth, under the lamp of the hotel, into the black night.

We three turned to our places in the parlour, with the big red fire and four clear candles; and as we recapitulated what had passed, the first chill of our surprise soon changed into a glow of curiosity. We sat late; it was the latest session I have known in the old George. Each man, before we parted, had his theory that he was bound to prove; and none of us had any nearer business in this world than to track out the past of our condemned companion, and surprise the secret that he shared with the great London doctor. It is no great boast, but I believe I was a better hand at worming out a story than either of my fellows at the George; and perhaps there is now no other man alive who could narrate to you the following foul and unnatural events.

In his young days Fettes studied medicine in the schools of Edinburgh. He had talent of a kind, the talent that picks up swiftly what it hears and readily retails it for its own. He worked little at home; but he was civil, attentive, and intelligent in the presence of his masters. They soon picked him out as a lad who listened closely and remembered well; nay, strange as it seemed to me when I first heard it, he was in those days well favoured, and pleased by his exterior. There was, at that period, a certain extramural teacher of anatomy, whom I shall here designate by the letter K. His name was subsequently too well known. The man who bore it skulked through the streets of Edinburgh in disguise, while the mob that applauded at the execution of Burke called loudly for the blood of his employer. But Mr. K – was then at the top of his vogue; he enjoyed a popularity due partly to his own talent and address, partly to the incapacity of his rival, the university professor. The students, at least, swore by his name, and Fettes believed himself, and was believed by others, to have laid the foundations of success when he acquired the favour of this meteorically famous man. Mr. K – was a *bon vivant* as well as an accomplished teacher; he liked a sly illusion no less than a careful preparation. In both capacities Fettes enjoyed and

deserved his notice, and by the second year of his attendance he held the half-regular position of second demonstrator, or sub-assistant in his class.

In this capacity the charge of the theatre and lecture-
room devolved in particular upon his shoulders. He had
to answer for the cleanliness of the premises and the conduct of the other students, and it was a part of his duty to
supply, receive, and divide the various subjects. It was
with a view to this last – at that time very delicate – affair
that he was lodged by Mr. K – in the same wynd, and at
last in the same building, with the dissecting-rooms.
Here, after a night of turbulent pleasures, his hand still
tottering, his sight still misty and confused, he would be
called out of bed in the black hours before the winter
dawn by the unclean and desperate interlopers who supplied the table. He would open the door to these men,
since infamous throughout the land. He would help
them with their tragic burden, pay them their sordid
price, and remain alone, when they were gone, with the
unfriendly relics of humanity. From such a scene he
would return to snatch another hour or two of slumber, to
repair the abuses of the night, and refresh himself for the
labours of the day.

Few lads could have been more insensible to the
impressions of a life thus passed among the ensigns of
mortality. His mind was closed against all general considerations. He was incapable of interest in the fate and fortunes of another, the slave of his own desires and low
ambitions. Cold, light, and selfish in the last resort, he
had that modicum of prudence, miscalled morality,
which keeps a man from inconvenient drunkenness or
punishable theft. He coveted, besides, a measure of consideration from his masters and his fellow-pupils, and he
had no desire to fail conspicuously in the external parts
of life. Thus he made it his pleasure to gain some distinction in his studies, and day after day rendered unim-
peachable eye-service to his employer, Mr. K – . For his
day of work he indemnified himself by nights of roaring,

blackguardly enjoyment; and when that balance had been struck, the organ that he called his conscience declared itself content.

The supply of subjects was a continual trouble to him as well as to his master. In that large and busy class, the raw material of the anatomist kept perpetually running out; and the business thus rendered necessary was not only unpleasant in itself, but threatened dangerous consequences to all who were concerned. It was the policy of Mr. K – to ask no questions in his dealings with the trade. "They bring the body, and we pay the price," he used to say, dwelling on the alliteration –"*quid pro quo*." And, again, and somewhat profanely, "Ask no questions," he would tell his assistants, "for conscience' sake." There was no understanding that the subjects were provided by the crime of murder. Had that idea been broached to him in words, he would have recoiled in horror; but the lightness of his speech upon so grave a matter was, in itself, an offence against good manners, and a temptation to the men with whom he dealt. Fettes, for instance, had often remarked to himself upon the singular freshness of the bodies. He had been struck again and again by the hangdog, abominable looks of the ruffians who came to him before the dawn; and pulling things together clearly in his private thoughts, he perhaps attributed a meaning too immoral and too categorical to the unguarded counsels of his master. He understood his duty, in short, to have three branches: to take what was brought, to pay the price, and to avert the eye from any evidence of crime.

One November morning this policy of silence was put sharply to the test. He had been awake all night with a racking toothache – pacing his room like a caged beast or throwing himself in fury on his bed – and had fallen at last into that profound, uneasy slumber that so often follows on a night of pain, when he was awakened by the third or fourth angry repetition of the concerted signal. There was a thin, bright moonshine; it was bitter cold, windy, and frosty; the town had not yet awakened, but an indefinable stir already preluded the noise and business of the day. The ghouls had come later than usual, and they seemed more than usually eager to be gone. Fettes, sick with sleep, lighted them upstairs. He heard their grumbling Irish voices through a dream; and as they stripped the sack from their sad merchandise he leaned dozing, with his shoulder propped against the wall; he had to shake himself to find the men their money. As he did so his eyes lighted on the dead face. He started; he took two steps nearer, with the candle raised.

"God Almighty!" he cried. "That is Jane Galbraith!"

The men answered nothing, but they shuffled nearer the door.

"I know her, I tell you," he continued. "She was alive and hearty yesterday. It's impossible she can be dead; it's impossible you should have got this body fairly."

"Sure, sir, you're mistaken entirely," said one of the men.

But the other looked Fettes darkly in the eyes, and demanded the money on the spot.

It was impossible to misconceive the threat or to exaggerate the danger. The lad's heart failed him. He stammered some excuses, counted out the sum, and saw his hateful visitors depart. No sooner were they gone than he hastened to confirm his doubts. By a dozen unquestionable marks he identified the girl he had jested with the day before. He saw, with horror, marks upon her body that might well betoken violence. A panic seized him, and he took refuge in his room. There he reflected at length over the discovery that he had made; considered soberly the bearing of Mr. K –'s instructions and the danger to himself of interference in so serious a business, and at last, in sore perplexity, determined to wait for the advice of his immediate superior, the class assistant.

This was a young doctor, Wolfe Macfarlane, a high favourite among all the reckless students, clever, dissipated, and unscrupulous to the last degree. He had travelled and studied abroad. His manners were agreeable and a little forward. He was an authority on the stage, skilful on the ice or the links with skate or golf-club; he dressed with nice audacity, and, to put the finishing touch upon his glory, he kept a gig and a strong trotting-horse. With Fettes he was on terms of intimacy; indeed, their relative positions called for some community of life; and when subjects were scarce the pair would drive far into the country in Macfarlane's gig, visit and desecrate some lonely graveyard, and return before dawn with their booty to the door of the dissecting-room.

On that particular morning Macfarlane arrived somewhat earlier than his wont. Fettes heard him, and met him on the stairs, told him his story, and showed him the cause of his alarm. Macfarlane examined the marks on her body.

"Yes," he said, with a nod, "it looks fishy."

"Well, what should I do?" asked Fettes.

"Do?" repeated the other. "Do you want to do anything? Least said soonest mended, I should say."

"Some one else might recognise her," objected Fettes. "She was as well known as the Castle Rock."

"We'll hope not," said Macfarlane, "and if anybody does – well, you didn't, don't you see, and there's an end. The fact is, this has been going on too long. Stir up the mud, and you'll get K – into the most unholy trouble; you'll be in a shocking box yourself. So will I, if you come to that. I should like to know how any one of us would look, or what the devil we should have to say for ourselves, in any Christian witness-box. For me, you know there's one thing certain – that, practically speaking, all our subjects have been murdered."

"Macfarlane!" cried Fettes.

"Come now!" sneered the other. "As if you hadn't suspected it yourself!"

"Suspecting is one thing – "

"And proof another. Yes, I know; and I'm as sorry as you are this should have come here," tapping the body with his cane. "The next best thing for me is not to recognise it; and," he added coolly, "I don't. You may, if you please. I don't dictate, but I think a man of the world would do as I do; and I may add, I fancy that is what K – would look for at our hands. The question is, Why did he choose us two for his assistants? And I answer, Because he didn't want old wives."

This was the tone of all others to affect the mind of a lad like Fettes. He agreed to imitate Macfarlane. The body of the unfortunate girl was duly dissected, and no one remarked or appeared to recognise her.

One afternoon, when his day's work was over, Fettes dropped into a popular tavern and found Macfarlane sitting with a stranger. This was a small man, very pale and dark, with coal-black eyes. The cut of his features gave a promise of intellect and refinement which was but feebly realised in his manners, for he proved, upon a nearer acquaintance, coarse, vulgar, and stupid. He exercised, however, a very remarkable control over Macfarlane; issued orders like the Great Bashaw; became inflamed at the least discussion or delay, and commented rudely on the servility with which he was obeyed. This most offensive person took a fancy to Fettes on the spot, plied him with drinks, and honoured him with unusual confidences on his past career. If a tenth part of what he confessed were true, he was a very loathsome rogue; and the lad's vanity was tickled by the attention of so experienced a man.

"I'm a pretty bad fellow myself," the stranger remarked, "but Macfarlane is the boy – Toddy Macfarlane I call him. Toddy, order your friend another glass." Or it might be, "Toddy, you jump up and shut the door." "Toddy hates me," he said again. "Oh, yes, Toddy, you do!"

"Don't you call me that confounded name," growled Macfarlane.

"Hear him! Did you ever see the lads play knife? He would like to do that all over my body," remarked the stranger.

"We medicals have a better way than that," said Fettes.

"When we dislike a dead friend of ours, we dissect him."

Macfarlane looked up sharply, as though this jest were scarcely to his mind.

The afternoon passed. Gray, for that was the stranger's name, invited Fettes to join them at dinner, ordered a feast so sumptuous that the tavern was thrown into commotion, and when all was done commanded Macfarlane to settle the bill. It was late before they separated; the man Gray was incapably drunk. Macfarlane, sobered by his fury, chewed the cud of the money he had been forced to squander and the slights he had been obliged to swallow. Fettes, with various liquors singing in his head, returned home with devious footsteps and a mind entirely in abeyance. Next day Macfarlane was absent from the class, and Fettes smiled to himself as he imagined him still squiring the intolerable Gray from tavern to tavern. As soon as the hour of liberty had struck he posted from place to place in quest of his last night's companions. He could find them, however, nowhere; so returned early to his rooms, went early to bed, and slept the sleep of the just.

At four in the morning he was awakened by the well-known signal. Descending to the door, he was filled with astonishment to find Macfarlane with his gig, and in the gig one of those long and ghastly packages with which he was so well acquainted.

"What?" he cried. "Have you been out alone? How did you manage?"

But Macfarlane silenced him roughly, bidding him turn to business. When they had got the body upstairs and laid it on the table, Macfarlane made at first as if he were going away. Then he paused and seemed to hesitate; and then, "You had better look at the face," said he, in tones of some constraint. "You had better," he repeated, as Fettes only stared at him in wonder.

"But where, and how, and when did you come by it?" cried the other.

"Look at the face," was the only answer.

Fettes was staggered; strange doubts assailed him. He looked from the young doctor to the body, and then back again. At last, with a start, he did as he was bidden. He had almost expected the sight that met his eyes, and yet the shock was cruel. To see, fixed in the rigidity of death and naked on that coarse layer of sackcloth, the man whom he had left well clad and full of meat and sin upon the threshold of a tavern, awoke, even in the thoughtless Fettes, some of the terrors of the conscience. It was a *cras tibi* which re-echoed in his soul, that two whom he had known should have come to lie upon these icy tables. Yet these were only secondary thoughts. His first concern regarded Wolfe. Unprepared for a challenge so momentous, he knew not how to look his comrade in the face. He durst not meet his eye, and he had neither words nor voice at his command.

It was Macfarlane himself who made the first advance. He came up quietly behind and laid his hand gently but firmly on the other's shoulder.

"Richardson," said he, "may have the head."

Now Richardson was a student who had long been anxious for that portion of the human subject to dissect. There was no answer, and the murderer resumed: "Talking of business, you must pay me; your accounts, you see, must tally."

Fettes found a voice, the ghost of his own: "Pay you!" he cried. "Pay you for that?"

"Why, yes, of course you must. By all means and on every possible account, you must," returned the other. "I dare not give it for nothing, you dare not take it for nothing; it would compromise us both. This is another case like Jane Galbraith's. The more things are wrong the more we must act as if all were right. Where does old K – keep his money?"

"There," answered Fettes hoarsely, pointing to a cupboard in the corner.

"Give me the key, then," said the other calmly, holding out his hand.

There was an instant's hesitation, and the die was cast. Macfarlane could not suppress a nervous twitch, the infinitesimal mark of an immense relief, as he felt the key between his fingers. He opened the cupboard, brought out pen and ink and a paper-book that stood in one compartment, and separated from the funds in a drawer a sum suitable to the occasion.

"Now, look here," he said, "there is the payment made – first proof of your good faith: first step to your security. You have now to clinch it by a second. Enter the payment in your book, and then you for your part may defy the devil."

The next few seconds were for Fettes an agony of thought; but in balancing his terrors it was the most immediate that triumphed. Any future difficulty seemed almost welcome if he could avoid a present quarrel with Macfarlane. He set down the candle which he had been carrying all this time, and with a steady hand entered the date, the nature, and the amount of the transaction.

"And now," said Macfarlane, "it's only fair that you should pocket the lucre. I've had my share already. By-the-bye, when a man of the world falls into a bit of luck, has a few shillings extra in his pocket – I'm ashamed to speak of it, but there's a rule of conduct in the case. No treating, no purchase of expensive class-books, no squaring of old debts; borrow, don't lend."

"Macfarlane," began Fettes, still somewhat hoarsely, "I have put my neck in a halter to oblige you."

"To oblige me?" cried Wolfe. "Oh, come! You did, as near as I can see the matter, what you downright had to do in self-defence. Suppose I got into trouble, where would you be? This second little matter flows clearly from the first. Mr. Gray is the continuation of Miss Galbraith. You can't begin and then stop. If you begin, you must keep on beginning; that's the truth. No rest for the wicked."

A horrible sense of blackness and the treachery of fate seized hold upon the soul of the unhappy student.

"My God!" he cried, "but what have I done? and when did I begin? To be made a class assistant – in the name of reason, where's the harm in that? Service wanted the position; Service might have got it. Would *he* have been where *I* am now!"

"My dear fellow," said Macfarlane, "what a boy you are! What harm *has* come to you? What harm *can* come to you if you hold your tongue? Why, man, do you know what this life is? There are two squads of us – the lions and the lambs. If you're a lamb, you'll come to lie upon these tables like Gray or Jane Galbraith; if you're a lion, you'll live and drive a horse like me, like K – , like all the world with any wit or courage. You're staggered at the first. But look at K – ! My dear fellow, you're clever, you have pluck. I like you, and K – likes you. You were born to lead the hunt; and I tell you, on my honour and my experience of life, three days from now you'll laugh at all these scarecrows like a High School boy at a farce."

And with that Macfarlane took his departure and drove off up the wynd in his gig to get under cover before daylight. Fettes was thus left alone with his regrets. He saw the miserable peril in which he stood involved. He saw, with inexpressible dismay, that there was no limit to his weakness, and that, from concession to concession, he had fallen from the arbiter of Macfarlane's destiny to his paid and helpless accomplice. He would have given the world to have been a little braver at the time, but it did not occur to him that he might still be brave. The secret of Jane Galbraith and the cursed entry in the day-book closed his mouth.

Hours passed; the class began to arrive; the members of the unhappy Gray were dealt out to one and to another, and received without remark. Richardson was made happy with the head; and before the hour of free-dom rang Fettes trembled with exultation to perceive how far they had already gone toward safety.

For two days he continued to watch, with increasing joy, the dreadful process of disguise.

On the third day Macfarlane made his appearance. He had been ill, he said; but he made up for lost time by the energy with which he directed the students. To Richardson in particular he extended the most valuable assistance and advice, and that student, encouraged by the praise of the demonstrator, burned high with ambitious hopes, and saw the medal already in his grasp.

Before the week was out Macfarlane's prophecy had been fulfilled. Fettes had outlived his terrors and had forgotten his baseness. He began to plume himself upon his courage, and had so arranged the story in his mind that he could look back on these events with an unhealthy pride. Of his accomplice he saw but little. They met, of course, in the business of the class; they received their orders together from Mr. K – . At times they had a word or two in private, and Macfarlane was from first to last particularly kind and jovial. But it was plain that he avoided any reference to their common secret; and even when Fettes whispered to him that he had cast in his lot with the lions and forsworn the lambs, he only signed to him smilingly to hold his peace.

At length an occasion arose which threw the pair once more into a closer union. Mr. K – was again short of subjects; pupils were eager, and it was a part of this teacher's pretensions to be always well supplied. At the same time there came the news of a burial in the rustic graveyard of Glencorse. Time has little changed the place in question. It stood then, as now, upon a cross road, out of call of human habitations, and buried fathom deep in the foliage of six cedar trees. The cries of the sheep upon the neighbouring hills, the streamlets upon either hand, one loudly singing among pebbles, the other dripping furtively from pond to pond, the stir of the wind in mountainous old flowering chestnuts, and once in seven days the voice of the bell and the old tunes of the precentor, were the only sounds that disturbed the silence around the rural church. The Resurrection Man – to use a by-name of the period – was not to be deterred by any of the sanctities of customary piety. It was part of his trade to despise and desecrate the scrolls and trumpets of old tombs, the paths worn by the feet of worshippers and mourners, and the offerings and the inscriptions of bereaved affection. To rustic neighbourhoods, where love is more than commonly tenacious, and where some bonds of blood or fellowship unite the entire society of a parish, the body-snatcher, far from being repelled by natural respect, was attracted by the ease and safety of the task. To bodies that had been laid in earth, in joyful expectation of a far different awakening, there came that hasty, lamplit, terror-haunted resurrection of the spade and mattock. The coffin was forced, the cerements torn, and the melancholy relics, clad in sackcloth, after being rattled for hours on moonless byways, were at length exposed to uttermost indignities before a class of gaping boys.

Somewhat as two vultures may swoop upon a dying lamb, Fettes and Macfarlane were to be let loose upon a grave in that green and quiet resting-place. The wife of a farmer, a woman who had lived for sixty years, and been known for nothing but good butter and a godly conversation, was to be rooted from her grave at midnight and carried, dead and naked, to that far-away city that she had always honoured with her Sunday's best; the place beside her family was to be empty till the crack of doom; her innocent and almost venerable members to be exposed to that last curiosity of the anatomist.

Late one afternoon the pair set forth, well wrapped in cloaks and furnished with a formidable bottle. It rained without remission – a cold, dense, lashing rain. Now and again there blew a puff of wind, but these sheets of falling water kept it down. Bottle and all, it was a sad and silent drive as far as Penicuik, where they were to spend the evening. They stopped once, to hide their implements in a thick bush not far from the churchyard, and once again at the Fisher's Tryst, to have a toast before the kitchen fire and vary their nips of whisky with a glass of ale. When they reached their journey's end the gig was housed, the horse was fed and comforted, and the two young doctors in a private room sat down to the best dinner and the best wine the house afforded. The lights, the fire, the beating rain upon the window, the cold, incongruous work that lay before them, added zest to their enjoyment of the meal. With every glass their cordiality increased. Soon Macfarlane handed a little pile of gold to his companion.

"A compliment," he said. "Between friends these little d – d accommodations ought to fly like pipe-lights."

Fettes pocketed the money, and applauded the sentiment to the echo. "You are a philosopher," he cried. "I was an ass till I knew you. You and K – between you, by the Lord Harry! but you'll make a man of me."

"Of course we shall," applauded Macfarlane. "A man? I tell you, it required a man to back me up the other morning. There are some big, brawling, forty-year-old cowards who would have turned sick at the look of the d – d thing; but not you – you kept your head. I watched you."

"Well, and why not?" Fettes thus vaunted himself. "It was no affair of mine. There was nothing to gain on the one side but disturbance, and on the other I could count on your gratitude, don't you see?" And he slapped his pocket till the gold pieces rang.

Macfarlane somehow felt a certain touch of alarm at these unpleasant words. He may have regretted that he had taught his young companion so successfully, but he had no time to interfere, for the other noisily continued in this boastful strain: –

"The great thing is not to be afraid. Now, between you and me, I don't want to hang – that's practical; but for all cant, Macfarlane, I was born with a contempt. Hell, God, Devil, right, wrong, sin, crime, and all the old gallery of curiosities – they may frighten boys, but men of the world, like you and me, despise them. Here's to the memory of Gray!"

It was by this time growing somewhat late. The gig, according to order, was brought round to the door with both lamps brightly shining, and the young men had to pay their bill and take the road. They announced that they were bound for Peebles, and drove in that direction till they were clear of the last houses of the town; then, extinguishing the lamps, returned upon their course, and followed a by-road toward Glencorse. There was no sound but that of their own passage, and the incessant, strident pouring of the rain. It was pitch dark; here and there a white gate or a white stone in the wall guided them for a short space across the night; but for the most part it was at a foot pace, and almost groping, that they picked their way through that resonant blackness to their solemn and isolated destination. In the sunken woods that traverse the neighbourhood of the burying-ground the last glimmer failed them, and it became necessary to kindle a match and re-illumine one of the lanterns of the gig. Thus, under the dripping trees, and environed by huge and moving shadows, they reached the scene of their unhallowed labours.

They were both experienced in such affairs, and powerful with the spade; and they had scarce been twenty minutes at their task before they were rewarded by a dull rattle on the coffin lid. At the same moment, Macfarlane, having hurt his hand upon a stone, flung it carelessly above his head. The grave, in which they now stood almost to the shoulders, was close to the edge of the plateau of the graveyard; and the gig lamp had been propped, the better to illuminate their labours, against a tree, and on the immediate verge of the steep bank descending to the stream. Chance had taken a sure aim with the stone. Then came a clang of broken glass; night fell upon them; sounds alternately dull and ringing announced the bounding of the lantern down the bank, and its occasional collision with the trees. A stone or two, which it had dislodged in its descent, rattled behind it into the profundities of the glen; and then silence, like night, resumed its sway; and they might bend their hearing to its utmost pitch, but naught was to be heard except the rain, now marching to the wind, now steadily falling over miles of open country.

They were so nearly at an end of their abhorred task that they judged it wisest to complete it in the dark. The coffin was exhumed and broken open; the body inserted in the dripping sack and carried between them to the gig; one mounted to keep it in its place, and the other, taking the horse by the mouth, groped along by wall and bush until they reached the wider road by the Fisher's Tryst. Here was a faint, diffused radiancy, which they hailed like daylight; by that they pushed the horse to a good pace and began to rattle along merrily in the direction of the town.

They had both been wetted to the skin during their operations, and now, as the gig jumped among the deep ruts, the thing that stood propped between them fell now upon one and now upon the other. At every repetition of the horrid contact each instinctively repelled it with the greater haste; and the process, natural although it was, began to tell upon the nerves of the companions. Macfarlane made some ill-favoured jest about the farmer's wife, but it came hollowly from his lips, and was allowed to drop in silence. Still their unnatural burden bumped from side to side; and now the head would be laid, as if in confidence, upon their shoulders, and now the drenching sackcloth would flap icily about their faces. A creeping chill began to possess the soul of Fettes. He peered at the bundle, and it seemed somehow larger than at first. All over the country-side, and from every degree of distance, the farm dogs accompanied their passage with tragic ululations; and it grew and grew upon his mind that some unnatural miracle had been accomplished, that some nameless change had befallen the dead body, and that it was in fear of their unholy burden that the dogs were howling.

"For God's sake," said he, making a great effort to arrive at speech, "for God's sake, let's have a light!"

Seemingly Macfarlane was affected in the same direction; for, though he made no reply, he stopped the horse, passed the reins to his companion, got down, and proceeded to kindle the remaining lamp. They had by that time got no farther than the cross-road down to Auchenclinny. The rain still poured as though the deluge were returning, and it was no easy matter to make a light in such a world of wet and darkness. When at last the flickering blue flame had been transferred to the wick and began to expand and clarify, and shed a wide circle of misty brightness round the gig, it became possible for the two young men to see each other and the thing they had along with them. The rain had moulded the rough sacking to the outlines of the body underneath; the head was distinct from the trunk, the shoulders plainly modelled; something at once spectral and human riveted their eyes upon the ghastly comrade of their drive.

For some time Macfarlane stood motionless, holding up the lamp. A nameless dread was swathed, like a wet sheet, about the body, and tightened the white skin upon the face of Fettes; a fear that was meaningless, a horror of what could not be, kept mounting to his brain. Another beat of the watch, and he had spoken. But his comrade forestalled him.

"That is not a woman," said Macfarlane, in a hushed voice.

"It was a woman when we put her in," whispered Fettes.

"Hold that lamp," said the other. "I must see her face."

And as Fettes took the lamp his companion untied the fastenings of the sack and drew down the cover from the head. The light fell very clear upon the dark, well-moulded features and smooth-shaven cheeks of a too familiar countenance, often beheld in dreams of both of these young men. A wild yell rang up into the night; each leaped from his own side into the roadway: the lamp fell, broke, and was extinguished; and the horse, terrified by this unusual commotion, bounded and went off toward Edinburgh at a gallop, bearing along with it, sole occupant of the gig, the body of the dead and long-dissected Gray.

A LODGING FOR THE NIGHT

A LODGING FOR THE NIGHT

A Story of Francis Villon

IT was late in November 1456. The snow fell over Paris with rigorous, relentless persistence; sometimes the wind made a sally and scattered it in flying vortices; sometimes there was a lull, and flake after flake descended out of the black night air, silent, circuitous, interminable. To poor people, looking up under moist eyebrows, it seemed a wonder where it all came from. Master Francis Villon had propounded an alternative that afternoon at a tavern window: was it only Pagan Jupiter plucking geese upon Olympus? or were the holy angels moulting? He was only a poor Master of Arts, he went on; and as the question somewhat touched upon divinity, he durst not venture to conclude. A silly old priest from Montargis, who was among the company, treated the young rascal to a bottle of wine in honour of the jest and the grimaces with which it was accompanied, and swore on his own white beard that he had been just such another irreverent dog when he was Villon's age.

The air was raw and pointed, but not far below freezing; and the flakes were large, damp, and adhesive. The whole city was sheeted up. An army might have marched from end to end and not a footfall given the alarm. If there were any belated birds in heaven, they saw the island like a large white patch, and the bridges like slim white spars, on the black ground of the river. High up overhead the snow settled among the tracery of the cathedral towers. Many a niche was drifted full; many a statue wore a long white bonnet on its grotesque or sainted head. The gargoyles had been transformed into great false noses, drooping towards the point. The crockets were like upright pillows swollen on one side.

In the intervals of the wind there was a dull sound of dripping about the precincts of the church.

The cemetery of St. John had taken its own share of the snow. All the graves were decently covered; tall white housetops stood around in grave array; worthy burghers were long ago in bed, be-nightcapped like their domiciles; there was no light in all the neighbourhood but a little peep from a lamp that hung swinging in the church choir, and tossed the shadows to and fro in time to its oscillations. The clock was hard on ten when the patrol went by with halberds and a lantern, beating their hands; and they saw nothing suspicious about the cemetery of St. John.

Yet there was a small house, backed up against the cemetery wall, which was still awake, and awake to evil purpose, in that snoring district. There was not much to betray it from without; only a stream of warm vapour from the chimney-top, a patch where the snow melted on the roof, and a few half-obliterated footprints at the door. But within, behind the shuttered windows, Master Francis Villon the poet, and some of the thievish crew with whom he consorted, were keeping the night alive and passing round the bottle.

A great pile of living embers diffused a strong and ruddy glow from the arched chimney. Before this straddled Dom Nicolas, the Picardy monk, with his skirts picked up and his fat legs bared to the comfortable warmth. His dilated shadow cut the room in half; and the firelight only escaped on either side of his broad person, and in a little pool between his outspread feet. His face had the beery, bruised appearance of the continual drinker's; it was covered with a network of congested veins, purple in ordinary circumstances, but now pale violet, for even with his back to the fire the cold pinched him on the other side. His cowl had half-fallen back, and made a strange excrescence on either side of his bull-neck. So he straddled, grumbling, and cut the room in half with the shadow of his portly frame.

On the right, Villon and Guy Tabary were huddled together over a scrap of parchment; Villon making a ballade which he was to call the "Ballade of Roast Fish," and Tabary spluttering admiration at his shoulder. The poet was a rag of a man, dark, little, and lean, with hollow cheeks and thin black locks. He carried his four-and-twenty years with feverish animation. Greed had made folds about his eyes, evil smiles had puckered his mouth. The wolf and pig struggled together in his face. It was an eloquent, sharp, ugly, earthly countenance. His hands were small and prehensile, with fingers knotted like a cord; and they were continually flickering in front of him in violent and expressive pantomime. As for Tabary, a broad, complacent, admiring imbecility breathed from his squash nose and slobbering lips: he had become a thief, just as he might have become the most decent of burgesses, by the imperious chance that rules the lives of human geese and human donkeys.

At the monk's other hand, Montigny and Thevenin Pensete played a game of chance. About the first there clung some flavour of good birth and training, as about a fallen angel; something long, lithe, and courtly in the person; something aquiline and darkling in the face. Thevenin, poor soul, was in great feather: he had done a good stroke of knavery that afternoon in the Faubourg St. Jacques, and all night he had been gaining from Montigny. A flat smile illuminated his face; his bald head shone rosily in a garland of red curls; his little protuberant stomach shook with silent chucklings as he swept in his gains.

"Doubles or quits?" said Thevenin.

Montigny nodded grimly.

"*Some may prefer to dine in state,*" wrote Villon, "*On bread and cheese on silver plate.* Or – or – help me out, Guido!"

Tabary giggled.

"*Or parsley on a golden dish,*" scribbled the poet.

The wind was freshening without; it drove the snow

before it, and sometimes raised its voice in a victorious whoop, and made sepulchral grumblings in the chimney. The cold was growing sharper as the night went on. Villon, protruding his lips, imitated the gust with something between a whistle and a groan. It was an eerie, uncomfortable talent of the poet's, much detested by the Picardy monk.

"Can't you hear it rattle in the gibbet?" said Villon. "They are all dancing the devil's jig on nothing, up there. You may dance, my gallants, you'll be none the warmer! Whew! what a gust! Down went somebody just now! A medlar the fewer on the three-legged medlar-tree! – I say, Dom Nicolas, it'll be cold to-night on the St. Denis Road?" he asked.

Dom Nicolas winked both his big eyes, and seemed to choke upon his Adam's apple. Montfaucon, the great grisly Paris gibbet, stood hard by the St. Denis Road, and the pleasantry touched him on the raw. As for Tabary, he laughed immoderately over the medlars; he had never heard anything more light-hearted; and he held his sides and crowed. Villon fetched him a fillip on the nose, which turned his mirth into an attack of coughing.

"Oh, stop that row," said Villon, "and think of rhymes to 'fish.' "

"Doubles or quits?" said Montigny doggedly.

"With all my heart," quoth Thevenin.

"Is there any more in that bottle?" asked the monk.

"Open another," said Villon. "How do you ever hope to fill that big hogshead, your body, with little things like bottles? And how do you expect to get to heaven? How many angels, do you fancy, can be spared to carry up a single monk from Picardy? Or do you think yourself another Elias – and they'll send the coach for you?"

"*Hominibus impossibile,*" replied the monk, as he filled his glass.

Tabary was in ecstasies.

Villon filliped his nose again.

"Laugh at my jokes, if you like," he said.

"It was very good," objected Tabary.

Villon made a face at him. "Think of rhymes to 'fish,'" he said. "What have you to do with Latin? You'll wish you knew none of it at the great assizes, when the devil calls for Guido Tabary, clericus – the devil with the hump-back and red-hot finger-nails. Talking of the devil," he added in a whisper, "look at Montigny!"

All three peered covertly at the gamester. He did not seem to be enjoying his luck. His mouth was a little to a side; one nostril nearly shut, and the other much inflated. The black dog was on his back, as people say, in terrifying nursery metaphor; and he breathed hard under the gruesome burden.

"He looks as if he could knife him," whispered Tabary, with round eyes.

The monk shuddered, and turned his face and spread his open hands to the red embers. It was the cold that thus affected Dom Nicolas, and not any excess of moral sensibility.

"Come now," said Villon – "about this ballade. How does it run so far?" And beating time with his hand, he read it aloud to Tabary.

They were interrupted at the fourth rhyme by a brief and fatal movement among the gamesters. The round was completed, and Thevenin was just opening his mouth to claim another victory, when Montigny leaped up, swift as an adder, and stabbed him to the heart. The blow took effect before he had time to utter a cry, before he had time to move. A tremor or two convulsed his frame; his hands opened and shut, his heels rattled on the floor; then his head rolled backwards over one shoulder with the eyes wide open; and Thevenin Pensete's spirit had returned to Him who made it.

Every one sprang to his feet; but the business was over in two twos. The four living fellows looked at each other in rather a ghastly fashion; the dead man contemplating a corner of the roof with a singular and ugly leer.

"My God!" said Tabary; and he began to pray in Latin.

Villon broke out into hysterical laughter. He came a step forward and ducked a ridiculous bow at Thevenin, and laughed still louder. Then he sat down suddenly, all of a heap, upon a stool, and continued laughing bitterly as though he would shake himself to pieces.

Montigny recovered his composure first.

"Let's see what he has about him," he remarked; and he picked the dead man's pockets with a practised hand, and divided the money into four equal portions on the table. "There's for you," he said.

The monk received his share with a deep sigh, and a single stealthy glance at the dead Thevenin, who was beginning to sink into himself and topple sideways off the chair.

"We're all in for it," cried Villon, swallowing his mirth. "It's a hanging job for every man jack of us that's here – not to speak of those who aren't." He made a shocking gesture in the air with his raised right hand, and put out his tongue and threw his head on one side, so as to counterfeit the appearance of one who has been hanged. Then he pocketed his share of the spoil, and executed a shuffle with his feet as if to restore the circulation.

Tabary was the last to help himself; he made a dash at the money, and retired to the other end of the apartment.

Montigny stuck Thevenin upright in the chair, and drew out the dagger, which was followed by a jet of blood.

"You fellows had better be moving," he said, as he wiped the blade on his victim's doublet.

"I think we had," returned Villon, with a gulp. "Damn his fat head!" he broke out. "It sticks in my throat like phlegm. What right has a man to have red hair when he is dead?" And he fell all of a heap again upon the stool, and fairly covered his face with his hands.

Montigny and Dom Nicolas laughed aloud, even Tabary feebly chiming in.

"Cry baby," said the monk.

"I always said he was a woman," added Montigny with a sneer. "Sit up, can't you?" he went on, giving another shake to the murdered body. "Tread out that fire, Nick!"

But Nick was better employed; he was quietly taking Villon's purse, as the poet sat, limp and trembling, on the stool where he had been making a ballade not three minutes before. Montigny and Tabary dumbly demanded a share of the booty, which the monk silently promised as he passed the little bag into the bosom of his gown. In many ways an artistic nature unfits a man for practical existence.

No sooner had the theft been accomplished than Villon shook himself, jumped to his feet, and began helping to scatter and extinguish the embers. Meanwhile Montigny opened the door and cautiously peered into the street. The coast was clear; there was no meddlesome patrol in sight. Still it was judged wiser to slip out severally; and as Villon was himself in a hurry to escape from the neighbourhood of the dead Thevenin, and the rest were in a still greater hurry to get rid of him before he should discover the loss of his money, he was the first by general consent to issue forth into the street.

The wind had triumphed and swept all the clouds from heaven. Only a few vapours, as thin as moonlight, fleeted rapidly across the stars. It was bitter cold; and by a common optical effect, things seemed almost more definite than in the broadest daylight. The sleeping city was absolutely still: a company of white hoods, a field full of little Alps, below the twinkling stars. Villon cursed his fortune. Would it were still snowing! Now, wherever he went, he left an indelible trail behind him on the glittering streets; wherever he went he was still tethered to the house by the cemetery of St. John; wherever he went he must weave, with his own plodding feet, the rope that bound him to the crime and would bind him to the gallows. The leer of the dead man came back to him with a new significance. He snapped his fingers as if to pluck up his own spirits, and choosing a street at random, stepped boldly forward in the snow.

Two things preoccupied him as he went: the aspect of the gallows at Montfaucon in this bright windy phase of the night's existence, for one; and for another, the look of the dead man with his bald head and garland of red curls. Both struck cold upon his heart, and he kept quickening his pace as if he could escape from unpleasant thoughts by mere fleetness of foot. Sometimes he looked back over his shoulder with a sudden nervous jerk; but he was the only moving thing in the white streets, except when the wind swooped round a corner and threw up the snow, which was beginning to freeze, in spouts of glittering dust.

Suddenly he saw, a long way before him, a black clump and a couple of lanterns. The clump was in motion, and the lanterns swung as though carried by men walking. It was a patrol. And though it was merely crossing his line of march, he judged it wiser to get out of eyeshot as speedily as he could. He was not in the humour to be challenged, and he was conscious of making a very conspicuous mark upon the snow. Just on his left hand there stood a great hotel, with some turrets and a large porch before the door; it was half-ruinous, he remembered, and had long stood empty; and so he made three steps of it and jumped into the shelter of the porch. It was pretty dark inside, after the glimmer of the snowy streets, and he was groping forward with outspread hands, when he stumbled over some substance which offered an indescribable mixture of resistances, hard and soft, firm and loose. His heart gave a leap, and he sprang two steps back and stared dreadfully at the obstacle. Then he gave a little laugh of relief. It was only a woman, and she dead. He knelt beside her to make sure upon this latter point. She was freezing cold, and rigid like a stick. A little ragged finery fluttered in the wind about her hair, and her cheeks had been heavily rouged that same afternoon. Her pockets were quite empty; but in

her stocking, underneath the garter, Villon found two of
the small coins that went by the name of whites. It was
little enough; but it was always something; and the poet
was moved with a deep sense of pathos that she should
have died before she had spent her money. That seemed
to him a dark and pitiable mystery; and he looked from
the coins in his hand to the dead woman, and back again
to the coins, shaking his head over the riddle of man's
life. Henry V. of England, dying at Vincennes just after
he had conquered France, and this poor jade cut off by a
cold draught in a great man's doorway, before she had
time to spend her couple of whites – it seemed a cruel
way to carry on the world. Two whites would have taken
such a little while to squander; and yet it would have
been one more good taste in the mouth, one more smack
of the lips, before the devil got the soul, and the body
was left to birds and vermin. He would like to use all his
tallow before the light was blown out and the lantern
broken.

While these thoughts were passing through his mind,
he was feeling, half mechanically, for his purse. Suddenly
his heart stopped beating; a feeling of cold scales passed
up the back of his legs, and a cold blow seemed to fall
upon his scalp. He stood petrified for a moment; then he
felt again with one feverish movement; and then his loss
burst upon him, and he was covered at once with perspiration. To spendthrifts money is so living and actual –
it is such a thin veil between them and their pleasures!
There is only one limit to their fortune – that of time;
and a spendthrift with only a few crowns is the Emperor
of Rome until they are spent. For such a person to lose
his money is to suffer the most shocking reverse, and fall
from heaven to hell, from all to nothing, in a breath. And
all the more if he has put his head in the halter for it; if
he may be hanged to-morrow for that same purse so
dearly earned, so foolishly departed! Villon stood and
cursed; he threw the two whites into the street; he shook
his fist at heaven; he stamped, and was not horrified to

find himself trampling the poor corpse. Then he began rapidly to retrace his steps towards the house beside the cemetery. He had forgotten all fear of the patrol, which was long gone by at any rate, and had no idea but that of his lost purse. It was in vain that he looked right and left upon the snow: nothing was to be seen. He had not dropped it in the streets. Had it fallen in the house? He would have liked dearly to go in and see; but the idea of the grisly occupant unmanned him. And he saw besides, as he drew near, that their efforts to put out the fire had been unsuccessful; on the contrary, it had broken into a blaze, and a changeful light played in the chinks of door and window, and revived his terror for the authorities and Paris gibbet.

He returned to the hotel with the porch, and groped about upon the snow for the money he had thrown away in his childish passion. But he could only find one white; the other had probably struck sideways and sunk deeply in. With a single white in his pocket, all his projects for a rousing night in some wild tavern vanished utterly away. And it was not only pleasure that fled laughing from his grasp; positive discomfort, positive pain, attacked him as he stood ruefully before the porch. His perspiration had dried upon him; and though the wind had now fallen, a binding frost was setting in stronger with every hour, and he felt benumbed and sick at heart. What was to be done? Late as was the hour, improbable as was success, he would try the house of his adopted father, the chaplain of St. Benoît.

He ran there all the way, and knocked timidly. There was no answer. He knocked again and again, taking heart with every stroke; and at last steps were heard approaching from within. A barred wicket fell open in the iron-studded door, and emitted a gush of yellow light.

"Hold up your face to the wicket," said the chaplain from within.

"It's only me," whimpered Villon.

"Oh, it's only you, is it?" returned the chaplain; and he

cursed him with foul unpriestly oaths for disturbing him at such an hour, and bade him be off to hell, where he came from.

"My hands are blue to the wrist," pleaded Villon; "my feet are dead and full of twinges: my nose aches with the sharp air; the cold lies at my heart. I may be dead before morning. Only this once, father, and before God I will never ask again!"

"You should have come earlier," said the ecclesiastic coolly. "Young men require a lesson now and then." He shut the wicket and retired deliberately into the interior of the house.

Villon was beside himself; he beat upon the door with his hands and feet, and shouted hoarsely after the chaplain.

"Wormy old fox!" he cried. "If I had my hand under your twist, I would send you flying headlong into the bottomless pit."

A door shut in the interior, faintly audible to the poet down long passages. He passed his hand over his mouth with an oath. And then the humour of the situation struck him, and he laughed and looked lightly up to heaven, where the stars seemed to be winking over his discomfiture.

What was to be done? It looked very like a night in the frosty streets. The idea of the dead woman popped into his imagination, and gave him a hearty fright; what had happened to her in the early night might very well happen to him before morning. And he so young! and with such immense possibilities of disorderly amusement before him! He felt quite pathetic over the notion of his own fate, as if it had been some one else's, and made a little imaginative vignette of the scene in the morning, when they should find his body.

He passed all his chances under review, turning the white between his thumb and forefinger. Unfortunately he was on bad terms with some old friends who would once have taken pity on him in such a plight. He had lampooned them in verses, he had beaten and cheated them; and yet now, when he was in so close a pinch, he thought there was at least one who might perhaps relent. It was a chance. It was worth trying at least, and he would go and see.

On the way, two little accidents happened to him which coloured his musings in a very different manner. For, first, he fell in with the track of a patrol, and walked in it for some hundred yards, although it lay out of his direction. And this spirited him up; at least he had confused his trail; for he was still possessed with the idea of people tracking him all about Paris over the snow, and collaring him next morning before he was awake. The other matter affected him very differently. He passed a street corner, where, not so long before, a woman and her child had been devoured by wolves. This was just the kind of weather, he reflected, when wolves might take it into their heads to enter Paris again; and a lone man in these deserted streets would run the chance of something worse than a mere scare. He stopped and looked upon the place with an unpleasant interest – it was a centre where several lanes intersected each other; and he looked down them all one after another, and held his breath to listen, lest he should detect some galloping black things on the snow, or hear the sound of howling between him and the river. He remembered his mother telling him the story and pointing out the spot, while he was yet a child. His mother! If he only knew where she lived, he might make sure at least of shelter. He determined he would inquire upon the morrow; nay, he would go and see her too, poor old girl! So thinking, he arrived at his destination – his last hope for the night.

The house was quite dark, like its neighbours, and yet after a few taps, he heard a movement overhead, a door opening, and a cautious voice asking who was there. The poet named himself in a loud whisper, and waited, not without some trepidation, the result. Nor had he to wait long. A window was suddenly opened, and a pailful of slops splashed down upon the doorstep. Villon had not been unprepared for something of the sort, and had put himself as much in shelter as the nature of the porch admitted; but for all that, he was deplorably drenched below the waist. His hose began to freeze almost at once. Death from cold and exposure stared him in the face; he remembered he was of phthisical tendency, and began coughing tentatively. But the gravity of the danger steadied his nerves. He stopped a few hundred yards from the door where he had been so rudely used, and reflected with his finger to his nose. He could only see one way of getting a lodging, and that was to take it. He had noticed a house not far away, which looked as if it might be easily broken into, and thither he betook himself promptly, entertaining himself on the way with the idea of a room still hot, with a table still loaded with the remains of supper, where he might pass the rest of the black hours, and whence he should issue, on the morrow, with an armful of valuable plate. He even considered on what viands and what wines he should prefer; and as he was calling the roll of his favourite dainties, roast fish presented itself to his mind with an odd mixture of amusement and horror.

"I shall never finish that ballade," he thought to himself; and then, with another shudder at the recollection, "Oh, damn his fat head!" he repeated fervently, and spat upon the snow.

The house in question looked dark at first sight; but as Villon made a preliminary inspection in search of the handiest point of attack, a little twinkle of light caught his eye from behind a curtained window.

"The devil!" he thought. "People awake! Some student or some saint, confound the crew! Can't they get drunk and lie in bed snoring like their neighbours! What's the good of curfew, and poor devils of bell-ringers jumping at a rope's-end in bell-towers? What's the use of day, if people sit up all night? The gripes to them!" He grinned as he saw where his logic was leading him.

"Every man to his business, after all," added he, "and if they're awake, by the lord, I may come by a supper honestly for this once, and cheat the devil."

He went boldly to the door and knocked with an assured hand. On both previous occasions, he had knocked timidly and with some dread of attracting notice; but now, when he had just discarded the thought of a burglarious entry, knocking at a door seemed a mighty simple and innocent proceeding. The sound of his blows echoed through the house with thin, phantasmal reverberations, as though it were quite empty; but these had scarcely died away before a measured tread drew near, a couple of bolts were withdrawn, and one wing was opened broadly, as though no guile or fear of guile were known to those within. A tall figure of a man, muscular and spare, but a little bent, confronted Villon. The head was in massive bulk, but finely sculptured; the nose blunt at the bottom, but refining upward to where it joined a pair of strong and honest eyebrows; the mouth and eyes surrounded with delicate markings, and the whole face based upon a thick white beard, boldly and squarely trimmed. Seen as it was by the light of a flickering hand-lamp, it looked perhaps nobler than it had a right to do; but it was a fine face, honourable rather than intelligent, strong, simple, and righteous.

"You knock late, sir," said the old man in resonant, courteous tones.

Villon cringed, and brought up many servile words of apology; at a crisis of this sort the beggar was uppermost in him, and the man of genius hid his head with confusion.

"You are cold," repeated the old man, "and hungry? Well, step in." And he ordered him into the house with a noble enough gesture.

"Some great seigneur," thought Villon, as his host setting down the lamp on the flagged pavement of the entry, shot the bolts once more into their places.

"You will pardon me if I go in front," he said, when

this was done; and he preceded the poet upstairs into a large apartment, warmed with a pan of charcoal and lit by a great lamp hanging from the roof. It was very bare of furniture: only some gold plate on a sideboard; some folios; and a stand of armour between the windows. Some smart tapestry hung upon the walls, representing the crucifixion of our Lord in one piece, and in another a scene of shepherds and shepherdesses by a running stream. Over the chimney was a shield of arms.

"Will you seat yourself," said the old man, "and forgive me if I leave you? I am alone in my house to-night, and if you are to eat I must forage for you myself."

No sooner was his host gone than Villon leaped from the chair on which he had just seated himself, and began examining the room, with the stealth and passion of a cat. He weighed the gold flagons in his hand, opened all the folios, and investigated the arms upon the shield, and the stuff with which the seats were lined. He raised the window curtains, and saw that the windows were set with rich stained glass in figures, so far as he could see, of martial import. Then he stood in the middle of the room, drew a long breath, and retaining it with puffed cheeks, looked round and round him, turning on his heels, as if to impress every feature of the apartment on his memory.

"Seven pieces of plate," he said. "If there had been ten, I would have risked it. A fine house, and a fine old master, so help me all the saints!"

And just then, hearing the old man's tread returning along the corridor, he stole back to his chair, and began humbly toasting his wet legs before the charcoal pan.

His entertainer had a plate of meat in one hand and a jug of wine in the other. He set down the plate upon the table, motioning Villon to draw in his chair, and going to the sideboard, brought back two goblets, which he filled.

"I drink to your better fortune," he said, gravely touching Villon's cup with his own.

"To our better acquaintance," said the poet, growing

bold. A mere man of the people would have been awed by the courtesy of the old seigneur, but Villon was hardened in that matter; he had made mirth for great lords before now, and found them as black rascals as himself. And so he devoted himself to the viands with a ravenous gusto, while the old man, leaning backward, watched him with steady, curious eyes.

"You have blood on your shoulder, my man," he said.

Montigny must have laid his wet right hand upon him as he left the house. He cursed Montigny in his heart.

"It was none of my shedding," he stammered.

"I had not supposed so," returned his host quietly. "A brawl?"

"Well, something of that sort," Villon admitted with a quaver.

"Perhaps a fellow murdered?"

"Oh, no – not murdered," said the poet, more and more confused. "It was all fair play – murdered by accident. I had no hand in it, God strike me dead!" he added fervently.

"One rogue the fewer, I daresay," observed the master of the house.

"You may dare to say that," agreed Villon, infinitely relieved. "As big a rogue as there is between here and Jerusalem. He turned up his toes like a lamb. But it was a nasty thing to look at. I daresay you've seen dead men in your time, my lord?" he added, glancing at the armour.

"Many," said the old man. "I have followed the wars, as you imagine."

Villon laid down his knife and fork, which he had just taken up again.

"Were any of them bald?" he asked.

"Oh yes, and with hair as white as mine."

"I don't think I should mind the white so much," said Villon. "His was red." And he had a return of his shuddering and tendency to laughter, which he drowned with a great draught of wine. "I'm a little put out when I think of it," he went on. "I knew him – damn him! And then the cold gives a man fancies – or the fancies give a man cold, I don't know which."

"Have you any money?" asked the old man.

"I have one white," returned the poet, laughing. "I got it out of a dead jade's stocking in a porch. She was as dead as Caesar, poor wench, and as cold as a church, with bits of ribbon sticking in her hair. This is a hard world in winter for wolves and wenches and poor rogues like me."

"I," said the old man, "am Enguerrand de la Feuillée, seigneur de Brisetout, bailly du Patatrac. Who and what may you be?"

Villon rose and made a suitable reverence. "I am called Francis Villon," he said, " a poor Master of Arts of this university. I know some Latin, and a deal of vice. I can make chansons, ballades, lais, virelais, and roundels, and I am very fond of wine. I was born in a garret, and I shall not improbably die upon the gallows. I may add, my lord, that from this night forward I am your lordship's very obsequious servant to command."

"No servant of mine," said the knight; "my guest for this evening, and no more."

"A very grateful guest," said Villon politely; and he drank in dumb show to his entertainer.

"You are shrewd," began the old man, tapping his forehead, "very shrewd; you have learning; you are a clerk; and yet you take a small piece of money off a dead woman in the street. Is it not a kind of theft?"

"It is a kind of theft much practised in the wars, my lord."

"The wars are the field of honour," returned the old man proudly. "There a man plays his life upon the cast; he fights in the name of his lord the king, his Lord God, and all their lordships the holy saints and angels."

"Put it," said Villon, "that I were really a thief, should I not play my life also, and against heavier odds?"

"For gain, but not for honour."

"Gain?" repeated Villon, with a shrug. "Gain! The poor fellow wants supper, and takes it. So does the soldier in a campaign. Why, what are all these requisitions we hear so much about? If they are not gain to those who take them, they are loss enough to the others. The men-at-arms drink by a good fire, while the burgher bites his nails to buy them wine and wood. I have seen a good many ploughmen swinging on trees about the country; ay, I have seen thirty on one elm, and a very poor figure they made; and when I asked some one how all these came to be hanged, I was told it was because they could not scrape together enough crowns to satisfy the men-at-arms."

"These things are a necessity of war, which the low-born must endure with constancy. It is true that some captains drive overhard; there are spirits in every rank not easily moved by pity; and indeed many follow arms who are no better than brigands."

"You see," said the poet, "you cannot separate the soldier from the brigand; and what is a thief but an isolated brigand with circumspect manners? I steal a couple of mutton chops, without so much as disturbing people's sleep; the farmer grumbles a bit, but sups none the less wholesomely on what remains. You come up blowing gloriously on a trumpet, take away the whole sheep, and beat the farmer pitifully into the bargain. I have no trumpet; I am only Tom, Dick, or Harry; I am a rogue and a dog, and hanging's too good for me – with all my heart; but just you ask the farmer which of us he prefers, just find out which of us he lies awake to curse on cold nights."

"Look at us two," said his lordship. "I am old, strong, and honoured. If I were turned from my house to-morrow, hundreds would be proud to shelter me. Poor people would go out and pass the night in the streets with their children if I merely hinted that I wished to be alone. And I find you up, wandering homeless, and picking farthings off dead women by the wayside! I fear no man and nothing; I have seen you tremble and lose countenance at a word. I wait God's summons contentedly in

my own house, or, if it please the king to call me out
again, upon the field of battle. You look for the gallows; a
rough, swift death, without hope or honour. Is there no
difference between these two?"

"As far as to the moon," Villon acquiesced. "But if I
had been born lord of Brisetout, and you had been the
poor scholar Francis, would the difference have been any
the less? Should not I have been warming my knees at
this charcoal pan, and would not you have been groping
for farthings in the snow? Should not I have been the soldier, and you the thief?"

"A thief!" cried the old man. "I a thief! If you understood your words, you would repent them."

Villon turned out his hands with a gesture of inim-
itable impudence. "If your lordship had done me the
honour to follow my argument!" he said.

"I do you too much honour in submitting to your presence," said the knight. "Learn to curb your tongue when
you speak with old and honourable men, or some one
hastier than I may reprove you in a sharper fashion." And
he rose and paced the lower end of the apartment, struggling with anger and antipathy. Villon surreptitiously
refilled his cup, and settled himself more comfortably in
the chair, crossing his knees and leaning his head upon
one hand and the elbow against the back of the chair. He
was now replete and warm; and he was in nowise frightened for his host, having gauged him as justly as was
possible between two such different characters. The
night was far spent, and in a very comfortable fashion after
all; and he felt morally certain of a safe departure on the
morrow.

"Tell me one thing," said the old man, pausing in his
walk. "Are you really a thief?"

"I claim the sacred rights of hospitality," returned the
poet. "My lord, I am."

"You are very young," the knight continued.

"I should never have been so old," replied Villon,
showing his fingers, "if I had not helped myself with

these ten talents. They have been my nursing-mothers and my nursing-fathers."

"You may still repent and change."

"I repent daily," said the poet. "There are few people more given to repentance than poor Francis. As for change, let somebody change my circumstances. A man must continue to eat, if it were only that he may continue to repent."

"The change must begin in the heart," returned the old man solemnly.

"My dear lord," answered Villon, "do you really fancy that I steal for pleasure? I hate stealing, like any other piece of work or of danger. My teeth chatter when I see a gallows. But I must eat, I must drink, I must mix in society of some sort. What the devil! Man is not a solitary animal – *Cui Deus fœminam tradit*. Make me king's pantler – make me abbot of St. Denis; make me bailly of the Patatrac; and then I shall be changed indeed. But as long as you leave me the poor scholar Francis Villon, without a farthing, why, of course, I remain the same."

"The grace of God is all-powerful."

"I should be a heretic to question it," said Francis. "It has made you lord of Brisetout and bailly of the Patatrac; it has given me nothing but the quick wits under my hat and these ten toes upon my hands. May I help myself to wine? I thank you respectfully. By God's grace, you have a very superior vintage."

The lord of Brisetout walked to and fro with his hands behind his back. Perhaps he was not yet quite settled in his mind about the parallel between thieves and soldiers; perhaps Villon had interested him by some cross-thread of sympathy; perhaps his wits were simply muddled by so much unfamiliar reasoning; but whatever the cause, he somehow yearned to convert the young man to a better way of thinking, and could not make up his mind to drive him forth again into the street.

"There is something more than I can understand in this," he said at length. "Your mouth is full of subtleties, and the devil has led you very far astray; but the devil is only a very weak spirit before God's truth, and all his subtleties vanish at a word of true honour, like darkness at morning. Listen to me once more. I learned long ago that a gentleman should live chivalrously and lovingly to God, and the king, and his lady; and though I have seen many strange things done, I have still striven to command my ways upon that rule. It is not only written in all noble histories, but in every man's heart, if he will take care to read. You speak of food and wine, and I know very well that hunger is a difficult trial to endure; but you do not speak of other wants; you say nothing of honour, of faith to God and other men, of courtesy, of love without reproach. It may be that I am not very wise – and yet I think I am – but you seem to me like one who has lost his way and made a great error in life. You are attending to the little wants, and you have totally forgotten the great and only real ones, like a man who should be doctoring a toothache on the Judgment Day. For such things as honour and love and faith are not only nobler than food and drink, but indeed I think that we desire them more, and suffer more sharply for their absence. I speak to you as I think you will most easily understand me. Are you not, while careful to fill your belly, disregarding another appetite in your heart, which spoils the pleasure of your life and keeps you continually wretched?"

Villon was sensibly nettled under all this sermonising. "You think I have no sense of honour!" he cried. "I'm poor enough, God knows! It's hard to see rich people with their gloves, and you blowing in your hands. An empty belly is a bitter thing, although you speak so lightly of it. If you had had as many as I, perhaps you would change your tune. Any way I'm a thief – make the most of that – but I'm not a devil from hell, God strike me dead! I would have you to know I've an honour of my own, as good as yours, though I don't prate about it all day long, as if it was a God's miracle to have any. It seems quite natural to me; I keep it in its box till it's wanted. Why now, look you here, how long have I been in this room with you? Did you not tell me you were alone in the house? Look at your gold plate! You're strong, if you like, but you're old and unarmed, and I have my knife. What did I want but a jerk of the elbow and here would have been you with the cold steel in your bowels, and there would have been me, linking in the streets, with an armful of gold cups! Did you suppose I hadn't wit enough to see that? And I scorned the action. There are your damned goblets, as safe as in a church; there are you, with your heart ticking as good as new; and here am I, ready to go out again as poor as I came in, with my one white that you threw in my teeth! And you think I have no sense of honour – God strike me dead!"

The old man stretched out his right arm. "I will tell you what you are," he said. "You are a rogue, my man, an impudent and a black-hearted rogue and vagabond. I have passed an hour with you. Oh! believe me, I feel myself disgraced! And you have eaten and drunk at my table. But now I am sick at your presence; the day has come, and the night-bird should be off to his roost. Will you go before, or after?"

"Which you please," returned the poet, rising. "I believe you to be strictly honourable." He thoughtfully emptied his cup. "I wish I could add you were intelligent," he went on, knocking on his head with his knuckles. "Age, age! the brains stiff and rheumatic."

The old man preceded him from a point of self-respect; Villon followed, whistling, with his thumbs in his girdle.

"God pity you," said the lord of Brisetout at the door.

"Good-bye, papa," returned Villon, with a yawn. "Many thanks for the cold mutton."

The door closed behind him. The dawn was breaking over the white roofs. A chill, uncomfortable morning ushered in the day. Villon stood and heartily stretched himself in the middle of the road.

"A very dull old gentleman," he thought. "I wonder what his goblets may be worth."

MARKHEIM

MARRIEN

MARKHEIM

"YES," said the dealer, "our windfalls are of various kinds. Some customers are ignorant, and then I touch a dividend on my superior knowledge. Some are dishonest," and here he held up the candle, so that the light fell strongly on his visitor, "and in that case," he continued, "I profit by my virtue."

Markheim had but just entered from the daylight streets, and his eyes had not yet grown familiar with the mingled shine and darkness in the shop. At these pointed words, and before the near presence of the flame, he blinked painfully and looked aside.

The dealer chuckled. "You come to me on Christmas Day," he resumed, "when you know that I am alone in my house, put up my shutters, and make a point of refusing business. Well, you will have to pay for that; you will have to pay for my loss of time, when I should be balancing my books; you will have to pay, besides, for a kind of manner that I remark in you to-day very strongly. I am the essence of discretion, and ask no awkward questions; but when a customer cannot look me in the eye, he has to pay for it." The dealer once more chuckled; and then, changing to his usual business voice, though still with a note of irony, "You can give, as usual, a clear account of how you came into the possession of the object?" he continued. "Still your uncle's cabinet? A remarkable collector, sir!"

And the little pale, round-shouldered dealer stood almost on tip-toe, looking over the top of his gold spectacles, and nodding his head with every mark of disbelief. Markheim returned his gaze with one of infinite pity, and a touch of horror.

133

"This time," said he, "you are in error. I have not come to sell, but to buy. I have no curios to dispose of; my uncle's cabinet is bare to the wainscot; even were it still intact, I have done well on the Stock Exchange, and should more likely add to it than otherwise, and my errand to-day is simplicity itself. I seek a Christmas present for a lady," he continued, waxing more fluent as he struck into the speech he had prepared; "and certainly I owe you every excuse for thus disturbing you upon so small a matter. But the thing was neglected yesterday; I must produce my little compliment at dinner; and, as you very well know, a rich marriage is not a thing to be neglected."

There followed a pause, during which the dealer seemed to weigh this statement incredulously. The ticking of many clocks among the curious lumber of the shop, and the faint rushing of the cabs in a near thoroughfare, filled up the interval of silence.

"Well, sir," said the dealer, "be it so. You are an old customer after all; and if, as you say, you have the chance of a good marriage, far be it from me to be an obstacle. – Here is a nice thing for a lady now," he went on, "this hand-glass – fifteenth-century, warranted; comes from a good collection, too; but I reserve the name, in the interests of my customer, who was just like yourself, my dear sir, the nephew and sole heir of a remarkable collector."

The dealer, while he thus ran on in his dry and biting voice, had stooped to take the object from its place; and, as he had done so, a shock had passed through Markheim, a start both of hand and foot, a sudden leap of many tumultuous passions to the face. It passed as swiftly as it came, and left no trace beyond a certain trembling of the hand that now received the glass.

"A glass," he said hoarsely, and then paused, and repeated it more clearly. "A glass? For Christmas? Surely not?"

"And why not?" cried the dealer. "Why not a glass?"

Markheim was looking upon him with an indefinable

expression. "You ask me why not?" he said. "Why, look here – look in it – look at yourself! Do you like to see it? No! nor I – nor any man."

The little man had jumped back when Markheim had so suddenly confronted him with the mirror; but now, perceiving there was nothing worse on hand, he chuckled. "Your future lady, sir, must be pretty hard favoured," said he.

"I ask you," said Markheim, "for a Christmas present, and you give me this – this damned reminder of years, and sins and follies – this hand-conscience. Did you mean it? Had you a thought in your mind? Tell me. It will be better for you if you do. Come, tell me about yourself. I hazard a guess now, that you are in secret a very charitable man?"

The dealer looked closely at his companion. It was very odd, Markheim did not appear to be laughing; there was something in his face like an eager sparkle of hope, but nothing of mirth.

"What are you driving at?" the dealer asked.

"Not charitable?" returned the other gloomily. "Not charitable? not pious; not scrupulous; unloving, un-beloved; a hand to get money, a safe to keep it. Is that all? Dear God, man, is that all?"

"I will tell you what it is," began the dealer, with some sharpness, and then broke off again into a chuckle. "But I see this is a love-match of yours, and you have been drinking the lady's health."

"Ah!" cried Markheim, with a strange curiosity. "Ah, have you been in love? Tell me about that."

"I," cried the dealer. "I in love! I never had the time, nor have I the time to-day for all this nonsense. – Will you take the glass?"

"Where is the hurry?" returned Markheim. "It is very pleasant to stand here talking; and life is so short and insecure that I would not hurry away from any pleasure – no, not even from so mild a one as this. We should rather cling, cling to what little we can get, like a man at a cliff's edge. Every second is a cliff, if you think upon it – a cliff a mile high – high enough, if we fall, to dash us out of every feature of humanity. Hence it is best to talk pleasantly. Let us talk of each other: why should we wear this mask? Let us be confidential. Who knows? – we might become friends."

"I have just one word to say to you," said the dealer. "Either make your purchase, or walk out of my shop!"

"True, true," said Markheim. "Enough fooling. To business. Show me something else."

The dealer stooped once more, this time to replace the glass upon the shelf, his thin blond hair falling over his eyes as he did so. Markheim moved a little nearer, with one hand in the pocket of his greatcoat: he drew himself up and filled his lungs; at the same time many different emotions were depicted together on his face – terror, horror, and resolve, fascination and a physical repulsion; and through a haggard lift of his upper lip his teeth looked out.

"This, perhaps, may suit," observed the dealer: and then, as he began to re-arise, Markheim bounded from behind upon his victim. The long, skewer-like dagger flashed and fell. The dealer struggled like a hen, striking his temple on the shelf, and then tumbled on the floor in a heap.

Time had some score of small voices in that shop, some stately and slow, as was becoming to their great age; others garrulous and hurried. All these told out the seconds in an intricate chorus of tickings. Then the passage of a lad's feet, heavily running on the pavement, broke in upon these smaller voices and startled Markheim into the consciousness of his surroundings. He looked about him awfully. The candle stood on the counter, its flame solemnly wagging in a draught; and by that inconsiderable movement the whole room was filled with noiseless bustle and kept heaving like a sea: the tall shadows nodding, the gross blots of darkness swelling and dwindling as with respiration, the faces of the portraits and the china gods changing and wavering like images in water. The inner door stood ajar, and peered into that leaguer of shadows with a long slit of daylight like a pointing finger.

From these fear-stricken rovings Markheim's eyes returned to the body of his victim, where it lay both humped and sprawling, incredibly small and strangely meaner than in life. In these poor, miserly clothes, in that ungainly attitude, the dealer lay like so much sawdust. Markheim had feared to see it, and, lo! it was nothing. And yet, as he gazed, this bundle of old clothes and pool of blood began to find eloquent voices. There it must lie; there was none to work the cunning hinges or direct the miracle of locomotion – there it must lie till it was found. Found! ay, and then? Then would this dead flesh lift up a cry that would ring over England, and fill the world with the echoes of pursuit. Ay, dead or not, this was still the enemy. "Time was that when the brains were out," he thought; and the first word struck into his mind. Time, now that the deed was accomplished – time, which had closed for the victim, had become instant and moment-ous for the slayer.

The thought was yet in his mind when, first one and then another, with every variety of pace and voice – one deep as the bell from a cathedral turret, another ringing on its treble notes the prelude of a waltz – the clocks began to strike the hour of three in the afternoon.

The sudden outbreak of so many tongues in that dumb chamber staggered him. He began to bestir him-self, going to and fro with the candle, beleaguered by moving shadows, and startled to the soul by chance reflections. In many rich mirrors, some of home design, some from Venice or Amsterdam, he saw his face repeated and repeated, as it were an army of spies; his own eyes met and detected him; and the sound of his own steps, lightly as they fell, vexed the surrounding quiet. And still, as he continued to fill his pockets, his mind accused him, with a sickening iteration, of the thousand faults of his design. He should have chosen a more quiet hour; he should have prepared an alibi; he should not have used a knife; he should have been more cautious, and only bound and gagged the dealer, and not killed him; he should have been more bold and killed the servant also; he should have done all things otherwise: poignant regrets, weary, incessant toiling of the mind to change what was unchangeable, to plan what was now useless, to be the architect of the irrevocable past. Meanwhile, and behind all this activity, brute terrors, like the scurrying of rats in a deserted attic, filled the more remote chambers of his brain with riot; the hand of the constable would fall heavy on his shoulder, and his nerves would jerk like a hooked fish; or he beheld, in galloping defile, the dock, the prison, the gallows, and the black coffin.

Terror of the people in the street sat down before his mind like a besieging army. It was impossible, he thought, but that some rumour of the struggle must have reached their ears and set on edge their curiosity; and now, in all the neighbouring house, he divined them sitting motionless and with uplifted ear – solitary people, condemned to spend Christmas dwelling alone on the memories of the past, and now startlingly recalled from that tender exercise; happy family parties, struck into silence round the table, the mother still with raised finger: every degree and age and humour, but all, by their own hearths, prying and hearkening and weaving the rope that was to hang him. Sometimes it seemed to him he could not move too softly; the clink of the tall Bohemian goblets rang out loudly like a bell; and alarmed by the bigness of the ticking, he was tempted to stop the clocks. And then, again, with a swift transition of his terrors, the very silence of the place appeared a source of peril, and a thing to strike and freeze the passer-by; and he would step more boldly, and bustle aloud among the contents of the shop, and imitate, with elaborate bravado, the movements of a busy man at ease in his own house.

But he was now so pulled about by different alarms, that, while one portion of his mind was still alert and cunning, another trembled on the brink of lunacy. One hallucination in particular took a strong hold on his credulity. The neighbour hearkening with white face beside his window, the passer-by arrested by a horrible surmise on the pavement – these could at worst suspect, they could not know; through the brick walls and shuttered windows only sounds could penetrate. But here, within the house, was he alone? He knew he was; he had watched the servant set forth sweethearting, in her poor best, "out for the day" written on every ribbon and smile. Yes, he was alone, of course; and yet, in the bulk of empty house above him, he could surely hear a stir of delicate footing – he was surely conscious, inexplicably conscious, of some presence. Ay, surely; to every room and corner of the house his imagination followed it; and now it was a faceless thing, and yet had eyes to see with; and again it was a shadow of himself; and yet again beheld the image of the dead dealer, reinspired with cunning and hatred.

At times, with a strong effort, he would glance at the open door which still seemed to repel his eyes. The house was tall, the skylight small and dirty, the day blind with fog; and the light that filtered down to the ground story was exceedingly faint, and showed dimly on the threshold of the shop. And yet, in that strip of doubtful brightness, did there not hang wavering a shadow?

Suddenly, from the street outside, a very jovial gentleman began to beat with a staff on the shop-door, accompanying his blows with shouts and railleries in which the dealer was continually called upon by name. Markheim, smitten into ice, glanced at the dead man. But no! he lay quite still; he was fled away far beyond ear-shot of these blows and shoutings; he was sunk beneath seas of silence; and his name, which would once have caught his notice above the howling of a storm, had become an empty sound. And presently the jovial gentleman desisted from his knocking and departed.

Here was a broad hint to hurry what remained to be done, to get forth from this accusing neighbourhood, to plunge into a bath of London multitudes, and to reach, on the other side of day, that haven of safety and apparent innocence – his bed. One visitor had come: at any moment another might follow and be more obstinate. To have done the deed, and yet not to reap the profit, would be too abhorrent a failure. The money, that was now Markheim's concern; and as a means to that, the keys.

He glanced over his shoulder at the open door; where the shadow was still lingering and shivering; and with no conscious repugnance of the mind, yet with a tremor of the belly, he drew near the body of his victim. The human character had quite departed. Like a suit half-stuffed with bran, the limbs lay scattered, the trunk doubled, on the floor; and yet the thing repelled him. Although so dingy and inconsiderable to the eye, he feared it might have more significance to the touch. He took the body by the shoulders and turned it on its back. It was strangely light and supple, and the limbs, as if they had been broken, fell into the oddest postures. The face was robbed of all expression; but it was as pale as wax, and shockingly smeared with blood about one temple. That was, for Markheim, the one displeasing circumstance. It carried him back, upon the instant, to a certain fair-day in a fishers' village: a grey day, a piping wind, a crowd upon the street, a blare of brasses, the booming of drums, the nasal voice of a ballad-singer; and a boy going to and fro, buried over-head in the crowd and divided between interest and fear, until, coming out upon the chief place of concourse, he beheld a booth and a great screen with pictures, dismally designed, garishly coloured: Brownrigg with her apprentice; the Mannings with their murdered guest; Weare in the death-grip of Thurtell; and a score besides of famous crimes. The thing was as clear as an illusion; he was once again that little boy; he was looking once again, and with the same sense of physical revolt, at these vile pictures; he was still stunned by the thumping of the drums. A bar of that day's music returned upon his memory; and at that, for the first time, a qualm came over him, a breath of nausea, a sudden weakness of the joints, which he must instantly resist and conquer.

He judged it more prudent to confront than to flee from these considerations; looking the more hardily in the dead face, bending his mind to realise the nature and greatness of his crime. So little a while ago that face had moved with every change of sentiment, that pale mouth had spoken, that body had been all on fire with governable energies; and now, and by his act, that piece of life had been arrested, as the horologist, with interjected finger, arrests the beating of the clock. So he reasoned in vain; he could rise to no more remorseful consciousness; the same heart which had shuddered before the painted effigies of crime looked on its reality unmoved. At best, he felt a gleam of pity for one who had been endowed in vain with all those faculties that can make the world a garden of enchantment, one who had never lived and who was now dead. But of penitence, no, not a tremor.

With that, shaking himself clear of these considerations, he found the keys and advanced towards the open door of the shop. Outside, it had begun to rain smartly; and the sound of the shower upon the roof had banished silence. Like some dripping cavern, the chambers of the house were haunted by an incessant echoing, which filled the ear and mingled with the ticking of the clocks. And, as Markheim approached the door, he seemed to hear, in answer to his own cautious tread, the steps of another foot withdrawing up the stair. The shadow still palpitated loosely on the threshold. He threw a ton's weight of resolve upon his muscles, and drew back the door.

The faint, foggy daylight glimmered dimly on the bare floor and stairs; on the bright suit of armour posted, halbert in hand, upon the landing: and on the dark wood-carvings, and framed pictures that hung against the yellow panels of the wainscot. So loud was the beating of the rain through all the house that, in Markheim's ears, it began to be distinguished into many different sounds. Footsteps and sighs, the tread of regiments marching in the distance, the chink of money in the counting, and the creaking of doors held stealthily ajar, appeared to mingle with the patter of the drops upon the cupola and the gushing of the water in the pipes. The sense that he was not alone grew upon him to the verge of madness. On every side he was haunted and begirt by presences. He heard them moving in the upper chambers; from the shop he heard the dead man getting to his legs; and as he began with a great effort to mount the stairs, feet fled quietly before him and followed stealthily behind. If he were but deaf, he thought, how tranquilly he would possess his soul! And then again, and hearkening with ever fresh attention, he blessed himself for that unresting sense which held the outposts and stood a trusty sentinel upon his life. His head turned continually on his neck; his eyes, which seemed starting from their orbits, scouted on every side, and on every side were half-rewarded as with the tail of something nameless vanishing. The four-and-twenty steps to the first floor were four-and-twenty agonies.

On that first story, the doors stood ajar, three of them like three ambushes, shaking his nerves like the throats of cannon. He could never again, he felt, be sufficiently immured and fortified from men's observing eyes; he longed to be home, girt in by walls, buried among bedclothes, and invisible to all but God. And at that thought he wondered a little, recollecting tales of other murderers and the fear they were said to entertain of heavenly avengers. It was not so, at least, with him. He feared the laws of nature, lest, in their callous and immutable procedure, they should preserve some damning evidence of his crime. He feared tenfold more, with a slavish, superstitious terror, some scission in the continuity of man's experience, some wilful illegality of nature. He played

a game of skill, depending on the rules, calculating consequence from cause; and what if nature, as the defeated
tyrant overthrew the chess-board, should break the
mould of their succession? The like had befallen
Napoleon (so writers said) when the winter changed the
time of its appearance. The like might befall Markheim:
the solid walls might become transparent and reveal his
doings like those of bees in a glass hive; the stout planks
might yield under his foot like quicksands and detain
him in their clutch; ay, and there were soberer accidents
that might destroy him: if, for instance, the house should
fall and imprison him beside the body of his victim; or
the house next door should fly on fire, and the firemen
invade him from all sides. These things he feared; and,
in a sense, these things might be called the hands of God
reached forth against sin. But about God Himself he was
at ease: his act was doubtless exceptional, but so were his
excuses, which God knew; it was there, and not among
men, that he felt sure of justice.

When he had got safe into the drawing-room, and shut
the door behind him, he was aware of a respite from
alarms. The room was quite dismantled, uncarpeted
besides, and strewn with packing-cases and incongruous
furniture; several great pier-glasses, in which he beheld
himself at various angles, like an actor on a stage; many
pictures, framed and unframed, standing with their faces
to the wall; a fine Sheraton sideboard, a cabinet of mar-
quetry, and a great old bed, with tapestry hangings. The
windows opened to the floor; but by great good fortune
the lower part of the shutters had been closed, and this
concealed him from the neighbours. Here, then, Markheim drew in a packing-case before the cabinet, and
began to search among the keys. It was a long business,
for there were many; and it was irksome besides; for,
after all, there might be nothing in the cabinet, and time
was on the wing. But the closeness of the occupation
sobered him. With the tail of his eye he saw the door –
even glanced at it from time to time directly, like a

besieged commander, pleased to verify the good estate of his defences. But in truth he was at peace. The rain falling in the street sounded natural and pleasant. Presently, on the other side, the notes of a piano were wakened to the music of a hymn, and the voices of many children took up the air and words. How stately, how comfortable was the melody! How fresh the youthful voices! Markheim gave ear to it smilingly, as he sorted out the keys; and his mind was thronged with answerable ideas and images; church-going children and the pealing of the high organ; children afield, bathers by the brook-side, ramblers on the brambly common, kite-flyers in the windy and cloud-navigated sky; and then, at another cadence of the hymn, back again to church, and the som-nolence of summer Sundays, and the high genteel voice of the parson (which he smiled a little to recall) and the painted Jacobean tombs, and the dim lettering of the Ten Commandments in the chancel.

And as he sat thus, at once busy and absent, he was startled to his feet. A flash of ice, a flash of fire, a bursting gush of blood went over him, and then he stood transfixed and thrilling. A step mounted the stair slowly and steadily, and presently a hand was laid upon the knob, and the lock clicked, and the door opened.

Fear held Markheim in a vice. What to expect he knew not, whether the dead man walking, or the official ministers of human justice, or some chance witness blindly stumbling in to consign him to the gallows. But when a face was thrust into the aperture, glanced round the room, looked at him, nodded and smiled as if in friendly recognition, and then withdrew again, and the door closed behind it, his fear broke loose from his con-trol in a hoarse cry. At the sound of this the visitant returned.

"Did you call me?" he asked pleasantly, and with that he entered the room and closed the door behind him.

Markheim stood and gazed at him with all his eyes. Perhaps there was a film upon his sight, but the outlines of the new-comer seemed to change and waver like those of the idols in the wavering candlelight of the shop; and at times he thought he knew him; and at times he thought he bore a likeness to himself; and always, like a lump of living terror, there lay in his bosom the conviction that this thing was not of the earth and not of God.

And yet the creature had a strange air of the commonplace, as he stood looking on Markheim with a smile; and when he added: "You are looking for the money, I believe?" it was in the tones of everyday politeness.

Markheim made no answer.

"I should warn you," resumed the other, "that the maid has left her sweetheart earlier than usual and will soon be here. If Mr. Markheim be found in this house, I need not describe to him the consequences."

"You know me?" cried the murderer.

The visitor smiled. "You have long been a favourite of mine," he said; "and I have long observed and often sought to help you."

"What are you?" cried Markheim, "the devil?"

"What I may be," returned the other, "cannot affect the service I propose to render you."

"It can," cried Markheim; "it does! Be helped by you? No, never; not by you! You do not know me yet; thank God, you do not know me!"

"I know you," replied the visitant, with a sort of kind severity, or rather firmness. "I know you to the soul."

"Know me!" cried Markheim. "Who can do so? My life is but a travesty and slander on myself. I have lived to belie my nature. All men do; all men are better than this disguise, that grows about and stifles them. You see each dragged away by life, like one whom bravos have seized and muffled in a cloak. If they had their own control – if you could see their faces, they would be altogether different, they would shine out for heroes and saints! I am worse than most; myself is more overlaid; my excuse is known to me and God. But, had I the time, I could disclose myself."

145

"To me?" inquired the visitant.

"To you before all," returned the murderer. "I supposed you were intelligent. I thought – since you exist – you would prove a reader of the heart. And yet you would propose to judge me by my acts! Think of it; my acts! I was born and I have lived in a land of giants; giants have dragged me by the wrists since I was born out of my mother – the giants of circumstance. And you would judge me by my acts! But can you not look within? Can you not understand that evil is hateful to me? Can you not see within me the clear writing of conscience, never blurred by any wilful sophistry, although too often disregarded? Can you not read me for a thing that surely must be common as humanity – the unwilling sinner?"

"All this is very feelingly expressed," was the reply, "but it regards me not. These points of consistency are beyond my province, and I care not in the least by what compulsion you may have been dragged away, so as you are but carried in the right direction. But time flies; the servant delays, looking in the faces of the crowd and at the pictures on the hoardings, but still she keeps moving nearer; and remember, it is as if the gallows itself was striding towards you through the Christmas streets! Shall I help you; I, who know all? Shall I tell you where to find the money?"

"For what price?" asked Markheim.

"I offer you the service for a Christmas gift," returned the other.

Markheim could not refrain from smiling with a kind of bitter triumph. "No," said he, "I will take nothing at your hands; if I were dying of thirst, and it was your hand that put the pitcher to my lips, I should find the courage to refuse. It may be credulous, but I will do nothing to commit myself to evil."

"I have no objection to a death-bed repentance," observed the visitant.

"Because you disbelieve their efficacy!" Markheim cried.

"I do not say so," returned the other; "but I look on these things from a different side, and when the life is done my interest falls. The man has lived to serve me, to spread black looks under colour of religion, or to sow tares in the wheat-field, as you do, in a course of weak compliance with desire. Now that he draws so near to his deliverance, he can add but one act of service – to repent, to die smiling, and thus to build up in confidence and hope the more timorous of my surviving followers. I am not so hard a master. Try me. Accept my help. Please yourself in life as you have done hitherto; please yourself more amply, spread your elbows at the board; and when the night begins to fall and the curtains to be drawn, I tell you, for your greater comfort, that you will find it even easy to compound your quarrel with your conscience, and to make a truckling peace with God. I came but now from such a death-bed, and the room was full of sincere mourners, listening to the man's last words: and when I looked into that face, which had been set as a flint against mercy, I found it smiling with hope."

"And do you, then, suppose me such a creature?" asked Markheim. "Do you think I have no more generous aspirations than to sin, and sin, and sin, and, at the last, sneak into heaven? My heart rises at the thought. Is this, then, your experience of mankind? or is it because you find me with red hands that you presume such baseness? and is this crime of murder indeed so impious as to dry up the very springs of good?"

"Murder is to me no special category," replied the other. "All sins are murder, even as all life is war. I behold your race, like starving mariners on a raft, plucking crusts out of the hands of famine and feeding on each other's lives. I follow sins beyond the moment of their acting; I find in all that the last consequence is death; and to my eyes, the pretty maid who thwarts her mother with such taking graces on a question of a ball, drips no less visibly with human gore than such a murderer as yourself. Do I say that I follow sins? I follow virtues also; they differ not by the thickness of a nail, they are both scythes for the reaping angel of Death. Evil, for which I live, consists not in action but in character. The bad man is dear to me; not the bad act, whose fruits, if we could follow them far enough down the hurtling cataract of the ages, might yet be found more blessed than those of the rarest virtues. And it is not because you have killed a dealer, but because you are Markheim, that I offer to forward your escape."

"I will lay my heart open to you," answered Markheim. "This crime on which you find me is my last. On my way to it I have learned many lessons; itself is a lesson, a momentous lesson. Hitherto I have been driven with revolt to what I would not; I was a bond-slave to poverty, driven and scourged. There are robust virtues that can stand in these temptations; mine was not so: I had a thirst of pleasure. But to-day, and out of this deed, I pluck both warning and riches – both the power and a fresh resolve to be myself. I become in all things a free actor in the world; I begin to see myself all changed, these hands the agents of good, this heart at peace. Something comes over me out of the past; something of what I have dreamed on Sabbath evenings to the sound of the church organ, of what I forecast when I shed tears over noble books, or talked, an innocent child, with my mother. There lies my life; I have wandered a few years, but now I see once more my city of destination."

"You are to use this money on the Stock Exchange, I think?" remarked the visitor; "and there, if I mistake not, you have already lost some thousands."

"Ah," said Markheim, "but this time I have a sure thing."

"This time, again, you will lose," replied the visitor quietly.

"Ah, but I will keep back the half!" cried Markheim.

"That also you will lose," said the other.

The sweat started upon Markheim's brow. "Well, then, what matter?" he exclaimed. "Say it be lost, say I am plunged again in poverty, shall one part of me, and

148

that the worse, continue until the end to override the better? Evil and good run strong in me, haling me both ways. I do not love the one thing, I love all. I can conceive great deeds, renunciations, martyrdoms; and though I be fallen to such a crime as murder, pity is no stranger to my thoughts. I pity the poor; who knows their trials better than myself? I pity and help them; I prize love, I love honest laughter; there is no good thing nor true thing on earth but I love it from my heart. And are my vices only to direct my life, and my virtues to lie without effect, like some passive lumber of the mind? Not so; good, also, is the spring of acts."

But the visitant raised his finger. "For six-and-thirty years that you have been in this world," said he, "through many changes of fortune and varieties of humour, I have watched you steadily fall. Fifteen years ago you would have started at a theft. Three years back you would have blenched at the name of murder. Is there any crime, is there any cruelty or meanness, from which you still recoil? – five years from now I shall detect you in the fact! Downward, downward lies your way; nor can anything but death avail to stop you."

"It is true," Markheim said huskily, "I have in some degree complied with evil. But it is so with all: the very saints, in the mere exercise of living, grow less dainty, and take on the tone of their surroundings."

"I will propound to you one simple question," said the other; "and as you answer, I shall read to you your moral horoscope. You have grown in many things more lax; possibly you do right to be so; and at any account, it is the same with all men. But granting that, are you in any one particular, however trifling, more difficult to please with your own conduct, or do you go in all things with a looser rein?"

"In any one?" repeated Markheim, with an anguish of consideration. "No," he added, with despair, "in none! I have gone down in all."

"Then," said the visitor, "content yourself with what

you are, for you will never change; and the words of your part on this stage are irrevocably written down."

Markheim stood for a long while silent, and indeed it was the visitor who first broke the silence. "That being so," he said, "shall I show you the money?"

"And grace?" cried Markheim.

"Have you not tried it?" returned the other. "Two or three years ago, did I not see you on the platform of revival meetings, and was not your voice the loudest in the hymn?"

"It is true," said Markheim; "and I see clearly what remains for me by way of duty. I thank you for these lessons from my soul; my eyes are opened, and I behold myself at last for what I am."

At this moment, the sharp note of the door-bell rang through the house; and the visitant, as though this were some concerted signal for which he had been waiting, changed at once in his demeanour.

"The maid!" he cried. "She has returned, as I fore-warned you, and there is now before you one more difficult passage. Her master, you must say, is ill; you must let her in, with an assured but rather serious countenance – no smiles, no overacting, and I promise you success! Once the girl within, and the door closed, the same dexterity that has already rid you of the dealer will relieve you of this last danger in your path. Thenceforward you have the whole evening – the whole night, if needful – to ransack the treasures of the house and to make good your safety. This is help that comes to you with the mask of danger. Up!" he cried; "up, friend; your life hangs trembling in the scales: up, and act!"

Markheim steadily regarded his counsellor. "If I be condemned to evil acts," he said, "there is still one door of freedom open – I can cease from action. If my life be an ill thing, I can lay it down. Though I be, as you say truly, at the beck of every small temptation, I can yet, by one decisive gesture, place myself beyond the reach of all. My love of good is damned to barrenness; it may, and let it be! But I have still my hatred of evil; and from that, to your galling disappointment, you shall see that I can draw both energy and courage."

The features of the visitor began to undergo a wonderful and lovely change: they brightened and softened with a tender triumph, and, even as they brightened, faded and dislimned. But Markheim did not pause to watch or understand the transformation. He opened the door and went downstairs very slowly, thinking to himself. His past went soberly before him; he beheld it as it was, ugly and strenuous like a dream, random as chancemedley – a scene of defeat. Life, as he thus reviewed it, tempted him no longer; but on the farther side he perceived a quiet haven for his bark. He paused in the passage, and looked into the shop, where the candle still burned by the dead body. It was strangely silent. Thoughts of the dealer swarmed into his mind, as he stood gazing. And then the bell once more broke out into impatient clamour.

He confronted the maid upon the threshold with something like a smile.

"You had better go for the police," said he: "I have killed your master."

THRAWN JANET

THRAWN JANET

THE Reverend Murdoch Soulis was long minister of the moorland parish of Balweary, in the vale of Dule. A severe, bleak-faced old man, dreadful to his hearers, he dwelt in the last years of his life, without relative or servant or any human company, in the small and lonely manse under the Hanging Shaw. In spite of the iron composure of his features, his eye was wild, scared, and uncertain; and when he dwelt, in private admonitions, on the future of the impenitent, it seemed as if his eye pierced through the storms of time to the terrors of eternity. Many young persons, coming to prepare themselves against the season of the Holy Communion, were dreadfully affected by his talk. He had a sermon on 1st Peter v. and 8th, "The devil as a roaring lion," on the Sunday after every seventeenth of August, and he was accustomed to surpass himself upon that text both by the appalling nature of the matter and the terror of his bearing in the pulpit. The children were frightened into fits, and the old looked more than usually oracular, and were, all that day, full of those hints that Hamlet deprecated. The manse itself, where it stood by the water of Dule among some thick trees, with the Shaw overhanging it on the one side, and on the other many cold, moorish hilltops rising towards the sky, had begun, at a very early period of Mr. Soulis's ministry, to be avoided in the dusk hours by all who valued themselves upon their prudence; and guidmen sitting at the clachan alehouse shook their heads together at the thought of passing late by that uncanny neighbourhood. There was one spot, to be more particular, which was regarded with especial awe. The manse stood between the high-road and the water of

Dule, with a gable to each; its back was towards the kirk-town of Balweary, nearly half a mile away; in front of it, a bare garden, hedged with thorn, occupied the land between the river and the road. The house was two stories high, with two large rooms on each. It opened not directly on the garden, but on a causewayed path, or passage, giving on the road on the one hand, and closed on the other by the tall willows and elders that bordered on the stream. And it was this strip of causeway that enjoyed among the young parishioners of Balweary so infamous a reputation. The minister walked there often after dark, sometimes groaning aloud in the instancy of his unspoken prayers; and when he was from home, and the manse door was locked, the more daring schoolboys ventured, with beating hearts, to "follow my leader" across that legendary spot.

This atmosphere of terror, surrounding, as it did, a man of God of spotless character and orthodoxy, was a common cause of wonder and subject of inquiry among the few strangers who were led by chance or business into that unknown, outlying country. But many even of the people of the parish were ignorant of the strange events which had marked the first year of Mr. Soulis's ministrations; and among those who were better informed, some were naturally reticent, and others shy of that particular topic. Now and again, only, one of the older folk would warm into courage over his third tumbler, and recount the cause of the minister's strange looks and solitary life.

Fifty years syne, when Mr. Soulis cam' first into Ba'weary, he was still a young man – a callant, the folk said – fu' o' book-learnin' an' grand at the exposition, but, as was natural in sae young a man, wi' nae leevin' experience in religion. The younger sort were greatly taken wi' his gifts an' his gab; but auld, concerned, serious men and women were moved even to prayer for the young man, whom they took to be a self-deceiver, an' the

parish that was like to be sae ill-supplied. It was before
the days o' the Moderates – weary fa' them; but ill things
are like guid – they baith come bit by bit, a pickle at a
time; an' there were folk even then that said the Lord
had left the college professors to their ain devices, an'
the lads that went to study wi' them wad hae done mair
an' better sittin' in a peat-bog, like their forbears o' the
persecution, wi' a Bible under their oxter an' a speerit o'
prayer in their heart. There was nae doubt, onyway, but
that Mr. Soulis had been ower lang at the college. He was
careful an' troubled for mony things besides the ae thing
needful. He had a feck o' books wi' him – mair than had
ever been seen before in a' that presbytery; and a sair
wark the carrier had wi' them, for they were a' like to
have smoored in the De'il's Hag between this an'
Kilmackerlie. They were books o' divinity, to be sure, or
so they ca'd them; but the serious were of opinion there
was little service for sae mony, when the hale o' God's
Word would gang in the neuk o' a plaid. Then he wad sit
half the day, an' half the nicht forbye, which was scant
decent – writin', nae less; an' first, they were feared he
wad read his sermons; an' syne it proved he was writin' a
book himsel', which was surely no' fittin' for ane o' his
years an' sma' experience.

   Onyway it behoved him to get an auld, decent wife to
keep the manse for him an' see to his bit denners; an' he
was recommended to an auld limmer – Janet M'Clour,
they ca'd her – an' sae far left to himself as to be ower
persuaded. There was mony advised him to the contrar,
for Janet was mair than suspeckit by the best folk in
Ba'weary. Lang or that, she had had a wean to a dragoon;
she hadna come forrit[1] for maybe thretty year; an' bairns
had seen her mumblin' to hersel' up on Key's Loan in
the gloamin', whilk was an unco time an' place for a God-
fearin' woman. Howsoever, it was the laird himsel' that
had first tauld the minister o' Janet; an' in thae days he

---

1 "To come forrit" – to offer oneself as a communicant.

wad hae gane a far gate to pleesure the laird. When folk tauld him that Janet was sib to the de'il, it was a' superstition by his way o' it; an' when they cast up the Bible to him an' the witch o' Endor, he wad threep it doun their thrapples that thir days were a' gane by, an' the de'il was mercifully restrained.

Weel, when it got about the clachan that Janet M'Clour was to be servant at the manse, the folk were fair mad wi' her an' him thegither; an' some o' the guidwives had nae better to dae than get round her doorcheeks and chairge her wi' a' that was ken't again' her, frae the sodger's bairn to John Tamson's twa kye. She was nae great speaker; folk usually let her gang her ain gate, an' she let them gang theirs, wi' neither Fair-guideen nor Fair-guid-day: but when she buckled to, she had a tongue to deave the miller. Up she got, an' there wasna an auld story in Ba'weary but she gart somebody lowp for it that day; they couldna say ae thing but she could say twa to it; till, at the hinder end, the guidwives up and claucht haud o' her, an' clawed the coats aff her back, an' pu'd her doun the clachan to the water o' Dule, to see if she were a witch or no, soom or droun. The carline skirled till ye could hear her at the Hangin' Shaw, an' she focht like ten; there was mony a guidwife bure the mark o' her neist day an' mony a lang day after; an' just in the hettest o' the collieshangie, wha suld come up (for his sins) but the new minister.

"Women," said he (and he had a grand voice), "I charge you in the Lord's name to let her go."

Janet ran to him – she was fair wud wi' terror – an' clang to him, an' prayed him, for Christ's sake, save her frae the cummers; an' they, for their pairt, tauld him a' that was ken't, an' maybe mair.

"Woman," says he to Janet, "is this true?"

"As the Lord sees me," says she, "as the Lord made me, no a word o't. Forbye the bairn," says she, "I've been a decent woman a' my days."

"Will you," says Mr. Soulis, "in the name of God, and

before me, His unworthy minister, renounce the devil and his works?"

Weel, it wad appear that when he askit that, she gave a girn that fairly frichtit them that saw her, an' they could hear her teeth play dirl thegither in her chafts; but there was naething for't but the ae way or the ither; an' Janet lifted up her hand an' renounced the de'il before them a'.

"And now," says Mr. Soulis to the guidwives, "home with ye, one and all, and pray to God for His forgiveness."

An' he gied Janet his arm, though she had little on her but a sark, an' took her up the clachan to her ain door like a leddy o' the land; an' her screighin' and laughin' as was a scandal to be heard.

There were mony grave folk lang ower their prayers that nicht; but when the morn cam' there was sic a fear fell upon a' Ba'weary that the bairns hid theirsels, an' even the men-folk stood an' keekit frae their doors. For there was Janet comin' doun the clachan – her or her likeness, nane could tell – wi' her neck thrawn, an' her heid on ae side, like a body that has been hangit, an' a girn on her face like an unstreakit corp. By an' by they got used wi' it, an' even speered at her to ken what was wrang; but frae that day forth she couldna speak like a Christian woman, but slavered an' played click wi' her teeth like a pair o' shears; an' frae that day forth the name o' God cam' never on her lips. Whiles she wad try to say it, but it michtna be. Them that kenned best said least; but they never gied that Thing the name o' Janet M'Clour; for the auld Janet, by their way o't, was in muckle hell that day. But the minister was neither to haud nor to bind; he preached about naething but the folk's cruelty that had gi'en her a stroke of the palsy; he skelpit the bairns that meddled her; an' he had her up to the manse that same nicht, an' dwalled there a' his lane wi' her under the Hangin' Shaw.

Weel, time gaed by: an' the idler sort commenced to

think mair lichtly o' that black business. The minister was weel thocht o'; he was aye late at the writing, folk wad see his can'le doon by the Dule water after twal' at e'en; an' he seemed pleased wi' himsel' an' upsitten as at first, though a' body could see that he was dwining. As for Janet she cam' an' she gaed; if she didna speak muckle afore, it was reason she should speak less then; she meddled naebody; but she was an eldritch thing to see, an' nane wad hae mistrysted wi' her for Ba'weary glebe.

About the end o' July there cam' a spell o' weather, the like o't never was in that countryside; it was lown an' het an' heartless; the herds couldna win up the Black Hill, the bairns were ower weariet to play; an' yet it was gousty too, wi' claps o' het wund that rumm'led in the glens, and bits o' shouers that slockened naething. We aye thocht it but to thun'er on the morn; but the morn cam', an' the morn's morning, an' it was aye the same uncanny weather, sair on folks and bestial. O' a' that were the waur, nane suffered like Mr. Soulis; he could neither sleep nor eat, he tauld his elders; an' when he wasna writin' at his weary book, he wad be stravaguin' ower a' the countryside like a man possessed, when a' body else was blithe to keep caller ben the house.

Abune Hangin' Shaw, in the bield o' the Black Hill, there's a bit enclosed grund wi' an iron yett; an' it seems, in the auld days, that was the kirkyaird o' Ba'weary, and consecrated by the Papists before the blessed licht shone upon the kingdom. It was a great howff o' Mr. Soulis's, onyway; there he wad sit an' consider his sermons; an' indeed it's a bieldy bit. Weel, as he cam' ower the wast end o' the Black Hill ae day, he saw first twa, an' syne fower, an' syne seeven corbie craws fleein' round an' round abune the auld kirkyaird. They flew laigh an' heavy, an' squawked to ither as they gaed; an' it was clear to Mr. Soulis that something had put them frae their ordinar'. He wasna easy fleyed, an' gaed straucht up to the wa's; an' what suld he find there but a man, or the appearance o' a man, sittin' in the inside upon a grave. He was of a great stature, an' black as hell, an' his e'en were singular to see.[1] Mr. Soulis had heard tell o' black men, mony's the time; but there was something unco about this black man that daunted him. Het as he was, he took a kind o' cauld grue in the marrow o' his banes; but up he spak for a' that; an' says he: "My friend, are you a stranger in this place?" The black man answered never a word; he got upon his feet, an' begoud to hirsle to the wa' on the far side; but he aye lookit at the minister; an' the minister stood an' lookit back; till a' in a meenit the black man was ower the wa' an' rinnin' for the bield o' the trees. Mr. Soulis, he hardly kenned why, ran after him; but he was fair forjeskit wi' his walk an' the het, unhalesome weather; an' rin as he likit, he got nae mair than a glisk o' the black man amang the birks, till he won doun to the foot o' the hillside, an' there he saw him ance mair, gaun hap-step-an'-lowp ower Dule water to the manse.

Mr. Soulis wasna weel pleased that this fearsome gangrel suld mak' sae free wi' Ba'weary manse; an' he ran the harder, an', wet shoon, ower the burn, an' up the walk; but the deil a black man was there to see. He stepped out upon the road, but there was naebody there; he gaed a' ower the gairden, but na, nae black man. At the hinder end, an' a bit feared, as was but natural, he lifted the hasp an' into the manse; an' there was Janet M'Clour before his een, wi' her thrawn craig, an' nane sae pleased to see him. An' he aye minded sinsyne, when first he set his een upon her, he had the same cauld and deidly grue.

"Janet," says he, "have you seen a black man?"

"A black man?" quo' she. "Save us a'! Ye're no wise, minister. There's nae black man in a' Ba'weary."

---

1 It was a common belief in Scotland that the devil appeared as a black man. This appears in several witch trials, and I think in Law's "Memorials," that delightful storehouse of the quaint and grisly.

But she didna speak plain, ye maun understand; but yam-yammered, like a powney wi' the bit in its moo.

"Weel," says he, "Janet, if there was nae black man, I have spoken with the Accuser of the Brethren."

An' he sat down like ane wi' a fever, an' his teeth chittered in his heid.

"Hoots," says she, "think shame to yoursel', minister"; an' gied him a drap brandy that she keept aye by her.

Syne Mr. Soulis gaed into his study amang a' his books. It's a lang, laigh, mirk chalmer, perishin' cauld in winter, an' no' very dry even in the tap o' the simmer, for the manse stands near the burn. Sae doun he sat, an' thocht o' a' that had come an' gane since he was in Ba'weary, an' his hame, an' the days when he was a bairn an' ran daffin' on the braes; an' that black man aye ran in his heid like the owercome o' a sang. Aye the mair he thocht, the mair he thocht o' the black man. He tried the prayer, an' the words wadna come to him; an' he tried, they say, to write at his book, but he couldna mak' nae mair o' that. There was whiles he thocht the black man was at his oxter, an' the swat stood upon him cauld as well-water; an' there was ither whiles when he cam' to himsel' like a christened bairn an' minded naething.

The upshot was that he gaed to the window an' stood glowrin' at Dule water. The trees are unco thick, an' the water lies deep an' black under the manse; an' there was Janet washin' the cla'es wi' her coats kilted. She had her back to the minister, an' he, for his pairt, hardly kenned what he was lookin' at. Syne she turned round, an' shawed her face; Mr. Soulis had the same cauld grue as twice that day afore, an' it was borne in upon him what folk said, that Janet was deid lang syne, an' this was a bogle in her clay-cauld flesh. He drew back a pickle and he scanned her narrowly. She was tramp-trampin' in the cla'es, croonin' to hersel'; and eh! Gude guide us, but it was a fearsome face. Whiles she sang louder, but there was nae man born o' woman that could tell the words o' her sang; an' whiles she lookit side-lang doun, but there was naething there for her to look at. There gaed a scunner through the flesh upon his banes; an' that was Heeven's advertisement. But Mr. Soulis just blamed himsel', he said, to think sae ill o' a puir, auld afflicted wife that hadna a freend forbye himsel'; an' he put up a bit prayer for him an' her, an' drank a little caller water – for his heart rose again' the meat – an' gaed up to his naked bed in the gloamin'.

That was a nicht that has never been forgotten in Ba'weary, the nicht o' the seeventeenth o' August, seeventeen hun'er' an' twal'. It had been het afore, as I hae said, but that nicht it was hetter than ever. The sun gaed doun amang unco-lookin' clouds; it fell as mirk as the pit; no' a star, no' a breath o' wund; ye couldna see your han' afore your face, an' even the auld folk cuist the covers frae their beds an' lay pechin' for their breath. Wi' a' that he had upon his mind, it was geyan unlikely Mr. Soulis wad get muckle sleep. He lay an' he tummled; the gude, caller bed that he got into brunt his very banes; whiles he slept, an' whiles he waukened; whiles he heard the time o' nicht, an' whiles a tyke yowlin' up the muir, as if somebody was deid; whiles he thocht he heard bogles claverin' in his lug, an' whiles he saw spunkies in the room. He behoved, he judged, to be sick; an' sick he was – little he jaloosed the sickness.

At the hinder end he got a clearness in his mind, sat up in his sark on the bed-side, an' fell thinkin' ance mair o' the black man an' Janet. He couldna weel tell how – maybe it was the cauld to his feet – but it cam' in upon him wi' a spate that there was some connection between thir twa, an' that either or baith o' them were bogles. An' just at that moment, in Janet's room, which was neist to his, there cam' a stramp o' feet as if men were wars'lin', an' then a loud bang; an' then a wund gaed reishling round the fower quarters o' the house; an' then a' was aince mair as seelent as the grave.

Mr. Soulis was feared for neither man nor deevil. He

163

got his tinder-box, an' lit a can'le, an' made three steps
o't ower to Janet's door. It was on the hasp, an' he pushed
it open, an' keekit bauldly in. It was a big room, as big as
the minister's ain, an' plenished wi' grand, auld, solid
gear, for he had naething else. There was a fower-posted
bed wi' auld tapestry; an' a braw cabinet o' aik, that was
fu' o' the minister's divinity books, an' put there to be
out o' the gate; an' a wheen duds o' Janet's lying here an'
there about the floor. But nae Janet could Mr. Soulis see;
nor ony sign o' a contention. In he gaed (an' there's few
that wad hae followed him) an' lookit a' round, an' listened. But there was naething to be heard, neither inside
the manse nor in a' Ba'weary parish, an' naething to be
seen but the muckle shadows turnin' round the can'le.
An' then a' at aince, the minister's heart played dunt an'
stood stock-still; an' a cauld wund blew amang the hairs
o' his heid. Whaten a weary sicht was that for the puir
man's een! For there was Janet hangin' frae a nail beside
the auld aik cabinet: her heid aye lay on her shouther,
her een were steekit, the tongue projected frae her
mouth, an' her heels were twa feet clear abune the floor.

"God forgive us all!" thocht Mr. Soulis; "poor Janet's
dead."

He cam' a step nearer to the corp; an' then his heart
fair whammled in his inside. For, by what cantrip it wad
ill beseem a man to judge, she was hingin' frae a single
nail an' by a single wursted thread for darnin' hose.

It's an awfu' thing to be your lane at nicht wi' siccan
prodigies o' darkness; but Mr. Soulis was strong in the
Lord. He turned an' gaed his ways oot o' that room, an'
lockit the door ahint him; an' step by step, doon the
stairs, as heavy as leed; an' set doon the can'le on the
table at the stairfoot. He couldna pray, he couldna think,
he was dreepin' wi' caul' swat, an' naething could he
hear but the dunt-dunt-duntin' o' his ain heart. He micht
maybe hae stood there an hour, or maybe twa, he minded
sae little; when a' o' a sudden, he heard a laigh, uncanny
steer upstairs; a foot gaed to an' fro in the chalmer whaur

the corp was hingin'; syne the door was opened, though he minded weel that he had lockit it; an' syne there was a step upon the landin', an' it seemed to him as if the corp was lookin' ower the rail an' doun upon him whaur he stood.

He took up the can'le again (for he couldna want the licht), an' as saftly as ever he could, gaed straucht out o' the manse an' to the far end o' the causeway. It was aye pit-mirk; the flame o' the can'le, when he set it on the grund, brunt steedy and clear as in a room; naething moved, but the Dule water seepin' an' sabbin' doun the glen, an' yon unhaly footstep that cam' ploddin' doun the stairs inside the manse. He kenned the foot ower weel, for it was Janet's; an' at ilka step that cam' a wee thing nearer, the cauld got deeper in his vitals. He commended his soul to Him that made an' keepit him; "and, O Lord," said he, "give me strength this night to war against the powers of evil."

By this time the foot was comin' through the passage for the door; he could hear a hand skirt alang the wa', as if the fearsome thing was feelin' for its way. The saughs tossed an' maned thegither, a lang sigh cam' ower the hills, the flame o' the can'le was blawn aboot; an' there stood the corp o' Thrawn Janet, wi' her grogram goun an' her black mutch, wi' the heid aye upon the shouther, an' the girn still upon the face o't – leevin', ye wad hae said – deid, as Mr. Soulis weel kenned – upon the threshold o' the manse.

It's a strange thing that the saul o' man should be that thirled into his perishable body; but the minister saw that, an' his heart didna break.

She didna stand there lang; she began to move again an' cam' slowly towards Mr. Soulis whaur he stood under the saughs. A' the life o' his body, a' the strength o' his speerit, were glowerin' frae his een. It seemed she was gaun to speak, but wanted words, an' made a sign wi' the left hand. There cam' a slap o' wund, like a cat's fuff; oot gaed the can'le, the slaughs skreighed like folk; and Mr.

Soulis kenned that, live or die, this was the end o't.

"Witch, beldame, devil!" he cried, "I charge you, by the power of God, begone – if you be dead, to the grave – if you be damned, to hell."

An' at that moment the Lord's ain hand out o' the Heevens struck the Horror whaur it stood; the auld, deid, desecrated corp o' the witch-wife, sae lang keepit frae the grave an' hirsled round by de'ils, lowed up like a brunstane spunk an' fell in ashes to the grund; the thunder followed, peal on dirlin' peal, the rairin' rain upon the back o' that; an' Mr. Soulis lowped through the garden hedge, an' ran, wi' skelloch upon skelloch, for the clachan.

That same mornin', John Christie saw the Black Man pass the Muckle Cairn as it was chappin' six; before eicht, he gaed by the change-house at Knockdow; an' no' lang after, Sandy M'Lellan saw him gaun linkin' doun the braes frae Kilmackerlie. There's little doubt but it was him that dwalled sae lang in Janet's body; but he was awa' at last; an' sinsyne the de'il has never fashed us in Ba'weary.

But it was a sair dispensation for the minister; lang, lang he lay ravin' in his bed; an' frae that hour to this he was the man ye ken the day.

THE MISADVENTURES OF
JOHN NICHOLSON

THE MISADVENTURES OF
JOHN NICHOLSON

Chapter 1
In which John sows the Wind

JOHN VAREY NICHOLSON was stupid; yet stupider men than he are now sprawling in Parliament, and lauding themselves as the authors of their own distinction. He was of a fat habit, even from boyhood, and inclined to a cheerful and cursory reading of the face of life; and possibly this attitude of mind was the original cause of his misfortunes. Beyond this hint philosophy is silent on his career, and superstition steps in with the more ready explanation that he was detested of the gods.

His father – that iron gentleman – had long ago enthroned himself on the heights of the Disruption Principles. What these are (and in spite of their grim name they are quite innocent) no array of terms would render thinkable to the merely English intelligence; but to the Scot they often prove unctuously nourishing, and Mr. Nicholson found in them the milk of lions. About the period when the churches convene at Edinburgh in their annual assemblies, he was to be seen descending the Mound in the company of divers red-headed clergymen: these voluble, he only contributing oracular nods, brief negatives, and the austere spectacle of his stretched upper lip. The names of Candlish and Begg were frequent in these interviews, and occasionally the talk ran on the Residuary Establishment and the doings of one Lee. A stranger to the tight little theological kingdom of Scotland might have listened and gathered literally nothing. And Mr. Nicholson (who was not a dull man) knew this, and raged at it. He knew there was a vast world outside to whom Disruption Principles were as the chatter of tree-top apes; the paper brought him chill whiffs from it; he had met Englishmen who had asked lightly if he did not belong to the Church of Scotland, and then had failed to be much interested by his elucidation of that nice point; it was an evil, wild, rebellious world, lying sunk in *dozenedness*, for nothing short of a Scots word will paint this Scotsman's feelings. And when he entered his own house in Randolph Crescent (south side), and shut the door behind him, his heart swelled with security. Here, at least, was a citadel unassailable by right-hand defections or left-hand extremes. Here was a family where prayers came at the same hour, where the Sabbath literature was unimpeachably selected, where the guest who should have leaned to any false opinion was instantly set down, and over which there reigned all the week, and grew denser on Sundays, a silence that was agreeable to his ear, and a gloom that he found comfortable.

Mrs. Nicholson had died about thirty, and left him with three children: a daughter two years and a son about eight years younger than John; and John himself, the unfortunate protagonist of the present history. The daughter, Maria, was a good girl – dutiful, pious, dull, but so easily startled that to speak to her was quite a perilous enterprise. "I don't think I care to talk about that, if you please," she would say, and strike the boldest speechless by her unmistakable pain; this upon all topics – dress, pleasure, morality, politics, in which the formula was changed to "my papa thinks otherwise," and even religion, unless it was approached with a particular whining tone of voice. Alexander, the younger brother, was sickly, clever, fond of books and drawing, and full of satirical remarks. In the midst of these, imagine that natural, clumsy, unintelligent and mirthful animal, John; mighty well-behaved in comparison with many lads, although not up to the standard of the house in Randolph Crescent; full of a sort of blundering affection, full of caresses which were never very warmly received; full of sudden and loud laughter which rang out in that still house like curses. Mr. Nicholson himself had a great fund of humour, of the Scots order – intellectual, turning on the observation of men; his own character, for instance – if he could have seen it in another – would have been a rare feast to him; but his son's empty guffaws over a broken plate, and empty, almost light-headed remarks, struck him with pain as the indices of a weak mind.

Outside the family John had early attached himself (much as a dog may follow a marquess) to the steps of Alan Houston, a lad about a year older than himself, idle, a trifle wild, the heir to a good estate which was still in the hands of a rigorous trustee, and so royally content with himself that he took John's devotion as a thing of course. The intimacy was gall to Mr. Nicholson; it took his son from the house, and he was a jealous parent; it kept him from the office, and he was a martinet; lastly, Mr. Nicholson was ambitious for his family (in which, and in the Disruption Principles, he entirely lived), and hated to see a son of his play second fiddle to an idler. After some hesitation, he ordered that the friendship should cease – an unfair command, though seemingly inspired by the spirit of prophecy and John, saying nothing, continued to disobey the order under the rose.

John was nearly nineteen when he was one day dismissed rather earlier than usual from his father's office, where he was studying the practice of the law. It was Saturday; and except that he had a matter of four hundred pounds in his pocket which it was his duty to hand over to the British Linen Company's Bank, he had the whole afternoon at his disposal. He went by Princes Street enjoying the mild sunshine, and the little thrill of easterly wind that tossed the flags along that terrace of palaces, and tumbled the green trees in the garden. The band was playing down in the valley under the Castle; and when it came to the turn of the pipers, he heard their wild sounds with a stirring of the blood. Something distantly martial woke in him; and he thought of Miss Mackenzie, the daughter of a retired captain of Highlanders, whom he was to meet that day at dinner in his father's house.

Now, it is undeniable that he should have gone directly to the bank; but right in the way stood the billiard-room of the hotel where Alan was almost certain to be found; and the temptation proved too strong. He entered the billiard-room, and was instantly greeted by his friend, cue in hand.

"Nicholson," said he, "I want you to lend me a pound or two till Monday."

"You've come to the right shop, haven't you?" returned John. "I have twopence"

"Nonsense," said Alan. "You can get some. Go and borrow at your tailor's; they all do it. Or I'll tell you what: pop your watch."

"O yes, I daresay," said John. "And how about my father?"

"How is he to know? He doesn't wind it up for you at night, does he?" inquired Alan, at which John guffawed. "No, seriously; I am in a fix," continued the tempter. "I have lost some money to a man here. I'll give it you to-night, and you can get the heirloom out again on Monday. Come; it's a small service, after all. I would do a good deal more for you."

Whereupon John went forth, and pawned his gold watch under the assumed name of John Froggs, 85 Pleasance. But the nervousness that assailed him at the door of that inglorious haunt, a pawnshop, and the effort necessary to invent the pseudonym (which somehow seemed to him a necessary part of the procedure), had taken more time than he imagined; and when he returned to the billiard-room with the spoils, the bank had already closed its doors.

This was a shrewd knock. "A piece of business had been neglected." He heard these words in his father's trenchant voice, and trembled, and then dodged the thought. After all, who was to know? He must carry four hundred pounds about with him till Monday, when the

neglect could be surreptitiously repaired; and meanwhile, he was free to pass the afternoon on the encircling
divan of the billiard-room, smoking his pipe, sipping a
pint of ale, and enjoying to the mast-head the modest
pleasures of admiration.

None can admire like a young man. Of all youth's passions and pleasures, this is the most common and least
alloyed; and every flash of Alan's black eyes; every aspect
of his curly head; every graceful reach and easy, stand-off
attitude of waiting; everything about him down even to
his shirt-sleeves and wrist-links, were seen by John
through a luxurious glory. He valued himself by the possession of that royal friend, hugged himself upon the
thought, and swam in warm azure; his own defects, like
vanquished difficulties, becoming things on which to
plume himself. Only when he thought of Miss
Mackenzie there fell upon his mind a shadow of regret;
that young lady was worthy of better things than plain
John Nicholson, still known among schoolmates by the
derisive name of "Fatty"; and he felt that if he could
chalk a cue, or stand at ease, with such a careless grace as
Alan, he could approach the object of his sentiments
with a less crushing sense of inferiority.

Before they parted, Alan made a proposal that was
startling in the extreme. He would be at Collette's that
night about twelve, he said. Why should not John come
there and get the money? To go to Collette's was to see
life indeed; it was wrong; it was against the laws; it par-
took, in a very dingy manner, of adventure. Were it
known, it was the sort of exploit that disconsidered a
young man for good with the more serious classes, but
gave him a standing with the riotous. And yet Collette's
was not a hell; it could not come, without vaulting hyper-
bole, under the description of a gilded saloon; and if it
was a sin to go there, the sin was merely local and muni-
cipal. Collette was simply an unlicensed publican, who
gave suppers after eleven at night, the Edinburgh hour of
closing. If you belonged to a club, you could get a much

better supper at the same hour, and lose not a jot in public esteem. But if you lacked that qualification, and were an-hungered, or inclined towards conviviality at unlawful hours, Collete's was your only port. You were very ill supplied. The company was not recruited from the Senate or the Church, though the Bar was very well represented on the only occasion on which I flew in the face of my country's laws, and, taking my reputation in my hand, penetrated into that grim supper-house. And Collette's frequenters, thrillingly conscious of wrong-doing and "that two-handed engine (the policeman) at the door," were perhaps inclined to somewhat feverish excess. But the place was in no sense a very bad one; and it is somewhat strange to me, at this distance of time, how it had acquired its dangerous repute.

In precisely the same spirit as a man may debate a project to ascend the Matterhorn or to cross Africa, John considered Alan's proposal, and greatly daring, accepted it. As he walked home, the thoughts of this excursion out of the safe places of life into the wild and arduous, stirred and struggled in his imagination with the image of Flora Mackenzie – incongruous and yet kindred thoughts, for did not each imply unusual tightening of the pegs of resolution? did not each woo him forth and warn him back again into himself?

Between these two considerations, at least, he was more than usually moved; and when he got to Randolph Crescent, he quite forgot the four hundred pounds in the inner pocket of his greatcoat, hung up the coat, with its rich freight, upon his particular pin of the hat-stand; and in the very action sealed his doom.

Chapter 2

In which John reaps the Whirlwind

ABOUT half-past ten it was John's brave good fortune to offer his arm to Miss Mackenzie, and escort her home. The night was chill and starry; and the way eastward the trees of the different gardens rustled and looked black. Up the stone gully of Leith Walk, when they came to cross it, the breeze made a rush and set the flames of the street-lamps quavering; and when at last they mounted to the Royal Terrace, where Captain Mackenzie lived, a great salt freshness came in their faces from the sea. These phases of the walk remained written on John's memory, each emphasised by the touch of that light hand on his arm; and behind all these aspects of the nocturnal city he saw, in his mind's eye, a picture of the lighted drawing-room at home where he had sat talking with Flora; and his father, from the other end, had looked on with a kind and ironical smile. John had read the signifi-cance of that smile, which might have escaped a stranger. Mr. Nicholson had remarked his son's entanglement with satisfaction, tinged with humour; and his smile, if it still was a thought contemptuous, had implied consent.

At the captain's door the girl held out her hand with a certain emphasis; and John took it and kept it a little longer, and said, "Good-night, Flora, dear," and was instantly thrown into much fear by his presumption. But she only laughed, ran up the steps and rang the bell; and while she was waiting for the door to open, kept close in the porch, and talked to him from that point as out of a fortification. She had a knitted shawl over her head; her blue Highland eyes took the light from the neighbouring street-lamp and sparkled; and when the door opened and closed upon her, John felt cruelly alone.

He proceeded slowly back along the terrace in a tender glow; and when he came to Greenside Church, he halted in a doubtful mind. Over the crown of the Calton Hill, to his left, lay the way to Collette's, where Alan would soon be looking for his arrival, and where he would now have no more consented to go than he would have wilfully wallowed in a bog; the touch of the girl's hand on his sleeve, and the kindly light in his father's eyes, both loudly forbidding. But right before him was the way home, which pointed only to bed, a place of little ease for one whose fancy was strung to the lyrical pitch, and whose not very ardent heart was just then tumultuously moved. The hill-top, the cool air of the night, the company of the great monuments, the sight of the city under his feet, with its hills and valleys and crossing files of lamps, drew him by all he had of the poetic, and he turned that way; and by that quite innocent deflection ripened the crop of his venial errors for the sickle of destiny.

On a seat on the hill above Greenside he sat for perhaps half an hour, looking down upon the lamps of Edinburgh, and up at the lamps of heaven. Wonderful were the resolves he formed; beautiful and kindly were the vistas of future life that sped before him. He uttered to himself the name of Flora in so many touching and dramatic keys that he became at length fairly melted with tenderness, and could have sung aloud. At that juncture a certain creasing in his greatcoat caught his ear. He put his hand into his pocket, pulled forth the envelope that held the money, and sat stupefied. The Calton Hill, about this period, had an ill name of nights; and to be sitting there with four hundred pounds that did not belong to him was hardly wise. He looked up. There was a man in a very bad hat, a little on one side of him, apparently looking at the scenery; from a little on the other a second night-walker was drawing very quietly near. Up jumped John. The envelope fell from his hands; he stooped to get it, and at the same moment both men ran in and closed with him.

A little after, he got to his feet very sore and shaken,

the poorer by a purse which contained exactly one penny postage-stamp, by a cambric handkerchief, and by the all-important envelope.

Here was a young man on whom, at the highest point of loverly exaltation, there had fallen a blow too sharp to be supported alone; and not many hundred yards away his greatest friend was sitting at supper – ay, and even expecting him. Was it not in the nature of man that he should run there? He went in quest of sympathy – in quest of that droll article that we all suppose ourselves to want when in a strait, and have agreed to call advice; and he went, besides, with vague but rather splendid expectations of relief. Alan was rich or would be so when he came of age. By a stroke of the pen he might remedy this misfortune, and avert that dreaded interview with Mr. Nicholson, from which John now shrank in imagination as the hand draws back from fire.

Close under the Calton Hill there runs a certain narrow avenue, part street, part by-road. The head of it faces the doors of the prison; its tail descends into the sunless slums of the Low Calton. On one hand it is overhung by the crags of the hill, on the other by an old graveyard. Between these two the roadway runs in a trench, sparsely lighted at night, sparsely frequented by day, and bordered, when it has cleared the place of tombs, by dingy and ambiguous houses. One of these was the house of Collette; and at his door our ill-starred John was presently beating for admittance. In an evil hour he satisfied the jealous inquiries of the contraband hotel-keeper; in an evil hour he penetrated into the somewhat unsavoury interior. Alan, to be sure, was there, seated in a room lit by by noisy gas-jets, beside a dirty table-cloth, engaged on a coarse meal, and in the company of several tipsy members of the junior Bar. But Alan was not sober; he had lost a thousand pounds upon a horse-race, had received the news at dinner-time, and was now, in default of any possible means of extrication, drowning the memory of his predicament. He to help John! The thing was impossible; he couldn't help himself.

"If you have a beast of a father," said he, "I can tell you I have a brute of a trustee."

"I'm not going to hear my father called a beast," said John, with a beating heart, feeling that he risked the last sound rivet of the chain that bound him to life.

But Alan was quite good-natured.

"All right, old fellow," said he. "Mos' respec'able man your father." And he introduced his friend to his companions as "old Nicholson the what-d'ye-call-um's son."

John sat in dumb agony. Collette's foul walls and spotted table-linen, everything even down to Collette's villainous casters, seemed like objects in a nightmare. And just then there came a knock and a scurrying: the police, so lamentably absent from the Calton Hill, appeared upon the scene; and the party, taken *flagrante delicto*, with their glasses at their elbow, were seized, marched up to the police office, and all duly summoned to appear as witnesses in the consequent case against that arch-shebeener, Collette.

It was a sorrowful and a mightily sobered company that came forth again. The vague terror of public opinion weighed generally on them all; but there were private and particular horrors on the minds of individuals. Alan stood in dread of his trustee, already sorely tried. One of the group was the son of a country minister, another of a judge; John, the unhappiest of all, had David Nicholson to father, the idea of facing whom on such a scandalous subject was physically sickening. They stood a while consulting under the buttresses of St. Giles'; thence they adjourned to the lodgings of one of the number in North Castle Street, where (for that matter) they might have had quite as good a supper, and far better drink, than in the dangerous paradise from which they had been routed. There, over an almost tearful glass, they debated their position. Each explained that he had the world to lose if the affair went on, and he appeared as a witness. It was remarkable what bright prospects were just then in the very act of opening before each of that little company of youths, and what pious consideration for the feelings of their families began now to well from them. Each, moreover, was in an odd state of destitution. Not one could bear his share of the fine; not one but evinced a wonderful twinkle of hope that each of the others (in succession) was the very man who could step in to make good the deficit. One took a high hand: he could not pay his share; if it went to a trial, he should bolt; he had always felt the English Bar to be his true sphere. Another branched out into touching details about his family, to which no one listened. John, in the midst of this disorderly competition of poverty and meanness, sat stunned, contemplating the mountain bulk of his misfortunes.

At last, upon a pledge that each should apply to his family with a common frankness, this convention of unhappy young asses broke up, went down the common stair, and in the grey of the spring morning, with the streets lying dead empty all about them, the lamps burning on into the daylight in diminished lustre, and the birds beginning to sound premonitory notes from the groves of the town gardens, went each his own way with bowed head and echoing footfall.

The rooks were awake in Randolph Crescent; but the windows looked down, discreetly blinded, on the return of the prodigal. John's pass-key was a recent privilege; this was the first time it had been used; and, O! with what a sickening sense of his unworthiness he now inserted it into the well-oiled lock and entered that citadel of the proprieties! All slept; the gas in the hall had been left faintly burning to light his return; a dreadful stillness reigned, broken by the deep ticking of the eight-day clock. He put the gas out, and sat on a chair in the hall, waiting and counting the minutes, longing for any human countenance. But when at last he heard the alarm-clock spring its rattle in the lower story, and the servants begin to be about, he instantly lost heart, and fled to his own room, where he threw himself upon the bed.

Chapter 3

In which John enjoys the Harvest Home

SHORTLY after breakfast, at which he assisted with a highly tragical countenance, John sought his father where he used to sit, presumably in religious meditation, on the Sabbath mornings. The old gentleman looked up with that sour inquisitive expression that came so near to smiling and was so different in effect.

"This is a time when I do not like to be disturbed," he said.

"I know that," returned John; "but I have – I want – I've made a dreadful mess of it," he broke out, and turned to the window.

Mr. Nicholson sat silent for an appreciable time while his unhappy son surveyed the poles in the back green, and a certain yellow cat that was perched upon the wall. Despair sat upon John as he gazed: and he raged to think of the dreadful series of his misdeeds, and the essential innocence that lay behind them.

"Well," said the father, with an obvious effort, but in very quiet tones, "what is it?"

"Maclean gave me four hundred pounds to put in the bank, sir," began John; "and I'm sorry to say that I've been robbed of it!"

"Robbed of it?" cried Mr. Nicholson, with a strong rising inflection. "Robbed? Be careful what you say, John!"

"I can't say anything else, sir; I was just robbed of it," said John, in desperation, sullenly.

"And where and when did this extraordinary event take place?" inquired the father.

"On the Calton Hill about twelve last night."

"The Calton Hill?" repeated Mr. Nicholson. "And what were you doing there at such a time of the night?"

"Nothing, sir," says John.

Mr. Nicholson drew in his breath.

"And how came the money in your hands at twelve last night?" he asked sharply.

"I neglected that piece of business," said John, anticipating comment; and then in his own dialect: "I clean forgot all about it."

"Well," said his father, "it's a most extraordinary story. Have you communicated with the police?"

"I have," answered poor John, the blood leaping to his face. "They think they know the men that did it. I daresay the money will be recovered, if that was all," said he, with a desperate indifference, which his father set down to levity; but which sprang from the consciousness of worse behind.

"Your mother's watch, too?" asked Mr. Nicholson.

"O, the watch is all right!" cried John. "At least, I mean I was coming to the watch – the fact is, I am ashamed to say, I – I had pawned the watch before. Here is the ticket; they didn't find that; the watch can be redeemed; they don't sell pledges." The lad panted out these phrases, one after another, like minute-guns; but at the last word, which rang in that stately chamber like an oath, his heart failed him utterly; and the dreaded silence settled on father and son.

It was broken by Mr. Nicholson picking up the pawnticket: "John Froggs, 85 Pleasance," he read; and then turning upon John, with a brief flash of passion and disgust, "Who is John Froggs?" he cried.

"Nobody," said John. "It was just a name."

"An *alias*," his father commented.

"O! I think scarcely quite that," said the culprit; "it's a form, they all do it, the man seemed to understand; and we had a great deal of fun over the name – "

He paused at that, for he saw his father wince at the picture like a man physically struck; and again there was silence.

"I do not think," said Mr. Nicholson at last, "that I am

an ungenerous father. I have never grudged you money within reason, for any avowable purpose; you had just to come to me and speak. And now I find that you have forgotten all decency and all natural feeling, and actually pawned – pawned – your mother's watch. You must have had some temptation; I will do you justice to suppose it was a strong one. What did you want with this money?"

"I would rather not tell you, sir," said John. "It will only make you angry."

"I will not be fenced with," cried his father. "There must be an end of disingenuous answers. What did you want with this money?"

"To lend it to Houston, sir," says John.

"I thought I had forbidden you to speak to that young man?" asked the father.

"Yes, sir," said John; "but I only met him."

"Where?" came the deadly question.

And "In a billiard-room" was the damning answer. Thus had John's single departure from the truth brought instant punishment. For no other purpose but to see Alan would he have entered a billiard-room; but he had desired to palliate the fact of his disobedience, and now it appeared that he frequented these disreputable haunts upon his own account.

Once more Mr. Nicholson digested the vile tidings in silence; and when John stole a glance at his father's countenance, he was abashed to see the marks of suffering.

"Well," said the old gentleman at last, "I cannot pretend not to be simply bowed down. I rose this morning what the world calls a happy man – happy, at least, in a son of whom I thought I could be reasonably proud – "

But it was beyond human nature to endure this longer, and John interrupted almost with a scream. "O, wheest!" he cried, "that's not all, that's not the worst of it – it's nothing! How could I tell you were proud of me? O! I wish, I wish that I had known; but you always said I was such a disgrace! And the dreadful thing is this: we were all taken up last night, and we have to pay Collette's fine among the six, or we'll be had up for evidence – she-beening it is. They made me swear to tell you; but for my part," he cried, bursting into tears, "I just wish that I was dead!" And he fell on his knees before a chair and hid his face.

Whether his father spoke, and whether he remained long in the room or at once departed, are points lost to history. A horrid turmoil of mind and body; bursting sobs; broken, vanishing thoughts, now of indignation, now of remorse; broken elementary whiffs of consciousness, of the smell of the horse-hair on the chair-bottom, of the jangling of church bells that now began to make day horrible throughout the confines of the city, of the hard floor that bruised his knees, of the taste of tears that found their way into his mouth: for a period of time, the duration of which I cannot guess, while I refuse to dwell longer on its agony, these were the whole of God's world for John Nicholson.

When at last, as by the touching of a spring, he returned again to clearness of consciousness and even a measure of composure, the bells had but just done ringing, and the Sabbath silence was still marred by the patter of belated feet. By the clock above the fire, as well as by these more speaking signs, the service had not long begun; and the unhappy sinner, if his father had really gone to church, might count on near two hours of only comparative unhappiness. With his father, the superlative degree returned infallibly. He knew it by every shrinking fibre in his body, he knew it by the sudden dizzy whirling of his brain, at the mere thought of that calamity. An hour and a half, perhaps an hour and three-quarters, if the Doctor was long-winded, and then would begin again that active agony from which, even in the dull ache of the present, he shrank as from the bite of fire. He saw, in a vision, the family pew, the somnolent cushions, the Bibles, the Psalm-books, Maria with her smelling-salts, his father sitting spectacled and critical; and at once he was struck with indignation, not unjustly.

It was inhuman to go off to church and leave a sinner in suspense, unpunished, unforgiven. And at the very touch of criticism, the paternal sanctity was lessened; yet the paternal terror only grew; and the two strands of feeling drew him in the same direction.

And suddenly there came upon him a mad fear lest his father should have locked him in. The notion had no ground in sense; it was probably no more than a reminiscence of similar calamities in childhood, for his father's room had always been the chamber of inquisition and the scene of punishment; but it stuck so rigorously in his mind that he must instantly approach the door and prove its untruth. As he went, he struck upon a drawer left open in the business table. It was the money-drawer, a measure of his father's disarray: the money-drawer – perhaps a pointing providence! Who is to decide, when even divines differ, between a providence and a temptation? or who, sitting calmly under his own vine, is to pass a judgment on the doings of a poor, hunted dog, slavishly afraid, slavishly rebellious, like John Nicholson on that particular Sunday? His hand was in the drawer almost before his mind had conceived the hope; and rising to his new situation, he wrote, sitting in his father's chair and using his father's blotting-pad, his pitiful apology and farewell –

"MY DEAR FATHER, – I have taken the money, but I will pay it back as soon as I am able. You will never hear of me again. I did not mean any harm by anything, so I hope you will try and forgive me. I wish you would say good-bye for me to Alexander and Maria, but not if you don't want to. I could not wait to see you, really. Please try to forgive me.

"Your affectionate son, JOHN NICHOLSON."

The coins abstracted and the missive written, he could not be gone too soon from the scene of these transgressions; and remembering how his father had once returned from church, on some slight illness, in the middle of the second psalm, he durst not even make a packet of a change of clothes. Attired as he was, he slipped from the paternal doors, and found himself in the cool spring air, the thin spring sunshine, and the great Sabbath quiet of the city, which was now only pointed by the cawing of the rooks. There was not a soul in Randolph Crescent, nor a soul in Queensferry Street; in this outdoor privacy and the sense of escape, John took heart again; and with a pathetic sense of leave-taking, he even ventured up the lane and stood a while, a strange peri at the gates of a quaint paradise, by the west end of St. George's Church. They were singing within; and by a strange chance the tune was "St. George's, Edinburgh," which bears the name, and was first sung in the choir, of that church. "Who is this King of Glory?" went the voices from within; and to John this was like the end of all Christian observances, for he was now to be a wild man like Ishmael, and his life was to be cast in homeless places and with godless people.

It was thus, with no rising sense of the adventurous, but in mere desolation and despair, that he turned his back on his native city, and set on foot for California – with a more immediate eye to Glasgow.

Chapter 4

The Second Sowing

IT is no part of mine to narrate the adventures of John Nicholson, which were many, but simply his more momentous misadventures, which were more than he desired, and by human standards, more than he deserved; how he reached California, how he was rooked, and robbed, and beaten, and starved; how he was at last taken up by charitable folk, restored to some degree of self-complacency, and installed as a clerk in a bank in San Francisco, it would take too long to tell; nor in these episodes were there any marks of the peculiar Nicholsonic destiny, for they were just such matters as befell some thousands of other young adventurers in the same days and places. But once posted in the bank, he fell for a time into a high degree of good fortune, which, as it was only a longer way about to fresh disaster, it behoves me to explain.

It was his luck to meet a young man in what is technically called a "dive," and, thanks to his monthly wages, to extricate this new acquaintance from a position of present disgrace and possible danger in the future. This young man was the nephew of one of the Nob Hill magnates, who run the San Francisco Stock Exchange much as more humble adventurers, in the corner of some public park at home, may be seen to perform the simple artifice of pea and thimble: for their own profit, that is to say, and the discouragement of public gambling. It was hence in his power – and, as he was of grateful temper, it was among the things that he desired – to put John in the way of growing rich; and thus, without thought or industry, or so much as even understanding the game at which he played, but by simply buying and selling what he was told to buy and sell, that plaything of fortune was presently at the head of between eleven and twelve thousand pounds, or, as he reckoned it, of upwards of sixty thousand dollars.

How he had come to deserve this wealth, any more than how he had formerly earned disgrace at home, was a problem beyond the reach of his philosophy. It was true that he had been industrious at the bank, but no more so than the cashier, who had seven small children and was visibly sinking in a decline. Nor was the step which had determined his advance – a visit to a dive with a month's wages in his pocket – an act of such transcendent virtue, or even wisdom, as to seem to merit the favour of the gods. From some sense of this and of the dizzy see-saw – heaven-high, hell-deep – on which men sit clutching; or perhaps fearing that the sources of his fortune might be insidiously traced to some root in the field of petty cash; he stuck to his work, said not a word of his new circumstances, and kept his account with a bank in a different quarter of the town. The concealment, innocent as it seems, was the first step in the second tragi-comedy of John's existence.

Meanwhile he had never written home. Whether from diffidence or shame, or a touch of anger, or mere procrastination, or because (as we have seen) he had no skill in literary arts, or because (as I am sometimes tempted to suppose) there is a law in human nature that prevents young men – not otherwise beasts – from the performance of this simple act of piety: – months and years had gone by, and John had never written. The habit of not writing, indeed, was already fixed before he had begun to come into his fortune; and it was only the difficulty of breaking this long silence that withheld him from an instant restitution of the money he had stolen or (as he preferred to call it) borrowed. In vain he sat before paper, attending on inspiration; that heavenly nymph, beyond suggesting the words "My dear father," remained obstinately silent; and presently John would crumple up the sheet and decide, as soon as he had " a good chance," to carry the money home in person. And this delay, which is indefensible, was his second step into the snares of fortune.

Ten years had passed, and John was drawing near to thirty. He had kept the promise of his boyhood, and was now of a lusty frame, verging towards corpulence; good features, good eyes, a genial manner, a ready laugh, a long pair of sandy whiskers, a dash of an American accent, a close familiarity with the great American joke, and a certain likeness to a R-y-l P-rs-n-ge, who shall remain nameless for me, made up the man's externals, as he could be viewed in society. Inwardly, in spite of his gross body and highly masculine whiskers, he was more like a maiden lady than a man of twenty-nine.

It chanced one day, as he was strolling down Market Street on the eve of his fortnight's holiday, that his eye was caught by certain railway bills, and in very idleness of mind he calculated that he might be home for Christmas if he started on the morrow. The fancy thrilled him with desire, and in one moment he decided to go.

There was much to be done: his portmanteau to be packed, a credit to be got from the bank where he was a wealthy customer, and certain offices to be transacted for that other bank in which he was a humble clerk; and it chanced, in conformity with human nature, that out of all this business it was the last that came to be neglected. Night found him not only only equipped with money of his own, but once more (as on that former occasion) saddled with a considerable sum of other people's.

Now it chanced there lived in the same boarding-house a fellow-clerk of his, an honest fellow, with what is called a weakness for drink – though it might, in this case, have been called a strength, for the victim had been drunk for weeks together without the briefest intermission. To this unfortunate John intrusted a letter with an inclosure of bonds, addressed to the bank manager. Even as he did so he thought he perceived a certain haziness of eye and speech in his trustee; but he was too hopeful to be stayed, silenced the voice of warning in his bosom, and with one and the same gesture committed the money to the clerk, and himself into the hands of destiny.

I dwell, even at the risk of tedium, on John's minutest errors, his case being so perplexing to the moralist; but we have done with them now, the roll is closed, the reader has the worst of our poor hero, and I leave him to judge for himself whether he or John has been the less deserving. Henceforth we have to follow the spectacle of a man who was a mere whip-top for calamity; on whose unmerited misadventures not even the humorist can look without pity, and not even the philosopher without alarm.

That same night the clerk entered upon a bout of drunkenness so consistent as to surprise even his intimate acquaintance. He was speedily ejected from the boarding-house; deposited his portmanteau with a perfect stranger, who did not even catch his name; wandered he knew not where, and was at last hove-to, all standing, in a hospital at Sacramento. There, under the impenetrable *alias* of the number of his bed, the crapulous being lay for some more days unconscious of all things, and of one thing in particular: that the police were after him. Two months had come and gone before the convalescent in the Sacramento hospital was identified with Kirkman, the absconding San Francisco clerk; even then, there must elapse nearly a fortnight more till the perfect stranger could be hunted up, the portmanteau recovered, and John's letter carried at length to its destination, the seal still unbroken, the inclosure still intact.

Meanwhile John had gone upon his holidays without a word, which was irregular; and there had disappeared with him a certain sum of money, which was out of all bounds of palliation. But he was known to be careless, and believed to be honest; the manager besides had a regard for him; and little was said, although something was no doubt thought, until the fortnight was finally at an end, and the time had come for John to reappear. Then, indeed, the affair began to look black; and when inquiries were made, and the penniless clerk was found to have amassed thousands of dollars, and kept them secretly in a rival establishment, the stoutest of his friends abandoned him, the books were overhauled for traces of ancient and artful fraud, and though none were found, there still prevailed a general impression of loss. The telegraph was set in motion; and the correspondent of the bank in Edinburgh, for which place it was understood that John had armed himself with extensive credits, was warned to communicate with the police.

Now this correspondent was a friend of Mr. Nicholson's; he was well acquainted with the tale of John's calamitous disappearance from Edinburgh; and putting one thing with another, hasted with the first word of this scandal, not to the police, but to his friend. The old gentleman had long regarded his son as one dead; John's place had been taken, the memory of his faults had already fallen to be one of those old aches, which awaken again indeed upon occasion, but which we can always vanquish by an effort of the will; and to have the long lost resuscitated in a fresh disgrace was doubly bitter.

"MacEwen," said the old man, "this must be hushed up, if possible. If I give you a cheque for this sum, about which they are certain, could you take it on yourself to let the matter rest?"

"I will," said MacEwen. "I will take the risk of it."

"You understand," resumed Mr. Nicholson, speaking precisely, but with ashen lips, "I do this for my family, not for that unhappy young man. If it should turn out that these suspicions are correct, and he has embezzled large sums, he must lie on his bed as he has made it." And then looking up at MacEwen with a nod, and one of his strange smiles: "Good-bye," said he; and MacEwen, perceiving the case to be too grave for consolation, took himself off, and blessed God on his way home that he was childless.

Chapter 5

The Prodigal's Return

By a little after noon on the eve of Christmas, John had
left his portmanteau in the cloak-room, and stepped
forth into Princes Street with a wonderful expansion of
the soul, such as men enjoy on the completion of long-
nourished schemes. He was at home again, incognito and
rich; presently he could enter his father's house by means
of the pass-key, which he had piously preserved through
all his wanderings; he would throw down the borrowed
money; there would be a reconciliation, the details of
which he frequently arranged; and he saw himself, during the next month, made welcome in many stately
houses at many frigid dinner-parties, taking his share in
the conversation with the freedom of the man and the
traveller, and laying down the law upon finance with the
authority of the successful investor. But this programme
was not to be begun before evening – not till just before
dinner, indeed, at which meal the re-assembled family
were to sit roseate, and the best wine, the modern fatted
calf, should flow for the prodigal's return.

Meanwhile he walked familiar streets, merry reminis-
cences crowding round him, sad ones also, both with the
same surprising pathos. The keen frosty air; the low, rosy,
wintry sun; the Castle, hailing him like an old acquaintance; the names of friends on door-plates; the sight of
friends whom he seemed to recognise, and whom he
eagerly avoided, in the streets; the pleasant chant of the
north-country accent; the dome of St. George's remind-
ing him of his last penitential moments in the lane, and
of that King of Glory whose name had echoed ever since
in the saddest corner of his memory; and the gutters
where he had learned to slide, and the shop where he

had bought his skates, and the stones on which he had trod, and the railings in which he had rattled his clacken as he went to school; and all those thousand and one nameless particulars which the eye sees without noting, which the memory keeps indeed yet without knowing, and which, taken one with another, build up for us the aspect of the place that we call home: all these besieged him, as he went, with both delight and sadness.

His first visit was for Houston, who had a house on Regent Terrace, kept for him in old days by an aunt. The door was opened (to his surprise) upon the chain, and a voice asked him from within what he wanted.

"I want Mr. Houston – Mr. Alan Houston," said he.

"And who are you?" said the voice.

"This is most extraordinary," thought John; and then aloud he told his name.

"No' young Mr. John?" cried the voice, with a sudden increase of Scottish accent, testifying to a friendlier feeling.

"The very same," said John.

And the old butler removed his defences, remarking only, "I thocht ye were that man." But his master was not there; he was staying, it appeared, at the house in Murrayfield; and though the butler would have been glad enough to have taken his place and given all the news of the family, John, struck with a little chill, was eager to be gone. Only, the door was scarce closed again, before he regretted that he had not asked about "that man."

He was to pay no more visits till he had seen his father and made all well at home; Alan had been the only possible exception, and John had not time to go as far as Murrayfield. But here he was on Regent Terrace; there was nothing to prevent him going round the end of the hill, and looking from without on the Mackenzies' house. As he went he reflected that Flora must now be a woman of near his own age, and it was within the bounds of possibility that she was married; but this dishonourable doubt he dammed down.

There was the house, sure enough; but the door was of another colour, and what was this – two door-plates? He drew nearer; the top one bore, with dignified simplicity, the words, "Mr. Proudfoot"; the lower one was more explicit, and informed the passer-by that here was likewise the abode of "Mr. J. A. Dunlop Proudfoot, Advocate." The Proudfoots must be rich, for no advocate could look to have much business in so remote a quarter; and John hated them for their wealth and for their name, and for the sake of the house they desecrated with their presence. He remembered a Proudfoot he had seen at school, not known: a little, whey-faced urchin, the despicable member of some lower class. Could it be this abortion that had climbed to be an advocate, and now lived in the birthplace of Flora and the home of John's tenderest memories? The chill that had first seized upon him when he heard of Houston's absence deepened and struck inward. For a moment, as he stood under the doors of that estranged house, and looked east and west along the solitary pavement of the Royal Terrace, where not a cat was stirring, the sense of solitude and desolation took him by the throat, and he wished himself in San Francisco.

And then the figure he made, with his decent portliness, his whiskers, the money in his purse, the excellent cigar that he now lit, recurred to his mind in consolatory comparison with that of a certain maddened lad who, on a certain spring Sunday ten years before, and in the hour of church-time silence, had stolen from that city by the Glasgow road. In the face of these changes it were impious to doubt fortune's kindness. All would be well yet; the Mackenzies would be found, Flora, younger and lovelier and kinder than before; Alan would be found, and would have so nicely discriminated his behaviour as to have grown, on the one hand, into a valued friend of Mr. Nicholson's, and to have remained, upon the other, of that exact shade of joviality which John desired in his companions. And so, once more, John fell to work discounting the delightful future: his first appearance in the family pew; his first visit to his uncle Greig, who thought himself so great a financier, and on whose purblind Edinburgh eyes John was to let in the dazzling daylight of the West; and the details in general of that unrivalled transformation scene, in which he was to display to all Edinburgh a portly and successful gentleman in the shoes of the derided fugitive.

The time began to draw near when his father would have returned from the office, and it would be the prodigal's cue to enter. He strolled westward by Albany Street, facing the sunset embers, pleased, he knew not why, to move in that cold air and indigo twilight, starred with street-lamps. But there was one more disenchantment waiting him by the way.

At the corner of Pitt Street he paused to light a fresh cigar; the vesta threw, as he did so, a strong light upon his features, and a man of about his own age stopped at sight of it.

"I think your name must be Nicholson," said the stranger.

It was too late to avoid recognition; and besides, as John was now actually on the way home, it hardly mattered, and he gave way to the impulse of his nature.

"Great Scott!" he cried, "Beatson!" and shook hands with warmth. It scarce seemed he was repaid in kind.

"So you're home again?" said Beatson. "Where have you been all this long time?"

"In the States," said John – "California. I've made my pile though; and it suddenly struck me it would be a noble scheme to come home for Christmas."

"I see," said Beatson. "Well, I hope we'll see something of you now you're here."

"I guess so," said John, a little frozen.

"Well, ta-ta," concluded Beatson, and he shook hands again and went.

This was a cruel first experience. It was idle to blink facts: here was John home again, and Beatson – Old

Beatson – did not care a rush. He recalled Old Beatson in the past – the merry and affectionate lad – and their joint adventures and mishaps, the window they had broken with a catapult in India Place, the escalade of the Castle rock, and many another inestimable bond of friendship; and his hurt surprise grew deeper. Well, after all, it was only on a man's own family that he could count: blood was thicker than water, he remembered; and the net result of this encounter was to bring him to the doorstep of his father's house with tenderer and softer feelings.

The night had come; the fanlight over the door shone bright; the two windows of the dining-room where the cloth was being laid, and the three windows of the drawing-room where Maria would be waiting dinner, glowed softer through yellow blinds. It was like a vision of the past. All this time of his absence, life had gone forward with an equal foot, and the fires and the gas had been lighted, and the meals spread, at the accustomed hours. At the accustomed hour, too, the bell had sounded thrice to call the family to worship. And at the thought a pang of regret for his demerit seized him; he remembered the things that were good and that he had neglected, and the things that were evil and that he had loved; and it was with a prayer upon his lips that he mounted the steps and thrust the key into the keyhole.

He stepped into the lighted hall, shut the door softly behind him, and stood there fixed in wonder. No surprise of strangeness could equal the surprise of that complete familiarity. There was the bust of Chalmers near the stair-railings, there was the clothes-brush in the accustomed place; and there, on the hat-stand, hung hats and coats that must surely be the same as he remembered. Ten years dropped from his life, as a pin may slip between the fingers; and the ocean and the mountains, and the mines, and the crowded marts and mingled races of San Francisco, and his own fortune and his own disgrace, became, for that one moment, the figures of a dream that was over.

He took off his hat, and moved mechanically towards the stand; and there he found a small change that was a great one to him. The pin that had been his from boyhood, where he had flung his balmoral when he loitered home from the Academy, and his first hat when he came briskly back from college or the office – his pin was occupied. "They might have at least respected my pin!" he thought, and he was moved as by a slight, and began at once to recollect that he was here an interloper, in a strange house, which he had entered almost by a burglary, and where at any moment he might be scandalously challenged.

He moved at once, his hat still in his hand, to the door of his father's room, opened it, and entered. Mr. Nicholson sat in the same place and posture as on that last Sunday morning; only he was older, and greyer, and sterner; and as he now glanced up and caught the eye of his son, a strange commotion and a dark flush sprang into his face.

"Father," said John steadily, and even cheerfully, for this was a moment against which he was long ago prepared, "Father, here I am, and here is the money that I took from you. I have come back to ask your forgiveness, and to stay Christmas with you and the children."

"Keep your money" said the father, "and go!"

"Father!" cried John; "for God's sake don't receive me this way. I've come for – "

"Understand me," interrupted Mr. Nicholson; "you are no son of mine; and in the sight of God, I wash my hands of you. One last thing I will tell you; one warning I will give you: all is discovered, and you are being hunted for your crimes; if you are still at large it is thanks to me; but I have done all that I mean to do; and from this time forth I would not raise one finger – not one finger – to save you from the gallows! And now," with a low voice of absolute authority, and a single weighty gesture of the finger, "and now – go!"

Chapter 6

The House at Murrayfield

How John passed the evening, in what windy confusion of mind, in what squalls of anger and lulls of sick collapse, in what pacing of streets and plunging into public-houses, it would profit little to relate. His misery, if it were not progressive, yet tended in no way to diminish; for in proportion as grief and indignation abated, fear began to take their place. At first, his father's menacing words lay by in some safe drawer of memory, biding their hour. At first, John was all thwarted affection and blighted hope; next bludgeoned vanity raised its head again, with twenty mortal gashes; and the father was disowned even as he had disowned the son. What was this regular course of life, that John should have admired it? what were these clock-work virtues, from which love was absent? Kindness was the test, kindness the aim and soul; and judged by such a standard, the discarded prodigal – now rapidly drowning his sorrows and his reason in successive drams – was a creature of a lovelier morality than his self-righteous father. Yes, he was the better man; he felt it, glowed with the consciousness, and entering a public-house at the corner of Howard Place (whither he had somehow wandered) he pledged his own virtues in a glass – perhaps the fourth since his dismissal. Of that he knew nothing, keeping no account of what he did or where he went; and in the general crashing hurry of his nerves, unconscious of the approach of intoxication. Indeed, it is a question whether he were really growing intoxicated, or whether at first the spirits did not even sober him. For it was even as he drained this last glass that his father's ambiguous and menacing words – popping from their hiding-place in memory – startled him like a hand laid upon his shoulder. "Crimes, hunted, the gallows." They were ugly words; in the ears of an innocent man, perhaps all the uglier; for if some judicial error were in act against him, who should set a limit to its grossness or to how far it might be pushed? Not John, indeed; he was no believer in the powers of innocence, his cursed experience pointing in quite other ways; and his fears, once wakened, grew with every hour and hunted him about the city streets.

It was perhaps nearly nine at night; he had eaten nothing since lunch, he had drunk a good deal, and he was exhausted by emotion, when the thought of Houston came into his head. He turned, not merely to the man as a friend, but to his house as a place of refuge. The danger that threatened him was still so vague, that he knew neither what to fear nor where he might expect it; but this much at least seemed undeniable, that a private house was safer than a public inn. Moved by these counsels, he turned at once to the Caledonian Station, passed (not without alarm) into the bright lights of the approach, redeemed his portmanteau from the cloak-room, and was soon whirling in a cab along the Glasgow road. The change of movement and position, the sight of the lamps twinkling to the rear, and the smell of damp and mould and rotten straw which clung about the vehicle, wrought in him strange alternations of lucidity and mortal giddiness.

"I have been drinking," he discovered; "I must go straight to bed, and sleep." And he thanked Heaven for the drowsiness that came upon his mind in waves.

From one of these spells he was awakened by the stoppage of the cab; and, getting down, found himself in quite a country road, the last lamp of the suburb shining some way below, and the high walls of a garden rising before him in the dark. The Lodge (as the place was named) stood, indeed, very solitary. To the south it adjoined another house, but standing in so large a garden as to be well out of cry; on all other sides, open fields stretched upward to the woods of Corstorphine Hill, or backward to the dells of Ravelston, or downward towards the valley of the Leith. The effect of seclusion was aided by the great height of the garden walls, which were, indeed, conventual, and, as John had tested in former days, defied the climbing schoolboy. The lamp of the cab threw a gleam upon the door and the not brilliant handle of the bell.

"Shall I ring for ye?" said the cabman, who had descended from his perch, and was slapping his chest, for the night was bitter.

"I wish you would," said John, putting his hand to his brow in one of his accesses of giddiness.

The man pulled at the handle, and the clanking of the bell replied from further in the garden; twice and thrice he did it, with sufficient intervals; in the great, frosty silence of the night the sounds fell sharp and small.

"Does he expect ye?" asked the driver, with that manner of familiar interest that well became his port-wine face; and when John had told him no, "Well, then," said the cabman, "if ye'll tak' my advice of it, we'll just gang back. And that's disinterested, mind ye, for my stables are in the Glesgie road."

"The servants must hear," said John.

"Hout!" said the driver. "He keeps no servants here, man. They're a' in the town house; I drive him often; it's just a kind of a hermitage this."

"Give me the bell," said John; and he plucked at it like a man desperate.

The clamour had not yet subsided before they heard steps upon the gravel, and a voice of singular nervous irritability cried to them through the door, "Who are you, and what do you want?"

"Alan," said John, "it's me – it's Fatty – John, you know. I'm just come home, and I've come to stay with you."

There was no reply for a moment, and then the door was opened.

"Get the portmanteau down," said John to the driver.

"Do nothing of the kind," said Alan; and then to John, "Come in here a moment. I want to speak to you."

John entered the garden, and the door was closed behind him. A candle stood on the gravel walk, winking a little in the draughts; it threw inconstant sparkles on the clumped holly, struck the light and darkness to and fro like a veil on Alan's features, and sent his shadow hovering behind him. All beyond was inscrutable; and John's dizzy brain rocked with the shadow. Yet even so, it struck him that Alan was pale, and his voice, when he spoke, unnatural.

"What brings you here to-night?" he began. "I don't want, God knows, to seem unfriendly; but I cannot take you in, Nicholson; I cannot do it."

"Alan," said John, "you've just got to! You don't know the mess I'm in; the governor's turned me out, and I daren't show face in an inn, because they're down on me for murder or something!"

"For what?" cried Alan, starting.

"Murder, I believe," says John.

"Murder!" repeated Alan, and passed his hand over his eyes. "What was that you were saying?" he asked again.

"That they were down on me," said John. "I'm accused of murder, by what I can make out; and I've really had a dreadful day of it, Alan, and I can't sleep on the roadside on a night like this – at least, not with a portmanteau," he pleaded.

"Hush!" said Alan, with his head on one side; and then, "Did you hear nothing?" he asked.

"No," said John, thrilling, he knew not why, with communicated terror. "No, I heard nothing; why?" And then, as there was no answer, he reverted to his pleading: "But I say, Alan, you've just got to take me in. I'll go right away to bed if you have anything to do. I seem to have been drinking; I was that knocked over. I wouldn't turn you away, Alan, if you were down on your luck."

"No?" returned Alan. "Neither will I you, then. Come and let's get your portmanteau."

The cabman was paid, and drove off down the long, lamp-lit hill, and the two friends stood on the side-walk beside the portmanteau till the last rumble of the wheels had died in silence. It seemed to John as though Alan attached importance to this departure of the cab; and John, who was in no state to criticise, shared profoundly in the feeling.

When the stillness was once more perfect, Alan shouldered the portmanteau, carried it in, and shut and locked the garden door; and then, once more, abstraction seemed to fall upon him, and he stood with his hand on the key, until the cold began to nibble at John's fingers.

"Why are we standing here?" asked John.

"Eh?" said Alan blankly.

"Why, man, you don't seem yourself," said the other.

"No, I'm not myself," said Alan; and he sat down on the portmanteau and put his face in his hands.

John stood beside him swaying a little, and looking about him at the swaying shadows, the flitting sparkles, and the steady stars overhead, until the windless cold began to touch him through his clothes on the bare skin. Even in his bemused intelligence, wonder began to awake.

"I say, let's come on to the house," he said at last.

"Yes, let's come on to the house," repeated Alan.

And he rose at once, re-shouldered the portmanteau, and, taking the candle in his other hand, moved forward to the Lodge. This was a long, low building, smothered in creepers; and now, except for some chinks of light between the dining-room shutters, it was plunged in darkness and silence.

In the hall Alan lit another candle, gave it to John, and opened the door of a bedroom.

"Here, said he; "go to bed. Don't mind me, John. You'll be sorry for me when you know."

"Wait a bit," returned John; "I've got so cold with all

that standing about. Let's go into the dining-room a minute. Just one glass to warm me, Alan."

On the table in the hall stood a glass, and a bottle with a whisky label on a tray. It was plain the bottle had been just opened, for the cork and corkscrew lay beside it.

"Take that," said Alan, passing John the whisky, and then with a certain roughness pushed his friend into the bedroom, and closed the door behind him.

John stood amazed; then he shook the bottle, and, to his further wonder, found it partly empty. Three or four glasses were gone. Alan must have uncorked a bottle of whisky and drunk three or four glasses one after the other, without sitting down, for there was no chair, and that in his own cold lobby on this freezing night! It fully explained his eccentricities, John reflected sagely, as he mixed himself a grog. Poor Alan! He was drunk; and what a dreadful thing was drink, and what a slave to it poor Alan was, to drink in this unsociable, uncomfortable fashion! The man who would drink alone, except for health's sake – as John was now doing – was a man utterly lost. He took the grog out, and felt hazier but warmer. It was hard work opening the portmanteau and finding his night-things; and before he was undressed, the cold had struck home to him once more. "Well," said he; "just a drop more. There's no sense in getting ill with all this other trouble." And presently dreamless slumber buried him.

When John awoke it was day. The low winter sun was already high in the heavens, but his watch had stopped, and it was impossible to tell the hour exactly. Ten, he guessed it, and made haste to dress, dismal reflections crowding on his mind. But it was less from terror than from regret that he now suffered; and with his regret there were mingled cutting pangs of penitence. There had fallen upon him a blow, cruel, indeed, but yet only the punishment of old misdoing; and he had rebelled and plunged into fresh sin. The rod had been used to chasten, and he had bit the chastening fingers. His father was right: John had justified him; John was no guest for decent people's houses, and no fit associate for decent people's children. And had a broader hint been needed, there was the case of his old friend. John was no drunkard, though he could at times exceed; and the picture of Houston drinking neat spirits at his hall-table struck him with something like disgust. He hung back from meeting his old friend. He could have wished he had not come to him; and yet, even now, where else was he to turn?

These musings occupied him while he dressed, and accompanied him into the lobby of the house. The door stood open on the garden; doubtless Alan had stepped forth; and John did as he supposed his friend had done. The ground was hard as iron, the frost still rigorous; as he brushed among the hollies, icicles jingled and glittered in their fall; and wherever he went, a volley of eager sparrows followed him. Here were Christmas weather and Christmas morning duly met, to the delight of children. This was the day of reunited families, the day to which he had so long looked forward, thinking to awake in his own bed in Randolph Crescent, reconciled with all men and repeating the footprints of his youth; and here he was alone, pacing the alleys of a wintry garden and filled with penitential thoughts.

And that reminded him: why was he alone? and where was Alan? The thought of the festal morning and the due salutations reawakened his desire for his friend, and he began to call for him by name. As the sound of his voice died away, he was aware of the greatness of the silence that environed him. But for the twittering of the sparrows and the crunching of his own feet upon the frozen snow, the whole windless world of air seemed to hang over him entranced, and the stillness weighed upon his mind with a horror of solitude.

Still calling at intervals, but now with a moderated voice, he made the hasty circuit of the garden, and finding neither man nor trace of man in all its evergreen coverts, turned at last to the house. About the house the silence seemed to deepen strangely. The door, indeed, stood open as before; but the windows were still shuttered, the chimneys breathed no stain into the bright air, there sounded abroad none of that low stir (perhaps audible rather to the ear of the spirit than to the ear of the flesh) by which a house announces and betrays its human lodgers. And yet Alan must be there – Alan locked in drunken slumbers, forgetful of the return of day, of the holy season, and of the friend whom he had so coldly received and was now so churlishly neglecting. John's disgust redoubled at the thought; but hunger was beginning to grow stronger than repulsion, and as a step to breakfast, if to nothing else, he must find and arouse the sleeper.

He made the circuit of the bedroom quarters. All, until he came to Alan's chamber, were locked from without, and bore the marks of a long disuse. But Alan's was a room in commission, filled with clothes, knick-knacks, letters, books, and the conveniences of a solitary man. The fire had been lit; but it had long ago burnt out, and the ashes were stone cold. The bed had been made, but it had not been slept in.

Worse and worse, then: Alan must have fallen where he sat, and now sprawled brutishly, no doubt, upon the dining-room floor.

The dining-room was a very long apartment, and was reached through a passage; so that John, upon his entrance, brought but little light with him, and must move towards the windows with spread arms, groping and knocking on the furniture. Suddenly he tripped and fell his length over a prostrate body. It was what he had looked for, yet it shocked him; and he marvelled that so rough an impact should not have kicked a groan out of the drunkard. Men had killed themselves ere now in such excesses, a dreary and degraded end that made John shudder. What if Alan were dead? There would be a Christmas Day!

By this, John had his hand upon the shutters, and

flinging them back, beheld once again the blessed face of
the day. Even by that light the room had a discomfort-
able air. The chairs were scattered, and one had been
overthrown; the table-cloth, laid as if for dinner, was
twitched upon one side, and some of the dishes had
fallen to the floor. Behind the table lay the drunkard, still
unaroused, only one foot visible to John.

But now that light was in the room, the worst seemed
over; it was a disgusting business, but not more than disgusting; and it was with no great apprehension that John
proceeded to make the circuit of the table: his last comparatively tranquil moment for that day. No sooner had
he turned the corner, no sooner had his eyes alighted on
the body, than he gave a smothered, breathless cry, and
fled out of the room and out of the house.

It was not Alan who lay there, but a man well up in
years, of stern countenance and iron-grey locks; and it
was no drunkard, for the body lay in a black pool of blood
and the open eyes stared upon the ceiling.

To and fro walked John before the door. The extreme
sharpness of the air acted on his nerves like an astrin-
gent, and braced them swiftly. Presently, he not relaxing
in his disordered walk, the images began to come clearer
and stay longer in his fancy; and next the power of
thought came back to him, and the horror and danger of
his situation rooted him to the ground.

He grasped his forehead, and staring on one spot of
gravel, pieced together what he knew and what he suspected. Alan had murdered some one: possibly "that
man" against whom the butler chained the door in
Regent Terrace; possibly another; some one at least: a
human soul, whom it was death to slay and whose blood
lay spilt upon the floor. This was the reason of the
whisky-drinking in the passage, of his unwillingness to
welcome John, of his strange behaviour and bewildered
words; this was why he had started at and harped upon
the name of murder; this was why he had stood and
hearkened, or sat and covered his eyes, in the black night.

And now he was gone, now he had basely fled; and to all his perplexities and dangers John stood heir.

"Let me think, let me think," he said aloud, impatiently, even pleadingly, as if to some merciless interrupter. In the turmoil of his wits, a thousand hints and hopes and threats and terrors dinning continuously in his ears, he was like one plunged in the hubbub of a crowd. How was he to remember – he, who had not a thought to spare – that he was himself the author, as well as the theatre, of so much confusion? But in hours of trial the junto of man's nature is dissolved, and anarchy succeeds.

It was plain he must stay no longer where he was, for here was a new Judicial Error in the very making. It was not so plain where he must go, for the old Judicial Error, vague as a cloud, appeared to fill the habitable world; whatever it might be, it watched for him, full-grown, in Edinburgh; it must have had its birth in San Francisco; it stood guard, no doubt, like a dragon, at the bank where he should cash his credit; and though there were doubtless many other places, who should say in which of them it was not ambushed? No, he could not tell where he was to go; he must not lose time on these insolubilities. Let him go back to the beginning. It was plain he must stay no longer where he was. It was plain, too, that he must not flee as he was, for he could not carry his portmanteau, and to flee and leave it was to plunge deeper in the mire. He must go, leave the house unguarded, find a cab, and return – return after an absence? Had he courage for that?

And just then he spied a stain about a hand's breadth on his trousers-leg, and reached his finger down to touch it. The finger was stained red: it was blood; he stared upon it with disgust, and awe, and terror, and in the sharpness of the new sensation fell instantly to act.

He cleansed his finger in the snow, returned into the house, drew near with hushed footsteps to the dining-room door, and shut and locked it. Then he breathed a little freer, for here at least was an oaken barrier between himself and what he feared. Next, he hastened to his room, tore off the spotted trousers, which seemed in his eyes a link to bind him to the gallows, flung them in a corner, donned another pair, breathlessly crammed his night-things into his portmanteau, locked it, swung it with an effort from the ground, and with a rush of relief came forth again under the open heavens.

The portmanteau, being of Occidental build, was no feather-weight; it had distressed the powerful Alan; and as for John, he was crushed under its bulk, and the sweat broke upon him thickly. Twice he must set it down to rest before he reached the gate; and when he had come so far, he must do as Alan did, and take his seat upon one corner. Here, then, he sat a while and panted; but now his thoughts were sensibly lightened; now, with the trunk standing just inside the door, some part of his dissociation from the house of crime had been effected, and the cabman need not pass the garden wall. It was wonderful how that relieved him; for the house, in his eyes, was a place to strike the most cursory beholder with suspicion, as though the very windows had cried murder.

But there was to be no remission of the strokes of fate. As he thus sat, taking breath in the shadow of the wall, and hopped about by sparrows, it chanced that his eye roved to the fastening of the door; and what he saw plucked him to his feet. The thing locked with a spring; once the door was closed, the bolt shot of itself; and without a key there was no means of entering from the road.

He saw himself compelled to one of two distasteful and perilous alternatives: either to shut the door altogether and set his portmanteau out upon the wayside, a wonder to all beholders; or to leave the door ajar, so that any thievish tramp or holiday schoolboy might stray in and stumble on the grisly secret. To the last, as the least desperate, his mind inclined; but he must first insure himself that he was unobserved. He peered out, and down the long road: it lay dead empty. He went to the corner of the by-road that comes by way of Dean; there also not a passenger was stirring. Plainly it was, now or never, the high tide of his affairs; and he drew the door as close as he durst, slipped a pebble in the chink, and made off downhill to find a cab.

Half-way down a gate opened, and a troop of Christmas children sallied forth in the most cheerful humour, followed more soberly by a smiling mother.

"And this is Christmas Day!" thought John; and could have laughed aloud in tragic bitterness of heart.

Chapter 7

A Tragi-Comedy in a Cab

IN front of Donaldson's Hospital, John counted it good fortune to perceive a cab a great way off, and by much shouting and waving of his arm, to catch the notice of the driver. He counted it good fortune, for the time was long to him till he should have done for ever with the Lodge; and the farther he must go to find a cab, the greater the chance that the inevitable discovery had taken place, and that he should return to find the garden full of angry neighbours. Yet when the vehicle drew up he was sensibly chagrined to recognise the port-wine cabman of the night before. "Here," he could not but reflect, "here is another link in the Judicial Error."

The driver, on the other hand, was pleased to drop again upon so liberal a fare; and as he was a man – the reader must already have perceived – of easy, not to say familiar, manners, he dropped at once into a vein of friendly talk, commenting on the weather, on the sacred season, which struck him chiefly in the light of a day of liberal gratuities, on the chance which had reunited him to a pleasing customer, and on the fact that John had been (as he was pleased to call it) visibly "on the randan" the night before.

"And ye look dreidful bad the-day, sir, I must say that," he continued. "There's nothing like a dram for ye – if ye'll take my advice of it; and bein' as it's Christmas, I'm no' saying," he added, with a fatherly smile, "but what I would join ye mysel'."

John had listened with a sick heart.

"I'll give you a dram when we've got through," said he, affecting a sprightliness which sat on him most unhandsomely, "and not a drop till then. Business first and pleasure afterwards."

With this promise the jarvey was prevailed upon to clamber to his place and drive, with hideous deliberation, to the door of the Lodge. There were no signs as yet of any public emotion; only, two men stood not far off in talk, and their presence, seen from afar, set John's pulses buzzing. He might have spared himself his fright, for the pair were lost in some dispute of a theological complexion, and, with lengthened upper lip and enumerating fingers, pursued the matter of their difference, and paid no heed to John.

But the cabman proved a thorn in the flesh. Nothing would keep him on his perch; he must clamber down, comment upon the pebble in the door (which he regarded as an ingenious but unsafe device), help John with the portmanteau, and enliven matters with a flow of speech, and especially of questions, which I thus condense: –

"He'll no' be here himsel', will he? No? Well, he's an eccentric man – a fair oddity – if ye ken the expression. Great trouble with his tenants, they tell me. I've driven the faim'ly for years. I drove a cab at his father's waddin'. What'll your name be? – I should ken your face. Baigrey, ye say? There were Baigreys about Gilmerton; ye'll be one of that lot? Then this'll be a friend's portmantie, like? Why? Because the name upon it's Nucholson! O, if ye're in a hurry, that's another job. Waverley Brig'? Are ye for away?"

So the friendly toper prated and questioned and kept John's heart in a flutter. But to this also, as to other evils under the sun, there came a period; and the victim of circumstances began at last to rumble towards the railway terminus at Waverley Bridge. During the transit he sat with raised glasses in the frosty chill and mouldy fœtor of his chariot, and glanced out sidelong on the holiday face of things, the shuttered shops, and the crowds along the pavement, much as the rider in the Tyburn cart may have observed the concourse gathering to his execution.

At the station his spirits rose again; another stage of

his escape was fortunately ended – he began to spy blue water. He called a railway porter, and bade him carry the portmanteau to the cloak-room: not that he had any notion of delay; flight, instant flight, was his design, no matter whither; but he had determined to dismiss the cabman ere he named, or even chose, his destination, thus possibly baulking the Judicial Error of another link. This was his cunning aim, and now with one foot on the roadway, and one still on the coach-step, he made haste to put the thing in practice, and plunged his hand into his trousers-pocket.

There was nothing there!

O, yes; this time he was to blame. He should have remembered, and when he deserted his blood-stained pantaloons, he should not have deserted along with them his purse. Make the most of his error, and then compare it with the punishment. Conceive his new position, for I lack words to picture it; conceive him condemned to return to that house, from the very thought of which his soul revolted, and once more to expose himself to capture on the very scene of the misdeed: conceive him linked to the mouldy cab and the familiar cabman. John cursed the cabman silently, and then it occurred to him that he must stop the incarceration of his portmanteau; that, at least, he must keep close at hand, and he returned to recall the porter. But his reflections, brief as they had appeared, must have occupied him longer than he supposed, and there was the man already returning with the receipt.

Well, that was settled; he had lost his portmanteau also; for the sixpence with which he had paid the Murrayfield Toll was one that had strayed alone into his waistcoat-pocket, and unless he once more successfully achieved the adventure of the house of crime, his portmanteau lay in the cloak-room in eternal pawn, for lack of a penny fee. And then he remembered the porter, who stood suggestively attentive, words of gratitude hanging on his lips.

John hunted right and left; he found a coin – prayed God that it was a sovereign – drew it out, beheld a halfpenny, and offered it to the porter.

The man's jaw dropped.

"It's only a halfpenny," he said, startled out of railway decency.

"I know that," said John piteously.

And here the porter recovered the dignity of man.

"Thank you, sir," said he, and would have returned the base gratuity. But John, too, would none of it; and as they struggled, who must join in but the cabman?

"Hoots, Mr. Baigrey," said he, "you surely forget what day it is!"

"I tell you I have no change!" cried John.

"Well," said the driver, "and what then? I would rather give a man a shillin' on a day like this than put him off with a derision like a bawbee. I'm surprised at the like of you, Mr. Baigrey!"

"My name is not Baigrey!" broke out John, in mere childish temper and distress.

"Ye told me it was yoursel'," said the cabman.

"I know I did; and what the devil right had you to ask?" cried the unhappy one.

"O very well," said the driver. "I know my place, if you know yours – if you know yours!" he repeated, as one who should imply grave doubts; and muttered inarticulate thunders, in which the grand old name of gentleman was taken seemingly in vain.

O to have been able to discharge this monster, whom John now perceived, with tardy clear-sightedness, to have begun betimes the festivities of Christmas! But far from any such ray of consolation visiting the lost, he stood bare of help and helpers, his portmanteau sequestered in one place, his money deserted in another and guarded by a corpse; himself, so sedulous of privacy, the cynosure of all men's eyes about the station; and, as if these were not enough mischances, he was now fallen in ill-blood with the beast to whom his poverty had linked him! In ill-blood, as he reflected dismally, with the witness who perhaps might hang or save him! There was no time to be lost; he durst not linger any longer in that public spot; and whether he had recourse to dignity or to conciliation, the remedy must be applied at once. Some happily surviving element of manhood moved him to the former.

"Let us have no more of this," said he, his foot once more upon the step. "Go back to where we came from."

He had avoided the name of any destination, for there was now quite a little band of railway folk about the cab, and he still kept an eye upon the court of justice, and laboured to avoid concentric evidence. But here again the fatal jarvey out-manœuvred him.

"Back to the Ludge?" cried he, in shrill tones of protest.

"Drive on at once!" roared John, and slammed the door behind him, so that the crazy chariot rocked and jingled.

Forth trundled the cab into the Christmas streets, the fare within plunged in the blackness of a despair that neighboured on unconsciousness, the driver on the box digesting his rebuke and his customer's duplicity. I would not be thought to put the pair in competition; John's case was out of all parallel. But the cabman, too, is worth the sympathy of the judicious; for he was a fellow of genuine kindliness and a high sense of personal dignity incensed by drink; and his advances had been cruelly and publicly rebuffed. As he drove, therefore, he counted his wrongs, and thirsted for sympathy and drink. Now, it chanced he had a friend, a publican in Queensferry Street, from whom, in view of the sacredness of the occasion, he thought he might extract a dram. Queensferry Street lies something off the direct road to Murrayfield. But then there is the hilly cross-road that passes by the valley of the Leith and the Dean Cemetery; and Queensferry Street is on the way to that. What was to hinder the cabman, since his horse was dumb, from choosing the cross-roads, and calling on his friend in passing? So it was decided; and the charioteer, already somewhat mollified, turned aside his horse to the right.

John, meanwhile, sat collapsed, his chin sunk upon his chest, his mind in abeyance. The smell of the cab was still faintly present to his senses, and a certain leaden chill about his feet; all else had disappeared in one vast oppression of calamity and physical faintness. It was drawing on to noon – two-and-twenty hours since he had broken bread; in the interval he had suffered tortures of sorrow and alarm, and had been partly tipsy; and though it was impossible to say he slept, yet when the cab stopped, and the cabman thrust his head into the window, his attention had to be recalled from depths of vacancy.

"If you'll no' *stand* me a dram," said the driver, with a well-merited severity of tone and manner, "I daresay ye'll have no objection to my taking one mysel'?"

"Yes – no – do what you like," returned John; and then, as he watched his tormentor mount the stairs and enter the whisky-shop, there floated into his mind a sense as of something long ago familiar. At that he started fully awake, and stared at the shop-fronts. Yes, he knew them; but when? and how? Long since, he thought; and then, casting his eye through the front glass, which had been recently occluded by the figure of the jarvey, he beheld the tree-tops of the rookery in Randolph Crescent. He was close to home – home, where he had thought, at that hour, to be sitting in the well-remembered drawing-room in friendly converse; and, instead – !

It was his first impulse to drop into the bottom of the cab; his next, to cover his face with his hands. So he sat, while the cabman toasted the publican, and the publican toasted the cabman, and both reviewed the affairs of the nation; so he still sat, when his master condescended to return, and drive off at last downhill, along the curve of Lynedoch Place; but even so sitting, as he passed the end of his father's street, he took one glance from between shielding fingers, and beheld a doctor's carriage at the door.

"Well, just so," thought he; "I'll have killed my father! And this is Christmas Day!"

If Mr. Nicholson died, it was down this same road he must journey to the grave; and down this road, on the same errand, his wife had preceded him years before; and many other leading citizens, with the proper trappings and attendance of the end. And now, in that frosty, ill-smelling, straw-carpeted, and ragged-cushioned cab, with his breath congealing on the glasses, towards what other destination was John himself advancing?

The thought stirred his imagination, which began to manufacture many thousand pictures, bright and fleeting like the shapes in a kaleidoscope; and now he saw himself, ruddy and comfortered, sliding in the gutter; and again a little woe-begone, bored urchin tricked forth in crape and weepers, descending this same hill at the foot's-pace of mourning coaches, his mother's body just preceding him; and yet again, his fancy, running far in front, showed him the house at Murrayfield – now standing solitary in the low sunshine, with the sparrows hopping on the threshold and the dead man within staring at the roof, and now, with a sudden change, thronged about with white-faced, hand-uplifting neighbours, the doctor bursting through their midst and fixing his stethoscope as he went, the policeman shaking a sagacious head beside the body. It was to this he feared that he was driving; in the midst of this he saw himself arrive, heard himself stammer faint explanations, and felt the hand of the constable upon his shoulder. Heavens! how he wished he had played the manlier part; how he despised himself that he had fled that fatal neighbourhood when all was quiet, and should now be tamely travelling back when it was thronging with avengers!

Any strong degree of passion lends, even to the dullest, the forces of the imagination. And so now as he dwelt on what was probably awaiting him at the end of this distressful drive – John, who saw things little, remembered them less, and could not have described them at all, beheld in his mind's eye the garden of the Lodge, detailed as in a map; he went to and fro in it, feeling his terrors; he saw the hollies, the snowy borders, the paths where he had sought Alan, the high, conventual walls, the shut door – what! was the door shut? Ay, truly, he had shut it – shut in his money, his escape, his future life – shut it with these hands, and none could now open it! He heard the snap of the spring-lock like something bursting in his brain, and sat astonied.

And then he woke again, terror jarring through his vitals. This was no time to be idle; he must be up and doing, he must think. Once at the end of this ridiculous cruise, once at the Lodge door, there would be nothing for it but to turn the cab and trundle back again. Why, then, go so far? why add another feature of suspicion to a case already so suggestive? why not turn at once? It was easy to say, turn, but whither? He had nowhere now to go to; he could never – he saw it in letters of blood – he could never pay that cab; he was saddled with that cab for ever. O that cab! his soul yearned to be rid of it. He forgot all other cares. He must first quit himself of this ill-smelling vehicle and of the human beast that guided it – first do that; do that at least; do that at once.

And just then the cab suddenly stopped, and there was his persecutor rapping on the front glass. John let it down, and beheld the port-wine countenance flamed with intellectual triumph.

"I ken wha ye are!" cried the husky voice. "I mind ye now. Ye're a Nucholson. I drove ye to Hermiston to a Christmas party, and ye came back on the box, and I let ye drive."

It was a fact. John knew the man; they had been even friends. His enemy, he now remembered, was a fellow of great good-nature – endless good-nature – with a boy; why not with a man? Why not appeal to his better side? He grasped at the new hope.

"Great Scott; and so you did," he cried, as if in a transport of delight, his voice sounding false in his own ears. "Well, if that's so, I've something to say to you. I'll just get out, I guess. Where are we, any way?"

The driver had fluttered his ticket in the eyes of the branch toll-keeper, and they were now brought to on the highest and most solitary part of the by-road. On the left, a row of field-side trees beshaded it; on the right it was bordered by naked fallows, undulating downhill to the Queensferry Road; in front, Corstorphine Hill raised its snow-bedabbled, darkling woods against the sky. John looked all about him, drinking the clear air like wine; then, his eyes returned to the cabman's face as he sat, not ungleefully, awaiting John's communication, with the air of one looking to be tipped.

The features of that face were hard to read, drink had so swollen them, drink had so painted them, in tints that varied from brick-red to mulberry. The small grey eyes blinked, the lips moved, with greed; greed was the ruling passion; and though there was some good-nature, some genuine kindliness, a true human touch, in the old toper, his greed was now so set afire by hope, that all other traits of character lay dormant. He sat there a monument of gluttonous desire.

John's heart slowly fell. He had opened his lips, but he stood there and uttered nought. He sounded the well of his courage, and it was dry. He groped in his treasury of words, and it was vacant. A devil of dumbness had him by the throat; a devil of terror babbled in his ears; and suddenly, without a word uttered, with no conscious purpose formed in his will, John whipped about, tumbled over the roadside wall, and began running for his life across the fallows.

He had not gone far, he was not past the midst of the first field, when his whole brain thundered within him, "Fool! You have your watch!" The shock stopped him and he faced once more towards the cab. The driver was leaning over the wall, brandishing his whip, his face

empurpled, roaring like a bull. And John saw (or thought)
that he had lost the chance. No watch would pacify the
man's resentment now; he would cry for vengeance also.
John would be under the eye of the police; his tale would
be unfolded, his secret plumbed, his destiny would close
on him at last, and for ever.

He uttered a deep sigh; and just as the cabman, taking
heart of grace, was beginning at last to scale the wall, his
defaulting customer fell again to running and disappeared into the farther fields.

Chapter 8

Singular Instance of the
Utility of Pass-Keys

WHERE he ran at first, John never very clearly knew; nor yet how long a time elapsed ere he found himself in the by-road near the lodge of Ravelston, propped against the wall, his lungs heaving like bellows, his legs leaden-heavy, his mind possessed by one sole desire – to lie down and be unseen. He remembered the thick coverts round the quarry-hole pond, an untrodden corner of the world where he might surely find concealment till the night should fall. Thither he passed down the lane; and when he came there, behold! he had forgotten the frost, and the pond was alive with young people skating, and the pond-side coverts were thick with lookers-on. He looked on awhile himself. There was one tall, graceful maiden, skating hand in hand with a youth, on whom she bestowed her bright eyes perhaps too patently; and it was strange with what anger John beheld her. He could have broken forth in curses; he could have stood there, like a mortified tramp, and shaken his fist and vented his gall upon her by the hour – or so he thought; and the next moment his heart bled for the girl. "Poor creature, it's little she knows!" he sighed. "Let her enjoy herself while she can!" But was it possible, when Flora used to smile at him on the Braid ponds, she could have looked so fulsome to a sick-hearted bystander?

The thought of one quarry, in his frozen wits, suggested another; and he plodded off towards Craigleith. A wind had sprung up out of the north-west; it was cruel keen, it dried him like a fire, and racked his finger-joints. It brought clouds, too; pale, swift, hurrying clouds, that blotted heaven and shed gloom upon the earth. He scrambled up among the hazelled rubbish-heaps that surround the cauldron of the quarry, and lay flat upon the stones. The wind searched close along the earth, the stones were cutting and icy, the bare hazels wailed about him; and soon the air of the afternoon began to be vocal with those strange and dismal harpings that herald snow. Pain and misery turned in John's limbs to a harrowing impatience and blind desire of change; now he would roll in his harsh lair, and when the flints abraded him was almost pleased; now he would crawl to the edge of the huge pit and look dizzily down. He saw the spiral of the descending roadway, the steep crags, the clinging bushes, the peppering of snow-wreaths, and, far down in the bottom, the diminished crane. Here, no doubt, was a way to end it. But it somehow did not take his fancy.

And suddenly he was aware that he was hungry; ay, even through the tortures of the cold, even through the frosts of despair, a gross, desperate longing after food, no matter what, no matter how, began to wake and spur him. Suppose he pawned his watch? But no, on Christmas Day – this was Christmas Day! – the pawn-shop would be closed. Suppose he went to the public-house close by at Blackhall, and offered the watch, which was worth ten pounds, in payment for a meal of bread and cheese? The incongruity was too remarkable; the good folks would either put him to the door, or only let him in to send for the police. He turned his pockets out one after another; some San Francisco tram-car checks, one cigar, no lights, the pass-key to his father's house, a pocket-handker-chief, with just a touch of scent: no – money could be raised on none of these. There was nothing for it but to starve; and after all, what mattered it! That also was a door of exit.

He crept close among the bushes, the wind playing round him like a lash; his clothes seemed thin as paper, his joints burned, his skin curdled on his bones. He had a vision of a high-lying cattle-drive in California, and the bed of a dried stream with one muddy pool, by which the vaqueros had encamped: splendid sun over all, the big bonfire blazing, the strips of cow browning and smoking on a skewer of wood; how warm it was, how savoury the steam of scorching meat! And then again he remembered his manifold calamities, and burrowed and wallowed in the sense of his disgrace and shame. And next he was entering Frank's restaurant in Montgomery Street, San Francisco; he had ordered a pan-stew and venison chops, of which he was immoderately fond, and as he sat waiting, Munroe, the good attendant, brought him a whisky-punch; he saw the strawberries float on the delectable cup, he heard the ice chink about the straws. And then he woke again to his detested fate, and found himself sitting, humped together, in a windy combe of quarry-refuse – darkness thick about him, thin flakes of snow lying here and there like rags of paper, and the strong shuddering of his body clashing his teeth like a hiccough.

We have seen John in nothing but the stormiest conditions; we have seen him reckless, desperate, tried beyond his moderate powers: of his daily self, cheerful, regular, not unthrifty, we have seen nothing; and it may thus be a surprise to the reader to learn that he was studiously careful of his health. This favourite pre-occupation now awoke. If he were to sit there and die of cold, there would be mighty little gained; better the police cell and the chances of a jury trial, than the miserable certainty of death at a dyke-side before the next winter's dawn, or death a little later in the gas-lit wards of an infirmary.

He rose on aching legs, and stumbled here and there among the rubbish-heaps, still circumvented by the yawning crater of the quarry; or perhaps he only thought so, for the darkness was already dense, the snow was growing thicker, and he moved like a blind man, and with a blind man's terrors. At last he climbed a fence, thinking to drop into the road, and found himself staggering, instead, among the iron furrows of a ploughland, endless, it seemed, as a whole county. And next he was in a wood, beating among young trees; and then he was aware of a house with many lighted windows, Christmas carriages waiting at the doors, and Christmas drivers (for Christmas has a double edge) becoming swiftly hooded with snow. From this glimpse of human cheerfulness he fled like Cain; wandered in the night, unpiloted, careless of whither he went; fell and lay, and then rose again and wandered farther; and at last, like a transformation scene, behold him in the lighted jaws of the city, staring at a lamp which had already donned the tilted night-cap of the snow. It came thickly now, a "Feeding Storm"; and while he yet stood blinking at the lamp, his feet were buried. He remembered something like it in the past, a street lamp crowned and caked upon the windward side with snow, the wind uttering its mournful hoot, himself looking on, even as now; but the cold had struck too sharply on his wits, and memory failed him as to the date and sequel of the reminiscence.

His next conscious moment was on the Dean Bridge; but whether he was John Nicholson of a bank in California Street, or some former John, a clerk in his father's office, he had now clean forgotten. Another blank, and he was thrusting his pass-key into the door-lock of his father's house.

Hours must have passed. Whether crouched on the cold stones or wandering in the fields among the snow, was more than he could tell; but hours had passed. The finger of the hall clock was close on twelve; a narrow peep of gas in the hall-lamp shed shadows; and the door of the back room – his father's room – was open and emitted a warm light. At so late an hour all this was strange; the lights should have been out, the doors locked, the good folk safe in bed. He marvelled at the irregularity, leaning on the hall table; and marvelled to himself there; and thawed and grew once more hungry in the warmer air of the house.

The clock uttered its premonitory catch; in five minutes Christmas Day would be among the days of the past – Christmas! – what a Christmas! Well, there was no use

waiting; he had come into that house, he scarce knew
how; if they were to thrust him forth again, it had best be
done at once; and he moved to the door of the back room
and entered.

O, well – then he was insane, as he had long believed.
There, in his father's room, at midnight, the fire was
roaring, and the gas blazing; the papers, the sacred
papers – to lay a hand on which was criminal – had all
been taken off and piled along the floor; a cloth was
spread, and a supper laid, upon the business table; and in
his father's chair a woman, habited like a nun, sat eating.
As he appeared in the doorway, the nun rose, gave a low
cry, and stood staring. She was a large woman, strong,
calm, a little masculine, her features marked with
courage and good sense; and as John blinked back at her,
a faint resemblance dodged about his memory, as when a
tune haunts us, and yet will not be recalled.

"Why, it's John!" cried the nun.

"I daresay I'm mad," said John, unconsciously following
King Lear; "but, upon my word, I do believe you're Flora."

"Of course I am," replied she.

And yet it is not Flora at all, thought John; Flora was
slender, and timid, and of changing colour, and dewy-
eyed; and had Flora such an Edinburgh accent? But he
said none of these things, which was perhaps as well.
What he said was, "Then why are you a nun?"

"Such nonsense!" said Flora. "I'm a sick-nurse; and I
am here nursing your sister, with whom, between you
and me, there is precious little the matter. But that is not
the question. The point is: How do you come here? and
are you not ashamed to show yourself?"

"Flora," said John sepulchrally, "I haven't eaten anything for three days. Or, at least, I don't know what day it
is; but I guess I'm starving."

"You unhappy man!" she cried. "Here, sit down and
eat my supper; and I'll just run upstairs and see my
patient; not but what I doubt she's fast asleep, for Maria
is a *malade imadginaire.*"

With this specimen of the French, not of Stratford-atte-Bowe, but of a finishing establishment in Moray Place, she left John alone in his father's sanctum. He fell at once upon the food; and it is to be supposed that Flora had found her patient wakeful, and been detained with some details of nursing, for he had time to make a full end of all there was to eat, and not only to empty the teapot, but to fill it again from a kettle that was fitfully singing on his father's fire. Then he sat torpid, and pleased, and bewildered; his misfortunes were then half forgotten; his mind considering, not without regret, this unsentimental return to his old love.

He was thus engaged when that bustling woman noiselessly re-entered.

"Have you eaten?" said she. "Then tell me all about it."

It was a long and (as the reader knows) a pitiful story; but Flora heard it with compressed lips. She was lost in none of those questionings of human destiny that have, from time to time, arrested the flight of my own pen; for women, such as she, are no philosophers, and behold the concrete only. And women, such as she, are very hard on the imperfect man.

"Very well," said she, when he had done; "then down upon your knees at once, and beg God's forgiveness."

And the great baby plumped upon his knees, and did as he was bid; and none the worse for that! But while he was heartily enough requesting forgiveness on general principles, the rational side of him distinguished, and wondered if, perhaps, the apology were not due upon the other part. And when he rose again from that becoming exercise, he first eyed the face of his old love doubtfully, and then, taking heart, uttered his protest.

"I must say, Flora," said he, "in all this business I can see very little fault of mine."

"If you had written home," replied the lady, "there would have been none of it. If you had even gone to Murrayfield reasonably sober, you would never have slept there, and the worst would not have happened.

Besides, the whole thing began years ago. You got into trouble, and when your father, honest man, was disappointed, you took the pet, or got afraid, and ran away from punishment. Well, you've had your own way of it, John, and I don't suppose you like it."

"I sometimes fancy I'm not much better than a fool," sighed John.

"My dear John," said she, "not much!"

He looked at her and his eye fell. A certain anger rose within him; here was a Flora he disowned: she was hard; she was of a set colour; a settled, mature, undecorative manner; plain of speech, plain of habit – he had come near saying, plain of face. And this changeling called herself by the same name as the many-coloured, clinging maid of yore; she of the frequent laughter, and the many sighs, and the kind, stolen glances. And to make all worse, she took the upper hand with him, which (as John well knew) was not the true relation of the sexes. He steeled his heart against this sick-nurse.

"And how do you come to be here?" he asked.

She told him how she had nursed her father in his long illness, and when he died, and she was left alone, had taken to nurse others, partly from habit, partly to be of some service in the world; partly, it might be, for amusement. "There's no accounting for taste," said she. And she told him how she went largely to the houses of old friends, as the need arose; and how she was thus doubly welcome, as an old friend first, and then as an experienced nurse, to whom doctors would confide the gravest case.

"And, indeed, it's a mere farce my being here for poor Maria," she continued; "but your father takes her ailments to heart, and I cannot always be refusing him. We are great friends, your father and I; he was very kind to me long ago – ten years ago."

A strange stir came in John's heart. All this while had he been thinking only of himself? All this while, why had he not written to Flora? In penitential tenderness, he took her hand, and, to his awe and trouble, it remained in

his, compliant. A voice told him this was Flora, after all –
told him so quietly, yet with a thrill of singing.

"And you never married?" said he.

"No, John; I never married," she replied.

The hall clock striking two recalled them to the sense
of time.

"And now," said she, "you have been fed and warmed,
and I have heard your story, and now it's high time to call
your brother."

"O!" cried John, chapfallen; "do you think that absolutely necessary?"

"I can't keep you here; I am a stranger," said she. "Do
you want to run away again? I thought you had enough of
that."

He bowed his head under the reproof. She despised
him, he reflected, as he sat once more alone; a monstrous
thing for a woman to despise a man; and, strangest of all,
she seemed to like him. Would his brother despise him,
too? And would his brother like him?

And presently the brother appeared, under Flora's
escort; and, standing afar off beside the doorway, eyed
the hero of this tale.

"So this is you?" he said at length.

"Yes, Alick, it's me – it's John," replied the elder
brother feebly.

"And how did you get in here?" inquired the younger.

"O, I had my pass-key," says John.

"The deuce you had!" said Alexander. "Ah, you lived
in a better world! There are no pass-keys going now."

"Well, father was always averse to them," sighed John.
And the conversation then broke down, and the brothers
looked askance at one another in silence.

"Well, and what the devil are we to do?" said
Alexander. "I suppose if the authorities got wind of you,
you would be taken up?"

"It depends on whether they've found the body or
not," returned John. "And then there's that cabman, to
be sure!"

"O, bother the body!" said Alexander. "I mean about the other thing. That's serious."

"Is that what my father spoke about?" asked John. "I don't even know what it is."

"About your robbing your bank in California, of course," replied Alexander.

It was plain, from Flora's face, that this was the first she had heard of it; it was plainer still, from John's, that he was innocent.

"I!" he exclaimed. "I rob my bank! My God! Flora, this is too much; even you must allow that."

"Meaning you didn't?" asked Alexander.

"I never robbed a soul in all my days," cried John: "except my father, if you call that robbery; and I brought him back the money in this room, and he wouldn't even take it!"

"Look here, John," said his brother; "let us have no misunderstanding upon this. MacEwen saw my father; he told him a bank you had worked for in San Francisco was wiring over the habitable globe to have you collared – that it was supposed you had nailed thousands; and it was dead certain you had nailed three hundred. So MacEwen said, and I wish you would be careful how you answer. I may tell you also, that your father paid the three hundred on the spot."

"Three hundred?" repeated John. "Three hundred pounds, you mean? That's fifteen hundred dollars. Why, then, it's Kirkman!" he broke out. "Thank Heaven! I can explain all that. I gave them to Kirkman to pay for me the night before I left – fifteen hundred dollars, and a letter to the manager. What do they suppose I would steal fifteen hundred dollars for? I'm rich; I struck it rich in stocks. It's the silliest stuff I ever heard of. All that's needful is to cable to the manager: Kirkman has the fifteen hundred – find Kirkman. He was a fellow-clerk of mine, and a hard case; but to do him justice I didn't think he was as hard as this."

"And what do you say to that, Alick?" asked Flora.

"I say the cablegram shall go to-night! " cried Alexander, with energy. "Answer prepaid, too. If this can be cleared away – and upon my word I do believe it can – we shall all be able to hold up our heads again. Here, you John, you stick down the address of your bank manager. You, Flora, you can pack John into my bed, for which I have no further use to-night. As for me, I am off to the post-office, and thence to the High Street about the dead body. The police ought to know, you see, and they ought to know through John; and I can tell them some rigmarole about my brother being a man of a highly nervous organisation, and the rest of it. And then; I'll tell you what, John – did you notice the name upon the cab?"

John gave the name of the driver, which, as I have not been able to commend the vehicle, I here suppress.

"Well," resumed Alexander, "I'll call round at their place before I come back, and pay your shot for you. In that way, before breakfast-time, you'll be as good as new."

John murmured inarticulate thanks. To see his brother thus energetic in his service moved him beyond expression; if he could not utter what he felt, he showed it legibly in his face; and Alexander read it there, and liked it the better in that dumb delivery.

"But there's one thing," said the latter, "cablegrams are dear; and I daresay you remember enough of the governor to guess the state of my finances."

"The trouble is," said John, "that all my stamps are in that beastly house."

"All your what?" asked Alexander.

"Stamps – money," explained John. "It's an American expression; I'm afraid I contracted one or two."

"I have some," said Flora. "I have a pound-note upstairs."

"My dear Flora," returned Alexander, "a pound-note won't see us very far; and besides, this is my father's business, and I shall be very much surprised if it isn't my father who pays for it."

"I would not apply to him yet; I do not think that can be wise," objected Flora.

"You have a very imperfect idea of my resources, and none at all of my effrontery," replied Alexander. "Please observe."

He put John from his way, chose a stout knife among the supper things, and with surprising quickness broke into his father's drawer.

"There's nothing easier when you come to try," he observed, pocketing the money.

"I wish you had not done that," said Flora. "You will never hear the last of it."

"O, I don't know," returned the young man; "the governor is human, after all. And now, John, let me see your famous pass-key. Get into bed, and don't move for any one till I come back. They won't mind you not answering when they knock; I generally don't myself."

Chapter 9

In which Mr. Nicholson concedes the Principle of an Allowance

IN spite of the horrors of the day and the tea-drinking of the night, John slept the sleep of infancy. He was wakened by the maid, as it might have been ten years ago, tapping at the door. The winter sunrise was painting the east; and as the window was to the back of the house, it shone into the room with many strange colours of refracted light. Without, the houses were all cleanly roofed with snow; the garden walls were coped with it a foot in height; the greens lay glittering. Yet strange as snow had grown to John during his years upon the Bay of San Francisco, it was what he saw within that most affected him. For it was to his own room that Alexander had been promoted; there was the old paper with the device of flowers, in which a cunning fancy might yet detect the face of Skinny Jim, of the Academy, John's former dominie; there was the old chest of drawers; there were the chairs – one, two, three – three as before. Only the carpet was new, and the litter of Alexander's clothes and books and drawing materials, and a pencil-drawing on the wall, which (in John's eyes) appeared a marvel of proficiency.

He was thus lying, and looking, and dreaming, hanging, as it were, between two epochs of his life, when Alexander came to the door, and made his presence known in a loud whisper. John let him in, and jumped back into the warm bed.

"Well, John," said Alexander, "the cablegram is sent in your name, and twenty words of answer paid. I have been to the cab office and paid your cab, even saw the old gentleman himself, and properly apologised. He was mighty placable, and indicated his belief you had been

232

drinking. Then I knocked up old MacEwen out of bed, and explained affairs to him as he sat and shivered in a dressing-gown. And before that I had been to the High Street, where they have heard nothing of your dead body, so that I incline to the idea that you dreamed it."

"Catch me!" said John.

"Well, the police never do know anything," assented Alexander; "and at any rate, they have despatched a man to inquire and to recover your trousers and your money, so that really your bill is now fairly clean; and I see but one lion in your path – the governor."

"I'll be turned out again, you'll see," said John dismally.

"I don't imagine so," returned the other; "not if you do what Flora and I have arranged; and your business now is to dress, and lose no time about it. Is your watch right? Well, you have a quarter of an hour. By five minutes before the half-hour you must be at table, in your old seat, under Uncle Duthie's picture. Flora will be there to keep you countenance; and we shall see what we shall see."

"Wouldn't it be wiser for me to stay in bed?" said John.

"If you mean to manage your own concerns, you can do precisely what you like," replied Alexander; "but if you are not in your place five minutes before the half-hour I wash my hands of you, for one."

And thereupon he departed. He had spoken warmly, but the truth is, his heart was somewhat troubled. And as he hung over the banisters, watching for his father to appear, he had hard ado to keep himself braced for the encounter that must follow.

"If he takes it well, I shall be lucky," he reflected. "If he takes it ill, why, it'll be a herring across John's tracks, and perhaps all for the best. He's a confounded muff, this brother of mine, but he seems a decent soul."

At that stage a door opened below with a certain emphasis, and Mr. Nicholson was seen solemnly to descend the stairs, and pass into his own apartment.

Alexander followed, quaking inwardly, but with a steady face. He knocked, was bidden to enter, and found his father standing in front of the forced drawer, to which he pointed as he spoke.

"This is a most extraordinary thing," said he; "I have been robbed!"

"I was afraid you would notice it," observed his son "it made such a beastly hash of the table."

"You were afraid I would notice it?" repeated Mr. Nicholson. "And, pray, what may that mean?"

"That I was the thief, sir," returned Alexander. "I took all the money in case the servants should get hold of it; and here is the change, and a note of my expenditure. You were gone to bed, you see, and I did not feel at liberty to knock you up; but I think when you have heard the circumstances you will do me justice. The fact is, I have reason to believe there has been some dreadful error about my brother John; the sooner it could be cleared up the better for all parties; it was a piece of business, sir – and so I took it, and decided, on my own responsibility, to send a telegram to San Francisco. Thanks to my quickness, we may hear to-night. There appears to be no doubt, sir, that John has been abominably used."

"When did this take place?" asked the father.

"Last night, sir, after you were asleep," was the reply.

"It's most extraordinary," said Mr. Nicholson. "Do you mean to say you have been out all night?"

"All night, as you say, sir. I have been to the telegraph and the police office, and Mr. MacEwen's. O, I had my hands full," said Alexander.

"Very irregular," said the father. "You think of no one but yourself."

"I do not see that I have much to gain in bringing back my elder brother," returned Alexander shrewdly.

The answer pleased the old man; he smiled. "Well, well, I will go into this after breakfast," said he.

"I'm sorry about the table," said the son.

"The table is a small matter; I think nothing of that," said the father.

"It's another example," continued the son, "of the awkwardness of a man having no money of his own. If I had a proper allowance, like other fellows of my age, this would have been quite unnecessary."

"A proper allowance!" repeated his father, in tones of blighting sarcasm, for the expression was not new to him. "I have never grudged you money for any proper purpose."

"No doubt, no doubt," said Alexander, "but then you see you aren't always on the spot to have the thing explained to you. Last night, for instance – "

"You could have wakened me last night," interrupted his father.

"Was it not some similar affair that first got John into a mess?" asked the son, skilfully evading the point.

But the father was not less adroit. "And pray, sir, how did you come and go out of the house?" he asked.

"I forgot to lock the door, it seems," replied Alexander.

"I have had cause to complain of that too often," said Mr. Nicholson. "But still I do not understand. Did you keep the servants up?"

"I propose to go into all that at length after breakfast," returned Alexander. "There is the half-hour going; we must not keep Miss Mackenzie waiting."

And, greatly daring, he opened the door.

Even Alexander, who, it must have been perceived, was on terms of comparative freedom with his parent – even Alexander had never before dared to cut short an interview in this high-handed fashion. But the truth is, the very mass of his son's delinquencies daunted the old gentleman. He was like the man with the cart of apples – this was beyond him! That Alexander should have spoiled his table, taken his money, stayed out all night, and then coolly acknowledged all, was something undreamed of in the Nicholsonian philosophy, and transcended comment. The return of the change, which the old gentleman still carried in his hand, had been a feature of imposing impudence; it had dealt him a staggering blow. Then there was the reference to John's original flight – a subject which he always kept resolutely curtained in his own mind; for he was a man who loved to have made no mistakes, and, when he feared he might have made one, kept the papers sealed. In view of all these surprises and reminders, and of his son's composed and masterful demeanour, there began to creep on Mr. Nicholson a sickly misgiving. He seemed beyond his depth; if he did or said anything, he might come to regret it. The young man, besides, as he had pointed out himself, was playing a generous part. And if wrong had been done – and done to one who was after, and in spite of, all, a Nicholson – it should certainly be righted.

All things considered, monstrous as it was to be cut short in his inquiries, the old gentleman submitted, pocketed the change, and followed his son into the dining-room. During these few steps he once more mentally revolted, and once more, and this time finally, laid down his arms: a still, small voice in his bosom having informed him authentically of a piece of news: that he was afraid of Alexander. The strange thing was that he was pleased to be afraid of him. He was proud of his son; he might be proud of him; the boy had character and grit, and knew what he was doing.

These were his reflections as he turned the corner of the dining-room door. Miss Mackenzie was in the place of honour, conjuring with a teapot and a cosy; and, behold! there was another person present, a large, portly, whiskered man of a very comfortable and respectable air, who now rose from his seat and came forward, holding out his hand.

"Good-morning, father," said he.

Of the contention of feeling that ran high in Mr. Nicholson's starched bosom, no outward sign was visible; nor did he delay long to make a choice of conduct. Yet in that interval he had reviewed a great field of possibilities both past and future: whether it was possible he had not been perfectly wise in his treatment of John; whether it was possible that John was innocent; whether, if he turned John out a second time, as his outraged authority suggested, it was possible to avoid a scandal; and whether, if he went to that extremity, it was possible that Alexander might rebel.

"Hum!" said Mr. Nicholson, and put his hand, limp and dead, into John's.

And then, in an embarrassed silence, all took their places; and even the paper – from which it was the old gentleman's habit to suck mortification daily, as he marked the decline of our institutions – even the paper lay furled by his side.

But presently Flora came to the rescue. She slid into the silence with a technicality, asking if John still took his old inordinate amount of sugar. Thence it was but a step to the burning question of the day; and in tones a little shaken, she commented on the interval since she had last made tea for the prodigal, and congratulated him on his return. And then addressing Mr. Nicholson, she congratulated him also in a manner that defied his ill-humour; and from that launched into the tale of John's misadventures, not without some suitable suppressions.

Gradually Alexander joined; between them, whether he would or no, they forced a word or two from John; and these fell so tremulously, and spoke so eloquently of a mind oppressed with dread, that Mr. Nicholson relented. At length even he contributed a question: and before the meal was at an end all four were talking even freely.

Prayers followed, with the servants gaping at this newcomer whom no one had admitted; and after prayers there came that moment on the clock which was the signal for Mr. Nicholson's departure.

"John," said he, "of course you will stay here. Be very careful not to excite Maria, if Miss Mackenzie thinks it desirable that you should see her. – Alexander, I wish to speak with you alone." And then, when they were both in the back-room: "You need not come to the office today," said he; "you can stay and amuse your brother, and I think it would be respectful to call on Uncle Greig. And, by-the-by" (this spoken with a certain – dare we say? – bashfulness), "I agree to concede the principle of an allowance; and I will consult Dr. Durie, who is quite a man of the world and has sons of his own, as to the amount. And, my fine fellow, you may consider yourself in luck!" he added, with a smile.

"Thank you," said Alexander.

Before noon a detective had restored to John his money, and brought news, sad enough in truth, but perhaps the least sad possible. Alan Houston had been found in his own house in Regent Terrace, under care of the terrified butler. He was quite mad, and instead of going to prison, had been taken to Morningside Asylum. The murdered man, it appeared, was an evicted tenant who had for nearly a year pursued his late landlord with threats and insults; and beyond this, the cause and details of the tragedy were lost.

When Mr. Nicholson returned for dinner they were able to put a despatch into his hands: – "John V. Nicholson, Randolph Crescent, Edinburgh. – Kirkman has disappeared; police looking for him. All understood. Keep mind quite easy. – AUSTIN." Having had this explained to him, the old gentleman took down the cellar key and departed for two bottles of the 1820 port. Uncle Greig dined there that day, and cousin Robina, and, by an odd chance, Mr. MacEwen; and the presence of these strangers relieved what might have been otherwise a somewhat strained relation. Ere they departed the family was welded once more into a fair semblance of unity.

In the end of April John led Flora – or, let us say, as more descriptive, Flora led John – to the altar, if altar that may be called which was indeed the drawing-room mantelpiece in Mr. Nicholson's house, the Reverend

Dr. Durie posted on the hearthrug in the guise of Hymen's priest.

The last I saw of them, on a recent visit to the north, was at a dinner-party in the house of my old friend Gellatly Macbride; and after we had, in classic phrase, "rejoined the ladies," I had an opportunity to overhear Flora conversing with another married woman on the much canvassed matter of a husband's tobacco.

"O yes!" said she; "I only allow Mr. Nicholson four cigars a day. Three he smokes at fixed times – after a meal, you know, my dear; and the fourth he can take when he likes with any friend."

"Bravo!" thought I to myself; "this is the wife for my friend John!"

LEO TOLSTOY
Collected Shorter Fiction (in 2 vols)
Anna Karenina
Childhood, Boyhood and Youth
The Cossacks
War and Peace

ANTHONY TROLLOPE
Barchester Towers
Can You Forgive Her?
Doctor Thorne
The Eustace Diamonds
Framley Parsonage
The Last Chronicle of Barset
Phineas Finn
The Small House at Allington
The Warden

IVAN TURGENEV
Fathers and Children
First Love and Other Stories
A Sportsman's Notebook

MARK TWAIN
Tom Sawyer
and Huckleberry Finn

JOHN UPDIKE
The Complete Henry Bech
Rabbit Angstrom

GIORGIO VASARI
Lives of the Painters, Sculptors and
Architects (in 2 vols)

JULES VERNE
Journey to the Centre of the Earth
Twenty Thousand Leagues under
the Sea
Round the World in Eighty Days

VIRGIL
The Aeneid

VOLTAIRE
Candide and Other Stories

EVELYN WAUGH
(US only)
Black Mischief, Scoop, The Loved
One, The Ordeal of Gilbert
Pinfold (in 1 vol.)
Brideshead Revisited
Decline and Fall
A Handful of Dust
The Sword of Honour Trilogy
Waugh Abroad: Collected Travel
Writing

EVELYN WAUGH (*cont.*)
(UK & US)
The Complete Short Stories

H. G. WELLS
The Time Machine,
The Invisible Man,
The War of the Worlds
(in 1 vol., US only)

EDITH WHARTON
The Age of Innocence
The Custom of the Country
Ethan Frome, Summer,
Bunner Sisters
(in 1 vol.)
The House of Mirth
The Reef

PATRICK WHITE
Voss

OSCAR WILDE
Plays, Prose Writings and Poems

P. G. WODEHOUSE
The Best of Wodehouse

MARY WOLLSTONECRAFT
A Vindication of the Rights of
Woman

VIRGINIA WOOLF
To the Lighthouse
Mrs Dalloway

WILLIAM WORDSWORTH
Selected Poems (UK only)

RICHARD YATES
Revolutionary Road
The Easter Parade
Eleven Kinds of Loneliness
(in 1 vol.)

W. B. YEATS
The Poems (UK only)

ÉMILE ZOLA
Germinal

This book is set in CASLON, designed and engraved by William Caslon of WILLIAM CASLON & SON, Letter-Founders in London, around 1740. In England at the beginning of the eighteenth century, Dutch type was probably more widely used than English. The rise of William Caslon put a stop to the importation of Dutch types and so changed the history of English typecutting.